the sex god

No Mud No Lotus

Ben Belenus

Copyright © 2012 by Ben Belenus

First Edition
Published by Belenus Publishing, 2012

ISBN 978-0-9572596-0-7

www.benbelenus.com

A CIP catalogue record for this title is available from the British Library

The Publisher has made every effort to use papers that are made from wood grown in sustainable forests.

Cover Photography: © Chi Chiu Chan | Dreamstime.com
Title Font: "Alice" K Erulevich, ©Cyreal

10 9 8 7 6 5 4 3 2 1

For my daughters,
for all daughters.
May all men worship
the beautiful feminine essence
in all women...

With deepest gratitude to the Divine Feminine,
soul mates,
intimate partners,
teachers
and those who chose to love, support
and walk with me
on this sweet journey in life.

Foreword

The book you are holding in your hands is like molten lava, reshaping the inner landscape of how we perceive and experience sexuality. In contemporary Western culture, no matter how blatant explicit advertising and pornography are, sex is still a private and often taboo subject. Ben goes to great lengths to crack open the most secret dimensions of male sexual thought and action. He opens up an important dialogue about the potent meaning of an activity which can be pleasurable, desperate, addictive, destructive, uplifting, euphoric, or spiritual, depending on how one plays the game.

Ben's innocence is overshadowed by his heightened libido, he simply loves women and sex. Ben is challenged to find his authentic self through the powerful forces of his sexual nature in a world with fixed social rules of sexual etiquette. Marriage vows couldn't really contain him and he finds himself impelled to play the field; maintaining security at the cost of his true nature by lying to his wife. Of course, the lying and cheating backfires, as it usually does, and he has hell to pay, learning many valuable lessons as a result. The story isn't unusual, but the way Ben dares to expose his innermost thoughts and feelings is deeply refreshing. At its heart 'the sex god' is a spiritual journey; and a revealing and passionate love story.

In our world today sex, pornography, sex addiction and the broken ways in the world are all highly charged subjects and 'the sex god' sits at the epicentre of them all. Something has warped in our relationship to sex and it is detrimentally affecting the way we honour men, women and the Earth. There has never been a better time for us all to take a good look at the assumptions that we make about our sexuality and how it affects our culture and all our relationships.

The book helps us take a step back from our conditioning and look at sex from a refreshing new perspective. I am reminded of how some other cultures have dealt with the subject of sexuality, and hope this book can support us all in opening up to new possibilities. For example, in Tahiti, when the first white men landed in their boats, they were dumbfounded when the native population sent boatloads of women to the ships. Gorgeous beauties swarmed onto the ships, lay down and invitingly opened their legs for the sailors to partake of their exquisite bounty. The sailors of course imagined that they had died and gone to heaven!

Over time, sailors began trying to possess individual women for themselves, as wives. There was a great congregation of Chiefs from the various Islands, who informed the sailors that the idea of possessing one woman for themselves was immoral and against nature. They told the sailors that if they did that, they would be destroying the refined culture of the Tahitians and the chiefs would be forced to expel the sailors. Unfortunately, Missionaries soon followed the sailors and did indeed destroy the refined culture of the Tahitians. To the religious or Victorian prudish mind the Tahitians appeared licentious. And yet, if you can look from another perspective they were aligned with truest nature. They were tuned into the truth of what it is to be human. Our sexuality doesn't in fact follow Victorian rules. Our bodies are not programmed for monogamy. On the other hand, because the Tahitians were completely in tune with their sexuality, heart and spirituality, their sexual expression was authentic; within a world view which honoured all that the human being is.

In ancient India, China and Japan, it was known that sexual energy is immensely powerful. It was considered imperative that mastery of the sexual arts be taught along with astronomy, astrology, architecture, spirituality, mathematics, languages and other refined aspects of learning. Young people were allowed to peek from behind curtains to witness amorous couples. In this way they got to understand the sixty-four positions of the Kama Sutra. Later as they became older they would go through initiations to learn about the subtle aspects of the arts of love and sex.

In ancient Celtic culture, people wisely found a way through the conundrum of one vs. multiple partners with the Beltane festival. It was held in early May each year. On the edge of the village, a line of fire was created between the tilled fields and the wild forest. Whoever wanted to participate in the fertility rites, would jump over the fire into the wild wood, and once there, spend hours or days in rapturous exploration of sex with whoever they liked. As everyone believed in this custom as being good and just, there wasn't any jealousy. Just as the tilled fields had been stolen from the wild, so it was believed that human nature also had a wild side which had been stolen by civilization. This wild side had to be honoured at least once in the year for there to be harmony in society. If any children were conceived during that time, they would be considered to be children of the Gods.

Ben, the hero of this book, eventually finds his way through the quagmire of sexual confusion, and tumbles into the world of Tantra. He finds that the human body is designed to know not only orgasm of the body, but orgasm of the heart and soul. Orgasm itself becomes his teacher, leading him to greater rewards than he could have ever dreamed were possible. He finds out that each cell of his body is part of the orgasm stream and that life itself is orgasmic, if we but know how to open up sufficiently. Love cracks him open so deeply, that he is forced to reinvent himself as a man. From sex and porn addiction, he finds there is much more powerful fulfilment waiting for him. His story reminds me of the Phoenix, the fabled bird who enters the fire and passes through it to rise again, flying free from the ashes of the old. In the same way Ben passes through the fire of lust and arises golden, victorious and redeemed into the dawning of wise love. He realises that a man who truly loves woman can bring peace on Earth and that an unconditionally loved man can love all peoples and the planet.

In my research into Tantra, I have found that there are two ways to play the game of love. In one scenario, many women can be experienced as one woman, as womankind so to speak. Or many men are experienced as one male principle. In the other scenario, one woman becomes all women, or one man becomes all men. In this book, Ben lives these two possibilities, and it is a true delight to be led on this journey into the ways of love and sex through his narrative.

It is part of my vocation to initiate couples into the art of Tantra. I have been privileged to be a witness to the revelations experienced by the author of this book as he has moved on the Tantra path with his Beloved. Teaching Tantra and the art of sexuality, love and relating, I am privileged to witness many miracles. Tantra is not so much a path of learning, as the art of remembering our true nature. Whatever was locked up behind walls of warped conditioning, finds space to breathe through the practice of Tantra. Exquisite nectar is contained in sexuality. We just need to know how to access it. Ben has found the way. And so can you.

Mahasatvaa Ma Ananda Sarita

Innocence - Passion

I remember that I am only Love.

May all beings be peaceful.

With healing intent...

Authentic

We fucked hard last night. It was body-connected real and six-sensory. No other women joined us in our shared fantasies. We were merged. We were one, beloved Angelica and I. A leaden night's sleep followed.

I awoke early this morning as day overcame darkness. I decided to forgo a walk in the fields, morning meditation and our usual love making. I was ready to step into the arena. Filled with a sense of mission, I crafted a hot mug of garrulous Kenyan AAA and settled down to write... a story about sex, fidelity and the search for wholeness; a book that advocates the worship of womankind.

The intimacy that arises between me and my lover is a truly sacred experience; the exact perfumed details to be known only to us. So to protect the sanctity of my many experiences I shall take creative licence to disguise exactitude. In endeavouring to preserve utmost juiciness though, I shall make use of a thinnest but highly sensitive membrane between truth and fiction. The essence of my evolution as a man *and* the erotically graphic descriptions will however remain intact.

Some say men are simple creatures, but I've no doubt that we are complex and multi-dimensional. This story will focus only on one of those dimensions, the sexual dimension. Sex will be explored in great depth and pursuant to my having testicles it will principally be from a man's perspective. I shall share much conquested-treasure and some occasional junk with you. I am a provocateur, so be open to my words and don't be fooled by your conditioned expectations of appropriate male behaviour.

Men you will be understood... and confronted.
Women you will be challenged... and adored.

Ancient teachings tell us that we all have a male and female essence within our psyche (as represented by the Tao symbol.)

Our highest-self contains balanced and positive blueprints for these sexual essences. For both men and women, early interactions with unbalanced men or women can warp, damage or steal our wholesome blueprints. In turn, our damaged blueprint then affects how we relate to each other *and* our World.

I have always longed to know and express my whole un-guarded self. We spend so much of our lives hiding behind roles and relating to others who are also playing roles. Through roles we darken our shadows and pretend to be what we are not. In recent years I broke trail and cast off the protective veneers that had me play the role of being an "average man", a small man. I was able to reveal an authentic Ben hiding inside.

As I am writing from an aware place, I am now sharing my authenticity with you. But sometimes a man's authenticity can be uncomfortable. Being honest, naked and uncompromising may be shocking... But shocking can be exciting. If you are a closed-one, at times you may not want to read any further for fear of what may be said next. But I'm sure that your sexual self will be curious, your intellectual self will be titillated, your spiritual self will be evolved... *and* you'll get wet.

Hopefully you will see past any selfish male arrogance and realise the gifted understandings that I shall share. If you indulge yourself in all my explicitly juicy retellings you shall see a richer psycho-spiritual story unfolding; a resplendent tapestry of the erotic and the sacred that can stealthily deliver its timely message. Beyond flippant dismissal, perhaps you will take some time to contemplate my messages in your own heart to assimilate their truth. Resonate with my authenticity if you will.

I come first and then love follows.

I am no prude, I shall be sexually frank. I shall be a naked, vulnerable man for you Reader. I have highest ambition, I trust myself so that I may bloom into peace.

Ha! Fear arises. An expose can rattle the ego. In spite of my authentic bravado, how much dare I tell of this one man's experience? How much shall I reveal about being a sexual man, a very sexual creature? When I'm naked, people can see the wrinkles that I would rather pretend weren't there. But I have a penis. And I have balls... Fear, I see you for what you are and I dance into the fire with you.

We have spent our entire lives being told who we are by people who do not know who they are. You have spent your entire life denying and dishonouring the formidably beautiful sexual energy that creation is trying to thrust through you. We must each honour our own sexuality.

My teacher says that repressed sexual energy has caused all the problems in the world. Is she right? Oh, did I mention my Tantra teacher? You shall meet her later, much later. We have some louche storytelling to do first...

Ready?

That Feeling

The billion-galaxied night sky makes me feel so small.
I look up and somehow the Universe swallows me.

I get the same feeling when I am absorbed into the chest of my open-hearted beloved Angelica. That's what it feels like to be consumed by her infinite Love.

Love is a gathering and celebration of what it means to be alive, it is to be everything and nothing all at once. Love IS life.

There's no doubt that one of the most amazing becomings of manifest Nature is to be embraced by the feminine essence of my lover. I become instilled by her and I enter a time where I cease wondering and I am allowed to just Be.

Soaking up and receiving the open heart of my lover is a place where I don't want protection. I feel strangely free, ageless and excited. I seldom know where I begin or end. The clock stops and time doesn't matter.

In embrace we can rest together as One. In this lonely existence.

In her I become nobody. No body and all things.
Two disappears.
The end of distinction.
No clouds, only sky.

It would be several decades before the sex god would lead me to her.

Emergence

The sex god emerged.

'C'mon round the side Ben, the gate is open,' she hollered.

I was visiting a school friend. I entered the back garden through a rusty, wrought iron gate and skipped my way down the gravel path lined with powder-blue forget-me-nots.

'Lance is upstairs packing his suitcase, he'll be down in a few minutes Ben. Help yourself to squash and fruitcake over there on the garden table then grab yourself a chair... And don't mind me, I'm catching some sun while I can... ready for our holidays in Spain. Lance is very excited as we're leaving tomorrow.' She shared a big smile and returned to her travel magazine. Spain was a long way away. I had never heard of anyone going to Spain before – they had money and could go to such places.

'Thank you Mrs. Honey,' came my voice-broken reply as I served myself the largest slab of cake.

I plonked down next to her on a nearby comfy chair. Its down cushion swallowed me. I looked around the garden, swinging my legs, as you did back then. As I gorged myself on the cake, I became fixated on Mrs. Honey's long body, her curves and her smallish powder-blue bikini. Perhaps I shouldn't have stared, but I didn't know how to stop. I couldn't quite see if her eyes were open through her apparently expensive sunglasses. Could she have seen me looking? ... Then she moved and turned away; it became permissible to hold a child's stare. As my curiosity became greater than my fear I decided to help myself to some more, perhaps indulge even. I feasted my eyes on her smooth skin. Certain parts of her shape aroused more than my interest. I shifted my pelvis. I looked at her, freely. I ate my cake slowly.

Women up until that moment had been mothers, aunts or women going about their everyday lives; there was no difference between them. They were just, well just women! Yet something impelled me to find Mrs. Honey attractive. That is to say, her body attracted me in much the same way that a lonesome garden flower would sexually attract a butterfly. I had never been attracted to a woman before, not in that magnetic way. But she was a different type of woman, for she was an "almost naked" woman. I hadn't ever stared at an almost-naked woman before.

Oh there was blessing in the gentle breezei. I was sure I could smell her, her perfume... and some other noble elixir. I felt drugged by her. She filled me with wonder. I licked the air.

My eyes toured her. She had large hammocked breasts, her nipples were hidden. She looked beautiful like an exotic flower; on display. A cleft could be seen in the fabric of her bikini. I couldn't quite see enough, I wanted more. I was in awe of how she captivated me. It was a timeless moment.

A yearning grew within me. I wanted to follow my yearning and go over to touch her. My touch would have been tender, wondrous and explorative. Something told me I would be cold-busted if I had done that though. I remembered being punished years back when I touched another girl at play-school. So I didn't follow my yearning.

She moved again, more was revealed. Perhaps I should have looked away... But no, I had all the time in the world, well at least until when Lance came down to go play go-kart. And that could be ages, he was always so tardy. Her bikini barely covered her hairy groin. I wondered what she would look like without a bikini.

New unfelt-before feelings emerged in me. They felt good. They had been awakened by the outermost aura of her femaleness.

A cause was set going. I had a lifetime ahead of me to learn about the feelings, longings and gifts of women.

---

i   Wordsworth - Prelude

Dark Room

Delicate beginnings. We were keen to see how our after-school nature-study photographs had panned out.

'This way Anna, we'll get back faster.' Eager to return to the dark room we skipped through a wooded shortcut avoiding the young brambles. We crashed through the art-annex doors and then skeeted across the wooden floor and into the dark room. Anna closed the door firmly behind the two of us – and then locked it. We became bathed in soft amber light and film-developer odour. The black and white chemistry was soon ready and we set about developing the prints for our photography project.

'Ben have you ever been with a girl?' Her candy perfume contrasted with her open blouse and tight pencil skirt.

'What do you mean?'

'Oh come on Ben, you know, been with a girl.'

'I am not sure I know what you mean Anna.'

'You know, like this...' She pushed me against the countertop, trapping me. I was uncomfortable at her forcefulness.

I felt as though she needed my permission to behave that way towards me. I didn't know about boundaries but I could feel that my boundary was being crossed. There was a NO in me that was trying to get expressed. But it wouldn't come out.

'Ben I want you, I have been waiting all week for this moment.'

I felt teenage bra wires poking through my shirt as she held herself firm against me. I felt my penis (or was it a Willy) swelling; it had a mind of its own and had rightly detected what was going on. She liked that. Anna was blossoming sixteen, wild haired, Romany-dark and brimming over with got-to-do-it teenage sexual energy. She was in her flow, on heat and was clawing at me like a black widow. She wanted it, had to have it. She groped between my legs. My sex god wasn't ready for this.

'NO'. The no was released. I tried to get away – she pulled me back. She knew what she was doing, I didn't. It was black and white.

'Ow! Not now Anna... What's happening, you're frightening me... What are you doing?' I tried to reason with her.

She trapped me again. 'I want you in me, I need you in me, I need the real thing Ben, I need you!' Her breath was hot, her amber smile cheeky. It was the stuff girls read about in Teenie mags. Not the kind of stuff in a boy's mag.

I managed to get out of check, ripping the collar of my school jumper. I wasn't ready for that. I didn't know what to do – I was shy and proper... and downright scared! The zeal in her hormones frightened me away, I had no idea a girl could be so primal.

'Come here Ben.' She moved to hold me back, grabbing my balls in a way that girls shouldn't – it hurt.

'Leave me alone Anna. We're not allowed,' I yelped, then scrambled to get the door open. Sweating, uncertain, confused, I ran to hide in the cycle sheds. I waited. I was shaken. I cried.

When I was sure she had left the school, I cycled home faster than I could. I don't remember how I explained my torn clothes to Mum, or for that matter the gouge on my shoulder.

And so my first "real" sexual encounter with a woman was complete.

I reminisce now and see that Anna was a tight flower-bud. She was willing to give away her outer female layers for free. She was willing to give away her puffy nipples and puppy curves, by force if necessary. Oh the innocence of those sapling years.

Oh to be able to shag her today.

I had had other encounters with women but they were encounters of the "unreal" kind. My sex education had thus far been "pretend-I-wasn't-looking" page-three girls. Oh and an inquisitive indulgence in the underwear section of mail order catalogues. I loved studying every photo for new anatomical insights, which was always a challenge as knickers in the seventies were spinnaker big. My studies were usually augmented with a good wank. I used those imaginary lovers to learn about the natural ways of my own body and to develop my own excellent masturbatory style. The onset of elixir caused my sight to dim and my hearing to muffle... and then came cosmic prisms; I loved to orgasm. Though these experiments were always quick and hidden so I didn't get caught. I would have died if I had been caught.

My sex god emerged further when I visited a friend's house. It was January 1972 when Playboy first published a fully naked woman. My friend had found one of his dad's copies of Penthouse which was always more educating. I wasn't sure why many of the stories involved cats. But the "full-frontals" were captivating indeed. I enjoyed the feelings in my body when I looked at those pictures. I didn't understand that the female essence was beckoning me through those pictures. Some of the pictures showed people doing things to each other that I didn't understand. They were disturbing to me, but why?

Like so many before, the men in my generation were denied a masterful education of how we should relate to a woman, to our sexuality or to honouring all that is. It was the same for women too. There's no wonder that sex is an emotive and challenging subject for most people. My youth was playing out against the human heritage of thousands of years of suppressed sexuality, oppressed women and sexually-damaged-men. I had arrived late into a party that was already happening. The pervasive devaluation of women, the repression of women and their values, has created significant social un-healthiness within us all. That un-healthiness is passed from abused generation to abused generation. And now it was my turn.

Ancient peoples knew of the workings of sexual energies, they knew that sex created the cosmos. They respected and understood our connectedness to all Nature. Those universal insights were buried in wisdoms throughout antiquity. Since all life and all men came from women, our ancestors also reverently understood the innate power of women-kind. In order to assume power for themselves my male ancestors decreed that sex, the creation-force of the Universe, was not important... and therefore women were not important. Structures of paternal power were born. Inevitably those power structures needed to be memorialised. So the task of preserving and documenting those sexual wisdoms was ceded to celibate monks. (Just imagine!) Wisdom about the creative force of the Universe was not suitable for the common man and woman. Sex liberates and a liberated population cannot be controlled. Sacred sexual teachings were to be kept secret. The sociopathic results of that folly can be witnessed all over the world today. We can witness how macho attitudes affect the lives of many women around us – mothers, wives, girl friends and daughters. What would our world be like if masculine dominance gave way to co-creation and the feminine were given fullest opportunity to express itself? It is only in the last hundred years or so that women have been given the freedom to vote, speak and think out loud. Five hundred years ago men thought that females were failed males. They were made to sniff lettuce as a test for their virginity. What was it like to be a woman a few thousand years ago when they were used as money? And even today, forced marriage is widespread and over one hundred and forty million women are living with genital mutilation.

Surely our collective consciousness has absorbed the wound.

My parents were "pretty normal" by any standard, some kids are raised in a more extreme world. I recently learned of a woman who years ago while at a Catholic school was made to wear a cape and neck-collar so that she didn't get sight of her body. What folly to believe that truest-nature can be "managed" by applying the right methods? And what message about sexuality did she have for her children? What message do sexually abused parents or an abusing parent have for their children? How might they educate their children to love and respect their bodies and sexuality?

I ponder, what is it like to be a woman today in this man's world? My man heart grieves.

There is no wonder that we are all growing up with such a complex relationship to being a man or a woman. Disrespect for the creative energy of the Universe is the origin of much that is wrong with our societies, our lack of respect for our Earth and our godlessness in bed.

Today, I love my body.

Rather than dark-room encounters, these days copious Internet pornography precedes sex-play for many young people.

Free access to thousands of images, of any taboo, are shaping the sexual unions of millions of people. And so the damage deepens. The propagation of unhealthy sexuality will continue until we wake up and see things as they truly are. All life and all men come from women. Men can choose to heal their shame and women can be worshipped back to open loving safe wholeness. Only then will our ancestors thank us, and our children bless us.

I bumped into Anna at school a few months later.

She was very pregnant.

Innocently not Knowing

No story that I shall share will be incompatible with inspiration. Truth and authenticity are themes that we shall dance with in this yarn. The innocent truth in this encounter was with a local girl. I was about to "be with a girl" for the first time. Virginity, lovely word, was to be lost.

It was sweltering as we sauntered home from school. We were still wearing our sweaters as required by the uniform rules. We arrived at the back door of her house, heated further by anticipation.

'Are your parents out?'

'They're usually out on a Thursday, I think we're in luck again Ben.' The back door was locked. She looked at me and smiled.

We let ourselves in.

'How long have we got together?' I asked as she embraced me in a way that was older than her years. When we share space with another person we often pick up on their subtle energies. Feeling how they feel. The sexy-heat in her energy was palpable.

'I think they'll be home at six thirty, so we have forty minutes to ourselves.'

We kissed. Our tongues entered each other. I was filled with a warm tingly spreading feeling as my sexual energy awakened and scintillated. I have always enjoyed the thrill of a first kiss.

We slid upstairs to her bedroom; where we most certainly weren't allowed to be. She put some Led Zep on. We kissed again. Our sexual engagement started. Our bodies writhed. In response to the presence of my maleness, her tightly closed flower started to open. She took her sweater off revealing her unfurled flower within. Its removal allowed stronger female essences to be known. The full mass of her wholesome breasts couldn't be missed through the opaque damp of her blouse. There was that look on her face, her movements became syrupy and sparkles arrived in her eyes.

'Have you been with a girl before Ben?' She was playing with her mousy-blond hair.

The rosiness in her cheeks spoke that she was ready. Nicola tended to overflow her bra. I fumbled to release her with the buckles at the back.

'Only a few times.' I attempted to assert my manliness. How does a man learn how to make love? Is his father supposed to hire him a hooker?

Nicola then deftly released her bra using the buckle at the front. Her breasts fell out. I stared at her smooth youthful nakedness. I had looked at and touched breasts before. But that night I sensed that we were going further, further than I had ever been before. She led the way, she knew what to do – as she also had an older boyfriend.

I saw a momentary lapse of uncertainty cross her face as she passed through a mini fear. It didn't feel right to stare any longer, so we cuddled. I loved the warmth of her body.

Maybe we weren't going further after all?

Her fear was soon overcome and she became more determined. Her sexual essence had a frank conversation with my essence. It said "I have more for you, come on inside". Innocently not knowing what to do next we lost ourselves in a purposeful flow. We kissed again, more passionately. My hands toured up her skirt and between her smooth thighs without any resistance on her part. I daren't explore higher.

After a while she pulled my hand up between her legs. I trembled nervously; I had a challenge on my hands. I felt her authority. She gave me more signals that I was moving too slowly. She pulled her knickers to one side; wafts of her youthful air swamped me. My long fingers slipped into her supple stickiness. She tensed, murmured then relaxed.

True happiness occurs when we are in contact with real life.

As I have a Y chromosome I am sharing insights into a man's mind. Reader, I am aware that today I have another challenge on my hands if you are to stay the course and receive my healing transmission – I need you to like me. My challenge, how to write a story that is accessible to men that may well alienate women or a story for women that men are too closed to receive? It would be easy for a man to read this book with his nuts, but my words are intended for his heart. Men must become vulnerable if they are to break through their conditioning. So yes, this writing is imbued with a man's perspective; men like to coif slowly on visual detail. A woman is significantly more qualified than me to write about a woman's point of view, as I know nothing. However, a woman may be wanton of heart, emotion and the psychology behind relationships (which is why most women still prefer a real man over a Rabbit dildo!) Fear not, there is plenty of that on its way too.

Nicola popped open my trousers and released a pinkish boyish erection out of my pants. Aliveness happens at the edge of comfort.

We were going to do "it", or something.

A woman was about to let me into her, a step deeper. My innocence during that moment was exquisite. Innocence is aliveness. Whenever we think we know or wrap life in meaning, we close and miss life itself. I knew nothing.

In a haze of consuming quivering botch, I climbed on top of her, groin to groin. It felt good.

But only good-ish. I moved around on instinct. It was so uncomfortable as her long dark pubes chaffed my virgin skin. Why was I shaking so much? Why was it making me sore? Why was everybody so into this? Maybe I should stick to playing with computers.

She took control again. 'Ben, what are you doing? You need to be inside me!'

My ignorance was innocent. I had sorely missed the mark, how humiliating. I couldn't muster a blush-saving response. My fibs to her that "I had done it before" were exposed as boy brag.

She gaped her pale legs wide. 'Come here sexy boy, I'll show you.' Using her fingers to open herself up, she slipped me in.

Fucking hell.

Experience got amplified. Good-ish became heaven. We became utterly extant. I daren't move. I was consumed by vital innocence while losing my innocence.

She wiggled and moaned. Was she in pain?

Several seconds later (I exaggerate) I ejaculated a youthful load.

Fuck that felt good.

Did I learn to ejaculate so fast from all those secret quick-wanks?

I lay there atop her for a while trembling and shaken. What fullness that girl gave me.

Perhaps a first experience is like that for everyone. She seemed to know what she was doing but maybe she didn't realise it had happened either!

Sex is so often the chemistry set for romantic love – delusion and disappointment. My virginity and my heart were taken for the first time. Over the next few months, Nicola became my "real" girlfriend. I felt very good.

I never understood why other girls said that she was a slut; she was beautiful to me. Sisters learn to disrespect each other at an early age.

One day, quite unexpectedly, she told me that she had decided to stay with her other "real" boyfriend. She had been dishonest with me to get what she needed.

I was dumped.

My eyes glazed. My fullness departed as my held breath seeped out. It felt like the end of the world as my heart broke closed.

I was off food for weeks. My soul wrinkled. I was confused as to how another person, a woman, could cause so much joy and yet so much pain in me. I was innocent with those feelings, and I suffered. A lesson was initiated that would take years to learn... That it is actually okay to suffer, okay to be vulnerable, okay to love, okay to be with whatever arises in life.

Fortunately a heartbroken man is attractive to other women.

PG-18

Reader, let's follow the tracks of my original wounding back into the forest with a sharpened curiosity.

We all have within us a sexual essence that has a masculine and a feminine principle. The health of these principles determines how we behave in the world. We could say that if our masculine-feminine are fully aligned then we have a healthy essence. If we are nurtured and educated by healthy masculine role models then all is well. I didn't receive love for my inner-masculine from any of the male elders of my youth. It was just how it was.

I grew up in a patriarchal religion. It deemed that highest power is vested in a formless masculine god and that being good required denial of the flesh. My parents inferred that the ways of my body were bad and I believed them. I was taught to be shameful, secretive and fearful of my sexual impulse, to be guilty about what it had me do. My parents hadn't mastered their own evolution. They had inherited their sex-opinions from their parents and so on. All damage is ancestral legacy.

Why didn't people talk openly about those beautiful parts of our nature? Who could I have turned to for healthy answers?

I didn't talk about sex with my mother. She had deferred herself to other women-kind to teach her son about sex and romantic love. I was to be initiated into the ways of sexual relations with women by boys and girls of my own age. It was all innocent, instinctual learning and growing but it was imbued with inherited mind-stuff and the shameful opinions of others.

War, illness or an addiction can cause a father to hide or be absent. My father was working too hard to keep his ship afloat; he was only occasionally present. I loved him but I was remote from him. As a teenager he shared his expectations of how I should relate to women. No son of my father should be an openly sexual being. He made fun of me for having girl friends and further ridiculed me for the broken hearts they left behind. Masturbation, girlfriends, the coursing of lusty-feelings weren't regarded as "well-functioning" behaviour. I felt bad for the way sexual energy manifested through me and did everything possible to avoid the blushing-beetroot embarrassments that he so relished. I needed to be free of his expectations. Attempts to communicate my sensitive feelings to the big people only resulted in more shame. A dad who is loving, interested and understanding in these matters is a rare man.

Unconsciously I decided to bury my treasures to keep them safe. Love of my sexuality was banished to the far flung provinces of my personality; where it was to stay for the next thirty years. What others, especially my parents and one day my wife, didn't know about me they couldn't judge. The repressed lives in the unconscious and gets manifested in the body, our adult eroticism and our politics. We then lose respect for women and the earth... and eventually ourselves. The seeds of subterfuge were planted.

So sex was where my wound lay. I was far from unique in a generation that is so disconnected from the feminine. For another it could be denial of love, loss, grief, joy or anger. The relationship I developed with my sex as a child was taken with me into adulthood.

Thus I was seamlessly integrated into the collective sexual numbness of my culture... A sexually repressed culture that is perpetually permeated by sexualised media imagery. No doubt it would have been different had I been a Latin or Thai. But doesn't every culture, every religion have a thing about sex?

What if we lived in a world where there were Sex Chefs on television? There are so many TV Chefs showing us how to have outrageously sensory experiences with food; but what about our sexuality, the most exquisite of sensory experiences. Where are the chefs to show us the recipes for being masterly lovers? Fine lovemaking is a high-art-form that requires dedication, mutual committed interest and a lot of practice.

I found myself at a college party under a sleeping bag cuddling and seducing little blond Alison. Her shyness had melted nicely. Alison was average, flossy-haired and innocent. We had no agenda; our sex gods were playing. When we play we aren't trying to accomplish anything. Thrilling feelings moved in me as I repeatedly caressed her warm navel and then slid down to give her a fingering. She was an unusually sensitive girl, sometimes having orgasms within a few seconds of being touched. Spine-wriggling, her legs quivered like jelly.

'I've never been touched this way,' she shared over a heated breath. I didn't let on that I had never touched that way. We were surrendered in sexual play. Sex without agenda was magical.

Dave appeared in the doorway. 'Ben, Jane wants you to go sleep with her. I think she's got the hots for you.'

Arrrgh, what to do? Jane was a gorgeous skinny brunette, daughter of landed Canadian ex-pats. She always (sexily) looked like she had just emerged from a long lie-in. She had seen me with Alison and had avoided me for most of the evening... What to do? Arrgh!

No gracious departure from Alison was possible.

The following morning, Jane wouldn't speak to me. She stood on my foot as she air-kissed a goodbye. That was an early insight into the competitive nature of woman.

I found Jane very attractive. She played on my mind; the ache of unsatisfied desire. A few days later I contacted her and arranged a meet.

We met. We kissed.

The ancients affirmed that our breath is our spirit, a kiss is the uniting of souls. A golden cording that would last a lifetime was woven into my life tapestry in that moment.

I was besotted with her. Within days we fell in love.

A week or so later Jane returned to her family in Montreal and we commenced a long-distance relationship.

Sex Ed

The essence of a woman, her magical energetic aura, is attractive to a man no matter how she is dressed. The subtle fragrance of her essence will fill a room, but not in the olfactory sense. It will be detected, tracked and followed by men – so that they can find their way back home, home to loved-wholeness. The home that men so unknowingly desire is deep inside a woman's heart. It is womb-like and filled with a universally radiant loving-mother presence. Directions to her home cannot be asked-for, as a woman does not know the way herself. A woman's inner-ways are too infinite and magical to be understood by a scheming mind, especially her own. Every woman is a mystery.

I was a playful spirit during my beach-town University days. Life was happening to me. I was out looking for a shag. We were soon partying-hard in a smoky basement cavern. Was it serendipity or fucking lucky that Suzie was at the club that night? Her tantalising presence had caught my eye and I proceeded to fancy her at a safe distance while posing with my friends. She looked "beyond reach" but her essence beckoned me. Her home called me to find a way in.

Momentarily bored of her posse of cool-guys, she took in the room. She dared me to look her in the eye. Wow, she was actually interested in me. It wasn't long before we struck up a banter. I shared stories with her about a 400 kilometre hike I had just completed. Going out into the world and accomplishing something, anything, makes you attractive to a woman. Perhaps the cool-guys had been too busy being cool to go and accomplish something. Seduction is always charm and persuasion. She let me get closer. She knew what would happen next, as her answers had become clever.

We were soon strolling in silence along the seafront. It was a perfect summer's evening and teen adventure.

Suzie was a fresh faced maiden with chocolate brown eyes. Her blue jeans hung off her hips, often exposing her fit midriff.

Our sauntering became a hug as we found our way to the arches by the pier. Happiness arose in me as we shared a lingering close-up, kissing and fondling experimentally. I liked the taste of ale and teenage-sweetness on her breath. I wasn't trembling from fear, it was from exhilaration. My hands wandered onto her creamy buttocks expressing both yearning and gratitude. Hers was an ass to behold, and behold I did. In that moment I became an ass man. Men have preference, tits or ass, why is that?

Opening my shirt buttons, she glided her small fingers over my chest hairs and then held her face against my heart. My excitement was apparent, yet her treasure was so concealed. We melted into the soundtrack of gently breaking waves.

It was late and we agreed to meet again.

A few days later we reconvened for a dinner date. We conversed about her problems with boyfriends and the meaning of the Universe. Torrential rain meant the walk home across town was a challenge. It was late and she offered shelter which was gratefully received. There were eighty four steps in the climb up to her rented attic room atop a seafront terrace.

We undressed as far as our underwear. Her knickers were small, turquoise and covered with love-hearts. I loved it when my girl stripped as far as her undies, much more could be anticipated. We lay under the duvet spooning for a while, to keep warm. We laughed about my knobbly knees. We cuddled until the wee hours smooching, stroking and fawning. I played with her necklace while listening to her dreams and woes. I gently voyaged over her pleasant body. She was touched almost everywhere, though not through the barrier of her knickers.

Persuaded by her aching curiosity her resolve fractured. She slipped her knickers off. Our time together had allowed her to feel safe; she had moved through some fears. It had been a long seduction and she had finally opened. Tired and exhausted, my energy dropped away. As a young man it is devastating to have a floppy dick when you most need it.

'It's okay Ben. Will you just hold me; just let me feel your warm body against mine.'

She was a far bigger woman than my squirming ego appreciated. I dropped my angst. In acceptance, a light is shone on experience and it is no longer dark. I was happy to oblige her simplest need and cuddle her for what was left of the night. A few more layers of her feminine essence were opened. I learned that the sex that a man can give to a woman does not always have to be penetrative or involve genitals.

A few days later we reconvened and she was in a playful mood. After a fun evening of flirty dance we retreated to her flat. She threw me a dirty smile as she locked the door behind us. We had nowhere to go and nothing to achieve.

Her short pleated skirt was off within minutes. She sat on a desk as we necked each other, kissing passionately. Her hands started to un-tuck me, she wasn't hanging around. Her halter top came off then her bra. Things were accelerating, I felt very dressed; she was way ahead of me. She stood up, leaving a moist streak on the blotting paper where she had been sitting. She tore her knickers off as she bridled me across the room. She fell back onto the bed and pulled my head between her legs. She was swollen and juicy. Holding me tightly in position she enforced my lick. It was my first taste – sweet like an apricot. Mouthing her soft lips, I knew what to do, it was innate.

Orgasm. I gave her an orgasm.

Then we flew together. That moment went on and on.

She laid there naked under white sheets bathed in the first gentle shafts of morning sunlight. Curves and shadows canvassed her high definition radiance; she was a work of art. Nakedness isn't erotic; Eros flows when nakedness is obscured.

She continued with her education of me.

'Ben, you aren't very experienced with women are you?'

I didn't know what I didn't know. If I wanted more of her I had to get over her directness and allow her to be the expert. Suzie was my first real teacher, but then every woman is a teacher, especially when she is giving from the hearth of love at her core.

Men can become great in the sack if women take the time to teach them about what feels good.

Suzie taught me that to be wholly vital is to be sexual. Over the next few months I had an education. Stripping, dancing, teaching, fucking. She was an orgasmic woman; I thought all women would be like her. She loved to help herself to several orgasms and with finessed timing she would deny me mine. She shared her expectations of my worship of her. Then when she was ready she would bring me off. I was in service to her. Make no mistake, I was there to serve. My reward for such duties was the unleashing of a youthful poet... And a sore cock.

To have been lost in my head when making love to Suzie would have been a fall from heaven. Though she got lost in her head several times in a different way... One night when laying in our after-glow she told me that she had cum so deeply because she had been fantasizing about her boyfriend back at home. Another layer of the gateau of woman was revealed and my ego was bruised. Fantasies about your absent lover hey? It would be years before I would do that.

The women of my early years were so confident and in their power. Perhaps they came to show me something about my own male essence? Each relationship I had revealed nuances about myself... When I cared to notice them. But sometimes what a woman had to show me would feel too-hot and I would bugger off. At least until life arranged for another teacher to appear and show me the same lesson. I now know that the completion of every lesson would allow me to return to peace.

Over the next few months Suzie and I almost fell in love.

Sadly our friendship fell apart with some high drama at a party. Suzie's glamour-pus friend Crystal came bursting into the bathroom while I was taking a pee. It was a blonde moment.

'Ooops... oooh, nice... I'll wait til you've finished darling... Sorry, my new pill is making me so psychotic Ben.'

While she waited, she let her diminutive cocktail dress fall to the floor... She had decided to upstage Suzie. Her eyes spoke "you want some of what I've got?"

'What do you think of my lingerie Ben?' Seeking approval, she postured her body suggestively as if doing a glamour shoot. 'I bought it all in the city today, lovely isn't... I need to buy lingerie for myself, until a real man comes into my life to buy me some.'

'You look stunning Crystal,' I drooled approvingly. She then proceeded to undo her bra to display her pert breasts and her perfect nipples. I stroked her as she arched herself towards me. 'Absolutely stunning.'

She was gagging for more. She smelt good. Some women may give their body away, they may even give you their pussy to sniff, lick and fuck. When they do that though they are usually disconnected from their bodies and their goddess nature. Many women are disconnected from their bodies during sex, especially a naive young woman unschooled or unaware of the magic of the feminine powers she contains. I shouldn't have been fooled by a woman who was giving away a fuck for she wasn't letting me get any closer to her inner sanctums of infinite love; she was just getting her hole filled.

Crystal's sex teeth dug in; some women love to bite. Some love to scratch. That kind of woman can get you found out.

'Mmmmm, you smell so good. I love the smell of a real man.' It was a hot evening.

'Lovely as you are, you need to stop baby.'

'Lemme just taste you baby, c'mon lemme, just a little taste, I can tell that you want me.' Competition amongst girls is subtle.

Suzie walked in.

We were complete.

Honesty

Some life events are turning points.

As a young man honesty was very important to me. It was in my nature to be true and say things for how I saw them. I had spoken truth through my childhood and learnt that adults often didn't want to hear it. They may have even responded violently causing feelings in me that I would have rather not felt.

Jane and I had become a long-distance item while I was at Uni. It was important to me that we had no secrets. Naively I decided to tell her about my fun times with Suzie. I told her that Suzie was a hot little lover and we had had much fun together. I shared how she had played with my heart... such was my innocence. It wasn't what she wanted to hear. Jane went *mental*. She was horrified and inconsolable with rage. Her beauty evaporated exposing her neediness and controlling possessiveness. She wasn't pretty. Honesty wasn't profitable. My words weren't violent, just true. I had seen that kind of rage years before when my dad blew up at me. Maybe Jane had learned how to do rage from her father? She told me in no uncertain terms to abandon my experiments with growing up and to love *only* her.

My innocence was crushed into an aching core of uncertainty with the world. As a child I learned that the best response to a violent onslaught was to not let it happen again – to disguise myself and my emotions and go underground.

Perhaps I should have left her then. I wasn't man enough or emotionally mature enough to be true to myself and continue to speak my mind; to set my boundaries. I reconfirmed that telling the truth gets you beaten up. That episode cast a long shadow over my life.

But teenage love had me, Jane had me. I went back in, I liked her love of me; even if it meant I had to lie to get it.

That was the end of truthfulness with women.

All is Sex

I noticed her close by. She sat on the edge of a granite water trough, beautiful glorious – creation. She was soon accompanied by her boyfriend. They shimmied for a while cooing and wooing. Her lover, was resplendent in fine plume, he danced big for her. She was soon ready to be laid, to be procreated with and by. Their Tao simply was.

He jumped her, and in a fluster the deed was done. She was done. No problem.

The two doves flew away. Some bees flew by.

The amber dawn continued its illumination.

Meaning is the domain of the mind; no dove-mind put meaning on that sexual act or even cared. Humans place meaning on sex. Sex is just a word.

Reader, as a grown man my yearning to engage fully with life has lead me to discover Tantra. I have become dedicated to uniting my heart, my sex and my consciousness; indeed this writing is an inherent part of that process.

Contrary to popular belief, Tantra isn't all licentious sex and genital utopia. It isn't a religion and there's nothing to believe. Tantra supports the unfolding of potential and teaches that *all* facets of life are stepping stones to the expansion of consciousness. It's a way of life, an experiential path of practice whereby we first work on ourselves, then our relationships and eventually our surroundings. Tantra is a matriarchal path. It is only when we redress our relationship to the feminine that we can heal our relationship to the Earth. Tantra is fully inclusive of every aspect of our being, including the body and all that it does.

Tantra is for everyone and doesn't require beards or robes. It is a powerfully transformative path for the bravest warriors of the heart, the most passionate seekers of Truth. It is a vehicle for realizing and experiencing who you truly are. It is a path of awareness, healing and pleasure. It isn't a well-trodden path.

Let's look at awareness. To become our true nature we must be aware of ourselves and our world. In awareness we can see that sex is all around us at all times, for sex *is* nature. It is intrinsic to all birth and all death. It is *the* phenomenon that brings us into being and then proceeds to shape our lives. Surely it makes sense for us to align with nature at all times? We *are* nature. It is our disconnection from nature that instils emptiness; when we live as an embodiment of nature we become interconnected and balanced with all life at all times. In awareness I can see that my body is my home, it is sacred and natural. My body is the place where I can experience myself as the pure nature that I am. My nature is Love.

Let's look at healing. The healing gifts of Tantric practice polishes away preference or disgust and exposes a joyous spacious equanimity with all of life. Peace is only possible when we have complete acceptance of all that is; including acceptance of ourselves. For us to meet our true nature we must be free from ourselves. Free of any pain and suffering that may be triggered by life, by reality, by this book.

Suffering arises when reality doesn't meet our expectations; we are all attached to reality being a certain way. Healing the psyche is a prerequisite to the freedom that Tantra offers. Reader, as we deepen our intimacy, you shall witness me grappling with guilt, judgement and right-relationship. They are locked psychic energies that need healing. For example, I might feel shame when sex wishes to be expressed, for my culture has told me that it is bad. Shame is the sensation that who I am is bad; it is secretive silent and judged. I might feel guilt when I share my sexual body with another and somebody else has deemed it unacceptable -- perhaps when somebody else has claimed dominion over my truest nature. Guilt is the sensation that I did something bad. The dark swamp of guilt and shame is epidemic in our peoples. Guilt and shame both restrict the flow of sexual energy.

Alchemy takes place when I shine light into the swamp of my soul. As I share hidden nooks and crannies of my male sexuality with you, any embarrassment or shame that *I* might have held is replaced with freedom. The more I reveal the more freedom

I have; with less to hide there's less worry about being found out. The critic doesn't matter as I become authentic. My authenticity then enriches intimacy with my beloved Angelica.

In healing we become aware of boundaries and asserting them. Tantra helps us attune to inner guidance on when and how to have sex. The shift in consciousness that Tantra offers could profoundly empower new generations of young people. It offers life-tools that radically change the way that people relate to each other. Imagine if every boy practiced ejaculatory-choice! How would that impact teen pregnancy statistics? So many teen sex stories are like my own and of the form, "it just happened" or "I was pushed into it" or "I had to be drunk". So sad, sex is such a beautiful thing.

Let's look at pleasure. For us to meet our truest nature we must realise our innate joy. **Tantra is a way of living whereby things are glorified just because they are.** It leads us to direct experience of and the purest realisation that we are Love... and Love is very yummy indeed. By expanding my love and my awareness, Tantra has enabled me to see the gifts that I bring to the world. It's beautiful teachings affect how I eat, make love and express my feelings. The path ultimately leads to pleasure. Tantric practice has often fried my circuits with pleasure-overwhelm.

Many of the stories I share could have been told by your father, your son, your partner or brother.

Reader, your own experiences as a sexual being will be different to mine. Nonetheless the tantric perspective I offer may support your own evolution as it is powerful medicine for all ills. Tantra has something for everybody, even if your sex god has departed or for whatever reason you don't do sex. Tantra requires that you change; but many people are uncomfortable with change, they don't want to get better. The momentum of mediocrity is what we have all grown used to. There's nothing mediocre about Tantra.

Why would a man want to read this book, for some titillation maybe? Or perhaps he thought he could learn how to be a Sex

God? Men will be curious of a teaching that shows them how they can make love all day, but they won't want to do the dedicated practice to attain such skill. Our culture has conditioned men to be attracted to acts that disrespect or abuse women in some way. Domination gives us men a sense of control over nature; it is non-cooperation. Our need to dominate is probably based on our insecurity, our emptiness. We don't know its root and most men are making little effort to discover it. Many of the ideas I share will be threatening to men, for Tantra calls men to engage with their healthiest essences... But, we men are being called to evolve; to wake up and embrace the highest potential of our masculinity. In the future men will no longer be able to use domination and war as proof of their masculinity. Masculinity will be measured by real courage, authentic communication and humility.

Man - you can feel that Mother Earth is calling, she's a damsel in distress. We know that the old ways are broken. Some brothers will step forwards to be counted in, but most will be fearful as Tantra requires that they are honest with themselves and their loved ones. Maybe they know that loads of shit and psychological vulnerability will come up. Men associate vulnerability with weakness, and we men don't like to be perceived as weak. I've recently learned that the only way we can find our way back to each other is to be vulnerable. Being vulnerable requires us to take emotional risk, to expose our true nature and to embrace uncertainty. Being vulnerable isn't weakness, it is courage. It is essential to wholehearted living.

So, most men will avoid Tantra. They will try to diffuse the momentum of this shift in consciousness. It is far easier to have a quick wank, go get a beer and watch a ball game instead. But men, what ties us is deeper than what divides us. Our hearts know that there is no business to be done on a dead planet. The rental tenancy we have on earth will come to an end if we do not change our ways.

What part of us is it that thinks we are not utterly connected to everything? What is its agenda?

Women too will be distrustful of my ideas as they aren't used to a man sharing so truthfully... But that would be their conditioning, born of being raised by unhealthy-masculine elders. But let's not deny our truest nature; surely it makes sense for us to align with nature at all times? If you have a tendency to outlaw ideas in your head without trying, read on.

I have been fortunate to have teachers along the way; masters who came into my life to share their core-splitting insights into the great wisdom traditions, teaching me to love myself and love women. The truths that they taught me were so true! Masters *are* Truth, not people. There were many teachers in my life; I refer to all those masters collectively as my teacher[ii].

But did they really teach me anything or was it all remembering?

Tantra is the marriage of energy and consciousness. Its teachings didn't appear in my life until my forties. The story that I'm sharing with you would have been very different if I had been taught that my body and my sex were sacred. The story for most men would be different.

I learned the hard way, I was a testosterone driven fucker...

---

ii   A full list of teachers, modern-day sages and wise people who influenced this writing can be found at the end of this book.

The Bar

Life calls us to dance with it. Our dance can embody a rejecting rigidity or it can be like an accepting liquid that flows with life. How do you dance with life Reader? During my days at the bar I experimented with acceptance. I flowed with whatever showed up in my life. My ease allowed me to grow up without damage.

Blondie was blaring above the din of the busier than usual bar. A warm summer evening brings both swarming ants and drinkers outdoors. It also brings parades of sweet young things in airy little dresses. Older women in summer dresses are alluring too – I saw one in town just yesterday, so noble and still very sexy. Though it's no substitute for warm bodied contact, I love to savour a woman in a pretty summer dress. Jiggling hugged buttocks and god given fine lines will attract every man not caught in his head. Perhaps it's the same kind of attraction a woman might get when she drives behind a fit young man on a bike.

I was caught in my head mixing cocktails at the bar. I hadn't noticed the two girls in scanty summer dresses sitting close by. They'd been having a right old laugh for most of the evening. Their perfume hit me in the face as they ordered another round of drinks.

'Hey gorgeous, would you like one too?' one of them said with a big white smile. 'We've been watching you, you look thirsty!'

I had to decline, the bar manager was around. 'I can't just yet lovely, maybe when we close?'

'Okay, we'll be here!'

Closing time eventually arrived with the usual herding of late night drinkers. I was tired and still recovering from a night with Katie. My body would have rather hit the hay.

'Let us take you for a little post-work drink,' the tall brunette declared.

Can a tired butterfly resist the nectar filled flower?

'Hi, my name's Tara and this is my friend Tiff.'

All they were selling was what they looked like.

You can never guess how your life may evolve by saying "yes" to life. I wasn't one to turn down gifts that showed up. I looked her over, I found the delicate bracelet on her small wrists attractive and I liked her forthright way.

'Sure, let's go, where do you have in mind?' I said smilingly.

Tiff was tall and slender with a dark perm. She worked in a fashion store. The somewhat stubborn Tara was a bank clerk and could have been her sister but with straight hair – *and* midnight blue eyeliner. Together they were an advert for tart high-fashion. My dick appeared to be attracted to tart energy, and I followed it.

Women, don't be fooled into thinking that this is a story about a self-indulgent man who just follows his dick. Men don't be fooled that this is a story that gives permission for you to abscond the fulfilment of your responsibilities, to go follow your dick. Remember, at that stage of life I was a young man unconsciously following my sexual and cultural programming.

There's something alluring about a tart. Tart or goddess, a woman chooses how she dresses. A woman has control over the outermost physical layers of her feminine essence; she can choose how that essence is displayed and radiated to the world around her. This outermost layer is given away for free. At different times of a woman's life she hides or gives away different aspects of herself to men and women around her. She may give it away in a bikini, a summer dress, goddess robes or a burqa. Some women give away free pictures of their breasts or perhaps even their gaping dry-vagina, but most are culturally tempered to only give away their precious outer layer. For example they may wear a business layer during the day (mimicking a male power dresser) and then a worn-out-woman-comfy-leisure-suit with pink fluffy slippers by night. But no matter what is given away, it is only ever the outermost layer.

I had a perm of my own-kind that night, a permanent and very stiff erection, which frankly couldn't be hidden through my white linen trousers. It was very embarrassing. The stiffy as he became known was adopted like a pet by the girls. He became a target of much amusement over the next few hours; he just wouldn't politely bow down. We drank and danced and drank and danced. They were all over me and their dresses beckoned me to be all over them.

It has always been peak pleasure to seduce a girl by slipping your hand down her trousers. Anticipation is such a pungent aphrodisiac and it's rarely stronger than in the access-freeing moment that a trouser button pops open or a zip is unpeeled. Breaths are held as the knicker-frontier is breached. But a slinky little dress, sheer and clingy requires a different approach whereby exposed smooth legs and inner thighs magnetically attract and guide you towards the treasure.

'You look tired Ben, let's take you home and get you tucked into bed!'

I sat between them for the ten minute jolly across town. We were all silent. My hands were fawning over hips and approving of their little buns. They responded by nursing the stiffy. We took it in turns to kiss each other. I could feel their fresh energy, it felt invigorating. Three musical notes played together allow so much more creative expression especially when harmonies are achieved.

We arrived back at their flat, entering via a flight of stairs, we passed various alcoves containing plastic flowers. I was to be their quarry for the night. Settling down, they let it be known that they were in charge. My arms were soon pinned down by Tiff's legs, as she knelt on me. Her crotch in my face smelt hot. They stripped me from the waist down. I didn't want to stop them. What a relief when the stiffy was freed.

I could feel their girl power, how they enjoyed ruling over me. They were great together. It was edgy, I'm certain there were subtle revenge issues playing out. I was naked and they were both fully dressed. They took it in turns to wank me hard and suck me. They felt aggressive in the way they were handling me; it was bondage without cuffs. I was having my first insights into the magic possible when being in bed with two girls. I am certain that such an intense threesome as this had magical properties that washed and bathed my soul. The seed was sown, and I had to learn more about this high-art of sexual joy in future years.

the sex god | 37

At times during their enforced wank I took what was rightfully mine, as sex is my own responsibility. I thought Tiff's damp pantied crotch was going to suffocate me – which was good. They worked me hard and I experienced a new level of sexual intensity. But a side effect of intense pleasure is fear. We can stop receiving if we feel we are having too much pleasure. They made me cum, pulling me off in unison. I was sweating and noisy. My ejaculation went everywhere... Didn't they know they should stop wanking me after I've cum? It was as if they had a plan all along! Geeez. Laughter broke out, it was too much. Like crying and orgasm, laughter allows energy to move. It was all fun after all. Nothing sinister.

Tiff and Tara negotiated with each other over who should have me first, they both wanted it. The tired spent boy-man that I was. It was begrudgingly agreed Tara would go first. Confirming her femininity, Tiff's demeanour changed like the wind.

'I think he's cheating on his bird Tara. He thinks that just because he's got a thing hangin' between his legs that he's so much better than us girls.'

'Oh come on Tiff, we agreed! Not again.' Tara was more interested in eating her desert.

'If he's going to cheat then why doesn't he do respectful cheating, I think women know how to respectfully cheat... I'm just going to get some air and a ciggy. I'll leave you two to it.' Tiff left the flat.

'I think she wanted you all to herself.... But now you are mine,' Tara added with a cheeky smile.

'... and there was me thinking you were both going to give me the privilege of a full on fucking threesome!'

We went to Tara's room. In the laughter and light things softened between us. We entered the unknown together. Sex is magic without structure. I removed her from her sticky lingerie, an action that leads to stronger drugs.

Using Suzie's teachings, I took up position between her thighs and suckled. She tasted delicious. She was very hairy. I liked it hairy. Hairy is natural, raw and primal, hairy is animal like.

We were irresistible for each other. I spent a long time giving and imbibing. The feedback of her groans confirmed to me when I had her in intensity. I liked it down there – I'm certain I got *high* down there.

She eventually sat up, exhausted. 'Ben aren't you going to fuck me?'

Oh yes, *that's* what she wants! I bent her over.

'Ow ow o wow o wow... you are hurting me!' Her face grimaced. I was in my own selfish groove and being too quick to lovingly open her up. I thought she just wanted a hard fuck.

'Slow down baby, go softly at first.' She grabbed my cock and took control.

We spent the next twenty minutes trying to fuck. She really gripped me. For some reason our thrusting geometry filled her up with air way too easily. We were dancing in union, but her farting pussy held us apart.

'Sorry baby.' We laughed so hard we crumpled into each other. I am certain that it was nature's way of balancing the energy of the moment. Every few thrusts of tight comfort and another spluttering fart.

'Sorry baby.' We couldn't find a position that worked and our flame was eventually blown out.

I lay down and Tara flopped naked on top of me, she was so light. I did wonder if I was going to have Tiff next, but alas it wasn't to be.

We had desperately tried to fuck like they did it in the movies. But laughter got in the way. Joy is experienced when we enter the lyrical with our lover. If we hadn't have laughed-hard the stuck energy of a primetime rejection would have wounded. Laughter heals in the bedroom and all of life. It came from a deep waters and it allowed us to both accept each other lovingly. Through laughter our authenticity was shared. Our acceptance of each other allowed us to avoid resistance, separateness and fear. The impersonal nature of sexual desire comes with the fantasised "promise" of perfection – how often is that promise fulfilled?

Let's remember that sex can sometimes lead to disappointment or disaffection or even disease.

Our incessant efforts to make things what they are not are the source of most suffering. Effort is required to swim against the flow of life as it arises. Accepting and adoring a woman for who she is, is the greatest gift a man can give her; even when she's being ordinary. Acceptance has great prizes for us in every aspect of our lives. Surrendering to what is present in every moment, being with whatever is arising in each moment, unconditionally, allows us to reconnect with the juicy flow of life. This is true whether we are going down on each other for the first time or waiting for a long-overdue train. When we come together as lovers, without any inner resistance to each other, the real experience of Love can shine through. Anytime we have expectation that differs from reality we shall suffer, and our connection and lovemaking shall suffer.

Tiff and Tara were a turning point in my relationship to women and sex – I felt at home as a sexual being. Those were fun, free times – though I must say that my innocence was starting to dissipate. I felt as though I was on auto-pilot. Beyond testosterone performing its function, I was driven to be sexually available for women. The sex god was a free spirit. Meeting, seducing, loving and fucking was all I really wanted to do; a nascent part of my being was starting to become conscious of that.

I saw Tara in a bar a few months later and we exchanged some polite though awkward words.

'Although you didn't get in touch again, Ben you were very influential in my life in a bizarre way – so thank you. I'll always think of you with affection... and perhaps regret.'

She left a smile behind as she departed with friends.

The sex god shapes our lives.

I'm certain she was pregnant.

the sex god

Who or what is "the sex god"? If the sex god were me then this book would be called The Sex God. In some of the stories herein you may think that I behaved like a Sex God or perhaps an asshole. But a Sex God persona I do not profess to be. I am simply Ben, an ordinary man, with plenty of sexual energy. Many people assume there is something wrong with being a sexual being and therein lies social malady.

For millions of years a primal urge of man was to shag as many women as they could. Life was dangerous, they needed to spread seed quickly and then return to the hunting grounds; to feed their women. It was better that they were unemotional else the constant departure, loneliness and killing of cute animals would render them useless. During that time women were left behind to eat; eating was good for ovulation, pregnancy and breast feeding; survival of our species. In the absence of men, women developed emotional intelligence that fostered community.

So here we are in the second millennia and our world is very different to the one that our ancestors inhabited. When we acknowledge that we have within us primal animal urges as well as sacred propensity we can embrace our whole self.

For years my sex god was adolescently benign, it brought fun, joy, gifts, growth, innocence and healing into my life. But as I grew older it became a reckless god, a force majeure.

If we are to become more intimate with the sex god I must study him deeply. I have been highly trained in meditation techniques and the art of witnessing the ever-changing subtle-phenomenon of the human condition. Let me share what I found...

I think about sex a lot. Perhaps the sex god comprises of thoughts – that are generally of a grasping or satiated nature. I have seen that thoughts are visitors, they come and go. I sometimes label my thoughts as good or bad.

But what is behind my sex god thoughts?

Feelings? I have witnessed sex god feelings that appear to precede my thoughts. Maybe the sex god is a feeling that brings about thought. The sex god gushes forth like a serpent to take its quarry and it will then retreat, drugged and engorged on its prey. The sex god felt most happy that I fucked Tara for example. I have the sense that the sex god feelings are not mine, they are not me. The sex god is a visitor that comes and goes like a wave with a rhythm all its own.

In the interests of taking a radical look at how I function, let's go deeper. Feelings are ever changing energy. I have seen that what might be called my personality is in fact many layers of energy — delicate, tender energies as well as powerful, dominating energies. When you pay attention to the energies within, you notice that you're not actually in charge of them; you don't have any choice except to be moved by them. I have sat down for several meditations to watch and suss the energies of the sex god. Reader, this is what I have found... The sex god is not who I am, rather it is an impersonal creative force. Like a glittering diamond it has many facets: healer, creator, animal, giver and receiver. It comes from that beyond-ness that thoughts and feelings originate from. You don't have to be a meditator to know what I mean. Energies within us affect our mood and feelings. You don't have to be a student of Buddhist metaphysics to sense this. I went deeper into those feelings looking for the origin of the sex god, my enquiry went to a place that is deeper than my own ability to reason. I was left simply as the witness of arising feelings, those adamant energies. But where do those energies come from?

To explain, I must use the concept of Source. The sex god arises from Source, the womb of all creation. Source is the mysterious source of all existence; that which has no name and is unimaginably wise and good. We don't know what it is, where it is going or why it is the way it is. As life arises from Source, the great Tao, life lives through us and thus Truth unfolds. For certain, we only ever pretend we have some control over it. We have no control over the energies that move within. If you are alive then energies will arise from Source to move and shape you. Those energies are like gods. It is as if we have many gods within us that animate us and live through us.

One of my gods, *my sex god,* is particularly omnipotent and it uses me to its own end. This unusual god is a motivational force that cannot be exiled. It's an irresistible urge for union with my opposite energy polarity. It's also a wonky force fuelled by nature itself, by karmic entanglements from the past or by wounded psychosis and addictive urgency. Sometimes the surging agenda of the sex god cannot be overcome. It causes dense identification with its need. Its agendas are many and varied including giving, addiction, healing, guiding my life and most importantly **taking me home to wholeness**; the sex god wishes to give to a woman so deeply that the hearth-flower of her soul is opened so she can take me home.

As a man I am perpetually one half of the whole, I long for the end of duality. The sex god propels me towards the end of duality and no power on earth will stop it. My heart's yearning to love and be loved can become one with my lovers' yearning to love and be loved – and so there may be wholeness.

Can I function autonomously and independent of the sex god that is so rooted into my soul? Can I function freely according to my own intrinsic nature? Perhaps, we shall see.

Polarity

As I reflected on what I was about to write, the urge surged. I couldn't resist it. I had to have a wank. I kidded myself that a carnal fantasy would prepare me to share such an honest story about sex.

My teacher says I shouldn't wank so often, she says I should exercise the choice to conserve my man-essence. She informs me that I should use an art-form to transform my sexual energy into a creative manifestation – for sexual energy is our rawest power. Well Reader, I'm a wayward erotic spirit and I wanked... So perhaps this particular story will not be as inspiringly pungent as it could have been. Sorry, it is my manner.

This body is all I have.

Unquestionably my body was designed to touch and be touched; by life. It is a body of sensory awareness through which all reality is tasted – through the lens of my conditioning.

My body has awareness; a formidable instrument. It is an instrument of engagement with the present moment. Reader, for so much of life the present moment is a parallel Universe, wouldn't you agree? I have a primal choice available to me so long as I am breathing and not in deepest sleep. I have the choice of where to direct my awareness. My energy flows where my attention goes. Whatever our awareness is pointed towards becomes real experience for us; very profound. That is how we touch life, and real life touches us. If my awareness is pointed towards my mind, then I have an unreal experience. Truest happiness can only be found in reality, from whatever is arriving through our senses in each moment. Any other happiness is an egoic approximation.

By coming into my body I can be with life. I can feel utterly alive, fully here. I can be. I can be fucking juicy.

Alcohol screws with your awareness and your senses. I had drunk more than I cared for. I needed some respite from the party revelry that was going off with a bang in the ballroom downstairs.

I found a quiet room where I could replenish myself. Sitting on the floor against a sofa, I dozed off to sleep...

I was awoken abruptly by her foot which had been caressing up the inside of my thigh. She sat reclined on the floor opposite me stroking my feet. She was a babe in her time and was enduring a golden autumn. I had a culturally determined reaction inside but was outwardly cool.

'Are you okay? I was worried about you and I thought I'd better come find you.' She smiled knowingly.

Almost an aunt to me, we looked at each other across our thirty-year gap. In spite of her age, the charm of her womanhood hadn't departed. I was caught in aroused aspic.

'Is there *anything* I can do for you?' It was the voice of a woman yearning to be touched. She wasn't pretty, but she was available.

Barbara's lusty manner was unexpected as she had always been so "proper". Women need a reason to have sex. Was she drugged up on chick-lit or were her husband's pants welded on? *She* was acting out; there was no disarming her. My gender was apparent. Her stockinged toes moved to knead my crotch. An uncomfortable pressure built there as my youthful cock swelled towards the unbelievable encounter that was evolving.

'Carry on, that feels nice.' Armouring petals around her heart unfurled. My heart raced. The door was ajar to the party.

Her older-woman's perfume was opiate and her soothing voice was entrancing. I had a flash back to the sights I stole from Mrs. Honey several years back. Would Barbra look like her? The young girls I had been with thus far were an education, but somehow I knew that an older woman would be exotic, a different education. I was generally comfortable with feeling uncomfortable especially in service of the sex god. But what if I was caught? We adjusted our positions, scissor like.

Most men don't have male teachers to educate them on the love-arts; this means that we all learn on the job. We are taught by porn or by women with all their issues; imprinted by their damaged parents, husbands and past lovers. Can you see the pattern here Reader? Unhealthy male-aspects propagate unhealthy male-aspects.

I slid my bare foot up her leg. It was soon bridled on her thigh against the top of her stockings. I was hot and restraining my fearful breath. Like any cool young man who can "handle it" would. Her foot stopped moving and started to press harder, enshrouding the hardness beneath my jeans. Dare I move my foot higher? She was overjoyed that I hadn't grassed or run away. So yes! It was my time to conquest deeper into a much older woman. It would be the same for any young man – at least those brave enough to have stuck around thus far.

Barbs was such a mystery for me. My foot transitioned from lace to the smooth clammy skin of her upper thigh. I love mystery. I rippled my toes. Her breath deepened. Higher still. She stopped moving her foot. The suspense was palpable; her smile dared me to go higher. Sex was shaping our lives. Her tender skin felt hotter the higher I went. I felt pubes at the edge of her knickers. Then my foot slid onto her. Stillness arose. In that moment my awareness was myopically focused on the sensory detail arriving through the sole of my foot. Pure presence. Somehow I had created the capacity to receive this experience.

Through the stillness and her steamy knickers I sensed her doughy mound. I'm certain my foot actually smelt her woody fragrance. We sat kneading each other at a safe distance for several minutes. My toes were skilful enough to have found a loose groove. She groaned, maybe even came. This body is all I have.

Snapping out of delirium we were uncertain as to what would happen next. It didn't feel safe to fuck. She stood up and surrounded me from behind, in one deft move her hand slid down my pubic abdomen and into my jeans. She gripped me tightly with her hand and mature odour. Her bosom against my back was much softer than I expected.

'Thank you,' she whispered, 'I needed that... Thank you for not running away.... it... it has been so long... He doesn't love me in that way anymore.... I really like you, I'm sorry.' She slowly withdrew her hand.

46 | the sex god

What was so alluring to me about an older woman? She had been written-off by her husband to sexually wither. It didn't have to be that way. I knew her husband to be a narrow minded and oppressive man. Such oppression might make a woman bitter to all men. But needs must I suppose. The sex god came to nourish her, and educate me.

I also learned that you can be insanely sexual just off the camera of others. There's something so sexy about exploring a woman at a party under everyone's noses. If the guests had smelt us, we'd have been found out. Encrusted with a psychosis of ethics and appropriate behaviour, I returned downstairs easing myself back into the party.

Rene was straight ahead of me. 'Hey you, you're back. Where have you been? Let's dance.'

Three months later unsatisfied desire conspired to bring Barb and I together again. We found ourselves alone and in the same room. A man is valued by the feelings he causes in a woman. Escalated by the sense of danger I was carrying a lot of nervous energy. I was unsure how to behave but curiosity wasn't going to kill that cat. Contrary to my self-centred ways, sex has never been just about me; she needed to make the first move away from our small-talk.

There is always a fifty-fifty split in any relationship, sexual or otherwise. There are always two realities coming together as two sets of emotions, histories, values, needs and aspirations. It is only through sex that we reveal ourselves fully whatever the energies that are moving through us. We always encounter parts of ourselves in sex. Barb's marital abandonment was meeting my fear of being consumed. But Source had its agenda and always perfectly balances any situation. Our two realities were about to meet and co-mingle. Barb had simple needs and she knew I could meet them. Nature *is* yin-yang manifest, always. There was an interesting and hot polarity between us but I wasn't so sure I should be there.

She fawned over me for a while. 'You have such beautiful eyes.'

Ignition. Sex shapes our lives. We were so quiet, if anyone heard us, what would have happened? There was no time to waste and her wanton whispers guided me to give her what she was aching for... YES, mystery met, my hand clasped between her legs, holding her weighty genitals. More innocence lost. We marinated in her heady fragrances. She whimpered.

'Ahhhhhhh.' Too loud.

Instinctively I explored her. The look on her face transitioned. Perhaps from passion to shame. She was a "proper" woman after all; and proper people don't do that kind of thing. I was shaking, too scared to say anything. She took control, unzipping me and widening her stance. I surrendered to her lust and she pulled me up deep inside her.

I breathed in and held a deep breath that had travelled to me from an enormous distance. Our breath reflects what is going on inside.

Fucking juicy hey Reader?

Fucking painful too perhaps? I am very aware that that sort of grasping, extra-marital dalliance is exactly how the sex god breaks up a family. Any child of a broken family will know the core-splitting pain that results.

But how many infidelities could be avoided if we all talked freely about our sex gods? Why does sex have such dirty-connotation? Why don't we celebrate sex?

Reader, unless we really understand the sex god, people will never heal and our families will forever carry pain... and the ancestral pattern shall repeat. Every generation is granted the power to heal something in its family legacy.

Love of my Life

The first rays of light started to warm our bones. It was a delicious time to make love and to further penetrate our incredibly close, even mystical, relationship. Jane was a sexually free being and sex was all we did when she was in town. There was a lot of sex god play in nature back then, churchyards, river banks, wheat fields and forests. She was often more than I could handle.

I loved her eyes, I loved her childlike heart. She possessed the classic silent beauty of the heroine in a 19th century painting. Our bi-continental love affair somehow defined us.

She was the love of my life.

There is wisdom that I know now, that I didn't know back then. To allow the flower of womankind to unfurl, a woman requires that her man must commit to her. When he shines the light of his committed presence onto her, she will turn to face him. Like a beautiful flower to sunlight with petals partially visible. In commitment a man is allowed to get a step closer to the hearth of her infinite love. There are many more steps to be taken though before he can finally arrive. He must commit to being in devoted service to his chosen one for that moment. She will surely ask that he commits for the next moment too. He must be ready to keep her safe and be ready to demonstrate how much he trusts himself. He must serve her, worship her and offer his manliness to her. She will share how others tried to take her buds and how she was hurt. She will reveal her deepest desires. Amidst a fragrance of love, she shall test him with unspoken words, ciphers and opposites. She will tell him how she needs to feel safe in order to unfurl more – she needs to trust that there will be infinite sunshine so that she may give him her utmost gift.

Commitment required that I take responsibility for myself. To give more, serve her more. It required that I devote to her and only to her.

Men have a warrior within; a woman loves our wild man. A woman can detect that you would die for her, defend your country and way of life for her. But many men back away when they encounter that womanly need. They would say that they are "commitment-phobes" or that she is stifling them. They back away because they don't trust themselves enough and they know that she would find them out.

To what extent do men trust themselves, how many young men trust themselves?

Jane needed me to commit to her. But I felt that she was trying to possess me. I could feel a willingness to commit to Jane someday, but I needed to do some growing up first. We were so young.

The sex gods of my ancestors gave life to Jane and I. All my ancestors were needed for our love affair to actualise. Perhaps it was divinely intended?

Freebies

Recently I was walking in dew-soaked woods. A jogger ran past in a small vest and even smaller latex hot pants. Those kinds of give-away signals can be confusing to a man. There is no wonder that some men paint radiant and beautiful Muslim flowers black.

Life and growing up continued apace. In every moment there is the potential to connect. I met a girl in a cafe named Rachel. I was caught by her black skin-tight leggings. I loved her gym-sculpted ass. The shape of her genitals well defined by black fabric beckoned me. She was promiscuous with the subtleties of her shape – was I supposed to ignore her, not be attracted to her. Did she know that men may look at her with grasping eyes? I was fascinated and attracted by what that Rachel-flower gave away so freely. Like a butterfly to buddleia I wanted her nectar.

Perpetually we choose communion or separation with whatever or whoever shows up in our world. I got to know Rachel, in spite of her letterbox smile. She got to know me in spite of my lechery. In every relationship at a very subtle level we choose actions that feel appropriate to us in each moment. Relationships deepen where both parties detect an underlying attraction. Attraction can become rejection at any time. This can even happen at a distance where for example a world-event might cause us to reject a whole culture or within deepest intimacy where we might reject a finger probing in any deeper.

Boundaries often play a role in the change of attraction into repulsion, assuming we know where they are *and* are comfortable enforcing them. The attractive / repulsive nature of relationship *always* changes. One day I might want to share Rachel's sweet juices and another day I might want her to be *a very long way away*!

My cupped hand moved into her knickers. She widened her legs to grant me access; Rachel kept saying "yes". I whispered how beautiful she was and how aroused the fullness of her pussy was making me. We soon found ourselves in bed.

Repulsion arose when Rachel squeamishly declared her fear of the sight of my erect cock. Bell-end all purple, throbbing and exposed, she couldn't look at it.

I understand why a woman might be shocked when seeing a man's cock for the first time. A man's member often isn't a pretty sight. Do women like the look of cock? Some do, but many report that it is a frightening sight, in the armed weaponry sense of the word. Men love to look at all of a woman; every little crease and protuberant. But for women, sexual relationship is more often about emotion and connection than what his genitals look like.

A boundary was met. Sleep suspended our frustration...

Innocently, I molested her in the night; I carefully and quietly relished her turned-on genitals.

But just because something feels good doesn't mean it's healthy. Boundaries are like membranes that keep out toxins and let in nutrients. I didn't know about boundaries back then but I knew that I was toxically crossing her boundary without permission. She was asleep and couldn't express her "No".

Though she was "not unresponsive".

Brothers we've all got the blood on our hands. You may well find that act erotic but relating to a woman in that way was damaged.

Dishonesty

Reader, perhaps I should share my main message now in case you put this book in the charity box... I have discovered that by loving many women I have always loved one Goddess-essence, through the many. My core yearns to bask in that essence. Together we are sharing my circuitous journey towards the discovery of the open secret that **one woman is all women**. Loving all women allows me to create peace and love the earth.

We can only be in authentic relationship with another when we have a healthy relationship to our sex god. **When sex is celebrated and freely discussed our world becomes beautiful.**

One rehabilitative evening after shagging Nicola back at my parents' house, the phone rang its invasive trill. It was Jane calling from Montreal. We chatted for a while; I missed her body and heart sorely.

'Ben, have you been seeing anybody else?' she asked, reasonably expecting the truth as a reply.

I sensed the heat from my feelings. I remembered that honesty had not been profitable. After an eternity of existential dilemma lasting less than a second, I replied.

'No.'

The sometimes-bitter of a man's ways, I lied to my woman.

I was like Pan living my nature in an unnatural world. I was transcendent of societal rules and mindsets. Sex is beautiful; perhaps my only stupidity was that I felt the need to lie.

Where do wayward behaviours come from? Perhaps from a sense of lack; from an ego that feels less than whole? Or from Karma and the lessons we need to learn? Or is the sex god an electro-chemical-hormonal outcome experienced through the distortions of human meaning?

Most of us have things about ourselves that we don't like, but I need to understand where my need to lie came from. Why was I so untrustworthy back then? Why did I let down the woman

I loved, what was wrong with me? Mum, Dad my incorrigible moralisers, what happened? How did I learn that it was reasonable behaviour? Where to start?

Did it *really* matter that I slept with other women? Was it really of consequence to Jane? Did she really need to know? Who or what was really affected by my deceit? When two lovers make love, they become the whole world and nothing else exists; why should those that don't exist in that moment actually care? Who or what is really affected?

Me. Me, because I could have been a big enough man to fearlessly speak my truth and then feel the feelings that resulted. My inner child didn't need to protect his wounds from the world anymore. So yes it did matter that I lied. How did I learn to lie?

Lying takes place when we make an un-true reference to a past event. Is it just mind-stuff? Several years ago I undertook some therapeutic work to try and discover the origins of my behaviours; what deeply veiled aspect of myself was at play? What childhood way of being did I protect with adult lies?

Perhaps I told the Truth many years ago to loved-ones four times my size. Maybe they didn't want to hear the truth and they lashed out at me. Perhaps violently? Maybe they made an insane judgement about me and I believed them.

Maybe I learned that if I lied I wouldn't have to feel ugly feelings *and* my loved-ones would continue to be happy. That's it! I lied because I was too scared of the response I would get if I told the truth. They were feelings that would be *too much* to feel if I were to tell the truth. At any expense, I made an enduring resolve to never feel those feelings again. I lied to Jane to avoid feeling those feelings. This revelation, this shedding of light onto shadow might be called a Big One.

How did you learn to lie Reader?

How did I learn to avoid feelings? That's easy. I was taught from a young age to suppress any feelings that may be seen as "negative", such as resentment, fear, anger and even sorrow. For example, if I witnessed my elders disrespecting their world, I wouldn't speak my truth. As a child I felt the ways that mother-

Earth was being harmed. I sensed that people were taking too many fish, destroying too many forests and having too many children. It felt wrong, but I daren't reveal my sadness or question their ways. I was conditioned to deny Truths that I witnessed and I was taught that "it isn't okay to ask for what you want" or to be true to yourself. I was conditioned to act as though I was in control by avoiding the display of overt emotion. The avoidance of feelings continued into my adult life where I often felt powerless in the presence of negative emotions. As an adult, if I didn't express "negative" feelings and emotions I probably redirected them into passive-aggressive behaviours. I may have used passive-aggression to veil the fact that I didn't know how to *simply be* in certain uncomfortable emotions.

Emotions are energy-in-motion. There are fluffy spiritual teachings that ask me to be free in emotions like gratitude and compassion. But back then I needed a fully encompassing teaching that showed me how inhabit *my truth, anger, sadness and fear* as well. If a master had appeared in a puff of smoke for me back then, she would have told me how to develop a new relationship to my emotions. She would have told me how to be *free from* my emotions. She would have told me how to be *free in my* emotions. It is okay to feel any feeling.

Thus lying is a simple strategy to avoid experiencing or showing certain feelings. Yet lying results in new feelings, deceit sat in my being like a dull aching welt. Masters didn't appear in my life for another twenty five years and I didn't anticipate that suppressed feelings all get banked for another day, with interest.

What if my elders had taught me to be at ease in my true nature; to be an authentic man who embodies his feelings? Taught me that authenticity would enable me to be open, transparent and enjoy bottomless intimacy. I could have chosen a path of licentious-variety and been honest about it. I could have said "this is how I behave", deal with it. Maybe it was that simple. But sex is never taken lightly; does a woman want to hear the truth?

When Jane asked me if I had seen anybody else, I should have been able to sit joyously in all the feelings that were showing up. I loved all my experiences with other girls after all. I could have hooked up actual experience with my speech and said:

"Oh lordy, have I been seeing anyone else? Well. I've so many crazy stories to share about my journey while we've been apart. Jane, there were loads of other women. There was Lexi, Heather, Katie, Tara... and Bouncy-Bouncy and more; I don't remember all their names just now. We've had so much fun together over the past few months and I've learned so much about women, making love and who I am. It was all safe and innocently motivated. There was never any intent to hurt anyone, not even you dear lover. They were all like trying on new clothes, for fun, with no intention to buy. I can't wait to see you in a few weeks when you are over. I'll be all yours and I can share a few sexy things that I've learnt that will make you just short of ecstatic."

...Or words to that effect. But I suspected that aggression would result from her "love", neediness and possessiveness of me if I had said that. Just like last time.

So I explained it all away with psychobabble. The fact is I wanted my cake and I wanted to eat it. I wanted it all.

So I lied. And I was prepared to do it again.

Black Room

One night with Collette, flaming-mother met virgin son. The universe can bring a man and woman together in infinite ways; two bodies, two histories, two psychologies, two sex gods, two circumstances, two vibrating energies of light. Sex play comes in many flavours. Thankfully, the darker, bitter and more challenging flavours haven't been part of my story. There is much pleasure to be had in experiencing the myriad combinations – the learning, healing and mirroring that is present in every concurrence.

Every woman is different, some are hot, some are cold and most are somewhere in between. If I slept with a hundred women, I would discover a hundred sexual experiences, all different. A woman will also be different on every day of her moon cycle. Nature provides variety. She will be different when her feminine archetypes reveal themselves. She could be a Mother, a Mistress or a Madonna. She could play with me as virgin or whore, flower or flame. Her pussy doesn't have an owner's manual; a skilled lover must have utmost sensitivity to her needs.

Men also meet women through their archetypes of Father, Son and Holy Spirit. At various times in my life I have been all of these. I can be all of these in a night, such is the dance of the sex god. The archetypes choose us as they desire. How sweet you are Nature!

Tarts in colourful Leotards were boogieing hard in various cages around the cavernous New York night club. Now 21, I felt as though I was a man of the world, living a jet set life. I had been trying my charm on some young-things, but hadn't had any lasting action. It was getting late and the night was losing its zing. As I prepared to retreat back to my hotel tower, an older woman, an enchantress, approached me. Older is always relative. We chatted for a while above the wump of a Duran track. She wasn't interested in dancing, just pulling.

We clicked. I couldn't believe my luck.

'I have a hotel room.' It was high up in a phallic skyscraper.

'So do I,' she said cheekily.

Collette was classy, petite and overly mature for her age; a thirty-something European. She told me she was a princess – married and out to play while she was comfortably distant from her aristocratic family back home. Her wanton mature nature met my wonder. Our meeting had an exhilarating polarity to it. The sex god bridled.

I was reduced to feeling like an inadequate toy-boy rather than a man of the world. Men are often become shy as she says "Yes" to sex. Surely such an elegant woman would somehow be different, I was fearful of how to perform. She was in a different league; alluring, confident and in charge. I think she loved it that I was just a boy – she had pulled a real young one. We kissed, slowly. The kiss worked. There was chemistry behind the fear. I was certain she could smell the stamina in my testosterone. Isn't that why an older woman picks up a young boy?

Back at the tower hotel she dropped her smoky clothes to the floor and showered. Secretly I was moved to inebriate with her clammy lingerie, I adored her smell.

Thrillingly she soon appeared in a gown ready to be taken. I say taken, as her submission was palpable. I couldn't tread any more water, I was about to drown in her.

'You look beautiful Collette, I feel very privileged.' It didn't come out right. When sex is performance we become self conscious.

We kissed again, slowly then fumbled around with nervous cuddles. In spite of my sex god and all my sexual experiences to date, Collette was confidently different. I continued to feel inadequate.

'Let me look, show what you have for me.' She released my belt and unzipped my trousers, pulling them open. I held my breath. Her hand felt into my pants.

'Very nice, Cheri, ooooh we going to have good time together.'

Maybe I wasn't inadequate.

Whispering submissively, 'You can do anything you like to me Cheri.'

My breath released. 'Anything, I questioned?' in a cracked voice.

'Anything, have me beauty, all of me is for you.'

The sex god has a rhythm all its own, it moves in infinite ways. Sometimes it needs to receive and it becomes submissive. Another time it needs to assert its power and it becomes dominant. The sex god and unabashed curiosity arose through me.

I led her to the bed and moved her onto all-fours, propping her chest up with the plentiful down pillows. I instructed her to arch her lower back, keeping her ass high in the air. She did as she was told. I parted her knees – just enough. Surrendered, she was wanton of being explored. Her gown draped down over her vanity. Older women were still mysterious to me. It was new territory and I assumed the techniques Suzie taught me would not work for her. She submitted to my naiveté, giving herself, as if to be of service to the growth of me. She was ready. What a gorgeous gift she was.

I wanted to explore her but a battle between embarrassment and lust ensued. My heart was racing, my breath was energised and my stomach butterflied. Scared is the same feeling as excited. It was a thrilling moment after all. I needed to see my fear as excitement. I wasn't feeling fear - I was feeling passion, excitement and curiosity. I loved those feelings, I got off on them. The more I played with my sexual energy, conquest and seduction, the more I could be comfortable with sexual fear. I could embrace the excitement as my sex god passion in action.

But not that night...

I turned the lights out. I can't believe I did that.

'Merde! Ben what is happening? Cheri, turn the lights back on... pleeease.'

The lights stayed off, it was hotel night-blind dark.

In the darkness, slowly and respectfully I disrobed her. Delaying access to her prize, I touched her adoringly from the tips of her toes, up her long legs. Touch brought me very close to her but intimacy isn't fusion. Touching in the dark revealed her in a way that light could not. It was a beautiful touch loaded with yearning thankfulness. My touch allowed me to penetrate reality, to penetrate her in ways that my vision couldn't; my senses awakened. I teased my fingers up her legs. I felt subtle temperature changes across her cheeks, soft skin and rougher skin. I felt downy hairs, then prickly hairs that gave way to coarser wiry hairs. I slid my fingers between her buttocks touching her arsehole. I moved my hands in long sensitive strokes up her back and into her thick soft hair. I reached under her chest and rolled her flat breasts and acorn nipples. My fingers ran through her soul. Sniffing behind her ear I then retraced the tour with my tongue. I was primal, I was animalistic. Reader, we all have that in us.

The discovery of her body was vivid and luminous in the darkness. I eventually arrived at her treasure. It felt so pronounced. Dry at first and then as I parted her I could feel she was ripe for penetration. She was warm and humid in the darkness.

I let out an involuntary 'Ahhhhhhhhhhhh.'

Nakedness needn't be shocking. Especially in the dark.

'I feel so exposed for you Cheri,' she purred, 'Your touch is beautiful, very special. Take your time, I am all for you Cheri, don't be shy or frightened. Can we turn the lights on?'

She was erect and much bigger than all the younger girls. I parted her and slipped my long finger deep inside her. Sophisticated. Sweet.

'Theeeere... Ahhhhhhhh.... this is so perfect.... take all the time you need.' She groaned and trembled. I'm certain the room filled with the sparkles of her feminine nature, perhaps she came?

Slowly I became my senses; my confidence returned through her giving acceptance of me. But I was still fearful of what I might see if I turned the lights on.

Soft mouthed, I gorged on her spread maturity; my face met her slow grind. She was Mrs. Honey.

Eventually, I mounted her from behind. Fusion.

In the darkness I became aware that my breath was intrinsic to my sex. The strong panting breath that charged my high-energy-fucking quickly became an exquisite breath-less-ness in orgasm.

Vertigo. I came way too soon.

Our sexual essences were spent; they had found their way through our innocent play into manifest reality. She didn't declare any disappointment at the haste of my fuck. We fell into an exhausted sleep.

I reflect for a moment; can I be sure that that the next breath *will* be provided when I'm lost in orgasm? What makes me so sure of that? What if the next breath never came, what if I died in orgasm!? It happens! We always believe that the next breath is coming; we unconsciously believe that we *are* going to get our next breath. The gap between my out-breath and in-breath is a moment of faith which is taken for granted like many other things in life.

A sucked cock makes a man smile. New York City was at full throttle twenty six floors below us as I was sucked out of my sleep by a mischievously smiling Colette. Bright morning sunshine pestered into the room; squinting I could see her gorgeous body, thick jiggling nipples, and dense dark bush... I love a natural woman.
        'Good Moring Collette... Don't stop... You look lovely... I shouldn't have turned the lights out last night, how could I?' I rasped.
        A finger slipped in my young ass, nobody had ever done that before. I liked it. She helped herself to more of what *she* needed. She had given herself freely to that curious young-thing in the dark the night before, and now it was *her* turn to take. I didn't resist.
        No passivity, Colette soon mounted me.
        'Ow, careful, don't scratch Colette. I'll get found out.' She was a scratcher lost in her sex. She didn't know she was doing it.
        'Sorry baby.' But she did it anyway.
        She took and I gave, and gave.
        The corridor-filling wail said it all.
        We completed and landed.

Sometimes, well often actually, life flows. Colette was pure flow. Flow is so easy. I said a resounding "Yes" to Life. Whenever I resist the flow of life, swim upstream to what creation has in store for me, life feels hard... But I was being deceitful to Jane and actively going out on the pull – was that still flow?

So Reader, what are these psychosexual psalms all about then, any clues? Well so far I've been setting the stage, a thankfully innocent one as it is still only my early years. This is no ordinary tale of soggy genitalia and feisty romps as sex makes Karma, it creates soul level attachments and psychic bonds. Karma is our obligation to move towards Spirit.

Not wishing to pander to your expectations of an easy read, the friction that has caused several sore cocks hopefully isn't the only friction around for you. Creativity creates friction. By now you will have witnessed much Creative Friction herein. The motive here all along has been to say things to provoke new thought. Maybe the conflicted or uncomfortable ideas I have presented can get new ideas and freedoms to form in you. As you drop your preference, control and expectation in life, you can experience the fullness of the miracle of all life. Alignment with nature is the only way to peace, for god is not ashamed of the truth. That is pure Tantra. Any aspect of the human experience both light and dark must be included, for it is all god.

Maybe my tales touch a yearning in you to have these kinds of experiences? As I know that the sex god energy runs through the whole Universe, even you dear Reader.

Perhaps if you're feeling titillated, now is a good time to go take a break?

Go have a wank.

Arousal Carousel

How many women can I love at once? My heart has always been vast enough to love several and all women, at once. My lovers have never understood my propensity; as they have always wanted me wholly to themselves.

Reader this is a long chapter, so make sure you have the staying power for it. It might be a nice one to read one evening when you are alone, as it may get you juicy.

In preparation for my writing today I decided to abstain from sex. My beloved must wait and not even a wank shall be indulged. Allow me to explain why I should be so restrained. My teacher has recently been instructing me about the creative opportunity that is available to a man who retains his semen. The practice of multiple non-ejaculatory orgasm is a pathway to bliss *and* utmost creativity she says. The sex god is foremost a creative god whose primal creative energy spouts into existence from the Mystery in the form of Eros. Eros is usually turned outward instead of inward; perhaps spurted towards the emptiness of lusty fantasy. Using conscious awareness to overrule my animal-cultural instinct to shed my load is a powerful and evolved choice. So today I am channelling my sexual energy inwards. The concentrated life-force contained in my salvo of three hundred million sperm is being retained. Its energy is being circulated within my body to imbue this creative writing. I circulate the energy from my groin to my head and then liberally through every cell of my body. In this practice I align with the creative propensity of the Universe – to write for *you* dear Reader. Let's see if it makes any difference!

I began life as an orgasm and sexuality is unrealised spirituality.

So I continued to discover myself as a sexual creature and I was blessed with abundance. The mystery of woman has many faces.

I had just awoken. I wandered downstairs to make tea, leaving Aija asleep under the duvet in recovery. I saw two letters waiting on the mat; one in a pink envelope and one yellow, both addressed to me. The pink letter was from Jane arranging our summer rendezvous. The yellow letter was from Germany, who could it be from? Oh yes, the lovely Klaudia who I had met a few weeks earlier in a club. Heavy petting was as far as she would go. But she was desperate to see me again.

I returned upstairs with two mugs of steaming tea. Aija propped herself up, smiling through a large amount of platinum blonde hair.

'There you go beautiful, I didn't expect you to be awake so soon.'

She was impeccable arm-candy. I loved her skin, tanned and dolphin smooth. I loved how her small breasts were so white against the rest of her sun kissed body.

'Vesihiisi sihisi hississä,' she said, giggling.

'Vessyhissy what?' I replied, feigning aghast.

'Vesi...hii...si...si...hi...si...hiss...issä, Vesihiisi sihisi hississä, it's a Finnish tongue twister and I'm saying it to check if my brain still works cos I think you fucked it out last night!'

'Say that again.' I laughed.

'Vesihiisi... sihisi... hississä.'

'Aha, your brain is working fine, maybe I need to lay you down to get the bits I didn't reach last night!' I jumped on her, pulling her down beneath me. 'Vessy...hissy hissy hissyhissy,' I enunciated.

'Again Ben.'

'Vessyhissy sihissy hissyhisser.'

'You've got it, that's very good, you get A+ again.' She thrust me over onto my back, she was strong! 'Lay down! I thought it you that has too many those brains mister.' Assertively she fed me into her already juiciness '...and it's *my* turn to fuck yours out.'

She *was* strong! Lusty zeal returned for the next few hours. Sex is so often better in the morning.

'Oh no, look at the time, it's almost twelve, I have to go, I have a class.'

I loved the strong smell of her sex.

She tripped across the room collating her clothes and hastily sweetened herself in the mirror. Sometimes it's a challenge to disguise a *just-been-fucked* hairdo.

'Are you coming to the party tonight Aija?'

'I can't, I'm got to working, remember?'

'Come along after work if you like, it would be lovely to see you...'

'I think I need an early night tonight, I have some those brains that need to be re-growing! Ciao baby, call me.' And she was gone.

Oh no, I won't have a girl with me tonight.

It was a special day. Summer recess was imminent and we were holding a party to celebrate the end of an era. The only decisions I needed to make were nice ones, what a blessing. So who should be my girl for the party as Jane was overseas and Aija was MIA?

En route to buy some crates of beer, I found a callbox to call Lexi. 'Hey Lex, are you still coming to our party tonight?'

'Ben, where have you been? I thought you'd forgotten me... I'd love to come, what time?'

'Great! See you in the bar at eight, and we'll go back to the party from there.'

A small swimming pool was inflated and placed auspiciously in the middle of the lounge. Three bales of ice and several crates of beer completed the house preparations. We could finally relax.

Lexi finally showed up. Her energy preceded her, she was having a girl-mood. Maybe her chemistry had been hijacked by her hormones? It's amazing how a woman's mood affects how she looks. She had lost her shine, but I told her she looked amazing – and she soon softened. We arrived late at the party which was already in full swing.

'I'm just going for a smoke, find us some drinks.' Lexi headed for the garden.

There were girls everywhere... Abundance is mine when I enjoy every moment, not in what I collect or try to make my own.

The doorbell chimed, it was Vivian. I greeted her with a connective kiss then she was enveloped by the party.

Heather, the nurse I had met a year before, was now going steady with James; but I was privy to each of their secret dalliances. Cheeks aflame, she took my hand. We sequestered ourselves upstairs.

'Where's Misaki tonight, I haven't seen her for ages? She's so beautiful, is she a super model or something?'

'Oh she's visiting her family in Japan right now.'

'Oh, that's a shame, is Jane here? Who are you with then? ... Where's James?'

'I think he's gone to get more beers. They're going fast. I saw him leave a few moments ago.'

The quiet room beyond beckoned. Heather was always such a benign influence on me – I didn't remember planning that one. The Tao had us enjoy a disconcerting embrace as we surveyed the street down below. There was no sign of James. Temptation took over, boundaries changed. Somehow we were making out. I knew Heather was a sexual creature as we were mutual confidants; we knew too much about each other. She loved black guys, very *avant* back then. Our meeting was to be swift, we shouldn't get caught – James wouldn't be happy. I loved James.

We grow when we shift our boundaries. I was crossing my boundary. I was afraid of saying "No" thus far. I felt her open. I didn't want to hurt her feelings. I had my hand between her legs; our heat was escalating. Expressing her heart's invitation, she laid back on the bed.

Was touching her through her knickers "having sex"?

'Ahhh. I'd just love to see what you look like this time Heather.' I pulled her knickers down, and pushed her legs apart. I breathed her in and plundered her with my eyes.

Was looking at her "having sex"?

'Fuck me Ben.' There was a long pause. We were on the precipice of betrayal and anticlimax.

'I can't Heather, it wouldn't be right, James is my best friend and I couldn't do that to him.'

I couldn't say "yes" just to please her. I had clear boundaries, but she was open to any outcome. I touched her as much as I dare before our procreative sex gods stepped in to consume our moral reason.

Rejection.

'What about Jane then? You shouldn't cheat on her either hey?' Was that blackmail?

Heather was onto me, how was it that I had honour with James but not with my long term girlfriend overseas? Where in my childhood did I learn that one? It was a life lesson to be learned.

'You know I've slept with Nick and *he* didn't seem so loyal,' she said trying to get me to acquiesce. I was very surprised to hear that. I thought there was a gentlemanly honour amongst close male housemates.

'Ha, unbelievable, you just can't trust any man can you?... Oh Heather, I've always fancied the pants off you. I love you, you know that. But I've always restrained myself; it has seemed the right thing to do. We have a special friendship,' I pleaded.

She softened. 'Please Ben, I hear great things from all the other girls, I want to know what it is that you do for them.'

Was tasting her "having sex"?

The deviant arose and I dived in and suckled on her open treasure; giving her what I could under exceptional circumstances. Wiping her sweet juice from my chin and lips, I looked up at her pleasured face. I always loved to see delight and elation on my girl's face. Our behaviour felt "acceptable" as it was only to be known by the two of us – but what of my friendship with James and what if Jane found out?

'Fuck me Ben.'

'Ben. Ben, are you up there?' Lexi was coming up the stairs.

'Gotta go Heather.' We chuckled, she knew me well.

'Next time I shall have your cock you lovely man.'

'Oh there you are, what have you been up to?'

Fucking hell Reader, I just re-read wot was writ. I'm starting to sound like I was god's gift to women or something! I'm not so sure I was.

I slipped out of the room and into Lexi's arms. I flustered out a distraction as we made our way downstairs. 'Is James back with the beer yet? Let's find James, he's been gone ages.'

'Haven't seen him. I'm just going to the loo Ben, see you in a mo.' Lexi motioned above the music that had gone high-energy disco.

James blustered in through the front door. He had a huge smile on his face. 'You wouldn't believe what just happened mate; such a laugh, and so unexpected. I just shagged Vivian didn't I I!'

'Really!' I startled, 'How, where?' There was no doubting my jealousy.

'She came with me to get the beers, we cut through the park and well mate, I think you'd have done the same!'

I should have fucked Heather.

'Where is she now?' I asked, thinking I might get a go too.

'Oh she'll be back later, she's gone to meet her man across town.' I was unlikely to get her tonight. 'And you wouldn't believe it, it turns out she's been shagging Nick as well!'

'REEEALY, I thought he was going steady with Katie.'

We were all doing it, shagging lying and cheating. It was the way of the world – lovers, friends and strangers. Driven by the needs of our sex gods, we were all at it. If the girls were doing it too, somehow it made it okay. Why were we all cheating? Was it our sex gods or did we all have childhood wounding playing out? Remember Reader, sex is a noble energy. Sex is natural. The one thing in common was that we all had a fear of telling our partners that we wanted more varietal sex than they could provide. Cheating was okay for everyone except my girlfriend.

I found Lexi sitting outside on a rickety oak bench under a bougainvillea. We turned pseudo-intellectual as we so often did. Our intimacy was with often with words rather than touch. The subject of cheating arose.

'Lexi, if we all do it then isn't it human nature? Should we resist human nature? Should we resist what happens anyway?' Are we choice-less passengers who have life happen to us?

'*No* that would be crazy.'

'Society expects good behaviour and we just follow our nature. The moralistic models don't match Nature's ways. Surely it's those morals that leave us feeling "bad".'

We were trying to work life out.

'Ha, great, maybe we should do away with morals then,' she surmised and then paused. 'But I guess the morals are there to help us avoid getting hurt when we have a fling and we get found out!... Cheating complicates the simplicity of love Ben.'

We paused to take in the stars. Her head fell onto my shoulder. How could we reconcile what happens when wild nature meets human nature? I felt paradoxed. There were no teachers back then.

'...So if we follow nature then morals make us feel bad and if we forget the morals we can feel great... but others will feel bad cos they have morals!'

'Enough already! Let's change the subject.'

I didn't let up. 'Yes, but the hurt we feel is born of jealousy and possession and such like... Women are possessive creatures. They want to *own* their man... it's all control drama Lexi...'

'Especially Jane!'

'Naughty.'

We kissed.

Deceit is sticky mud. It is always loaded with a fear of being found out. Fear made my world shrink; it diminished my potential to see magic everywhere. Why couldn't we all be honest about our sex gods and what those gods had us do? If we loved our sex gods and they were socially acceptable then lies wouldn't be necessary.

I had so much love for Jane; I lied to protect her from my ways. I lied to give her good feelings. I believed that if she felt good then I would feel good. Surely it's foolish to protect loved ones by withholding the truth. The truth is, when I lie, I feel like shit. That shit accumulates over the years. It accumulates and becomes a stinking shit heap that I must carry around. Eventually I have to choose to either live neck-deep in shit, or fess up and dump my shit on others; who then have a shit-fit.

No mud, no Lotus.

I left Lexi in the garden having a smoke. It's easy to attract another girl when you already have a pretty woman on your arm. It's playing I know. It takes advantage of the suitors underlying rivalry or jealousy. She wants what the other already has.

Mission Creep, I was playing the tart and soon found myself in Minnie's bedroom. Minnie was our sole female housemate. She was a ballsy girl with way too much hair.

She closed the door; I was captive.

Minnie had often told me tales of her religious upbringing. She wore an imprint that had left her tragically uncomfortable with and within her own body – and what it sexually required of her. Such is the toxic container of joyless dogma that so many souls are placed in by their imposed religion. The repression of her own experience in favour of what was "acceptable" surely led to deep wounding. Repression eventually becomes perversion. Most religions put considerable efforts to inculcate shame at sex, in spite of it being a beautiful form of shared-life celebration. Mary bore a child without being dirtied by sex after all. The separation of spirit and flesh is an original divide that wounds the planet's psyche. Religions have a vested interest in controlling people. Yet how many of us men and women stand up to tell religious zealots that they are wrong? Some say that there *is* a way to respect womankind, it is called atheism.

If we peek into our own truth we can see that even religious doctrine is *for purpose.* Any time there is an inner feeling of unhappiness towards some external situation; that unhappiness is simply asking us to step towards our own truth, our own power, our birthright. Unhappiness is the compass. All that's needed is the courage to follow it... and another sunrise.

'I don't feel sexy Ben. I don't like what I'm wearing; I need something more party-like. The other girls look so pretty in their little dresses. Be a darling would you and help me decide what to wear.' She proceeded to peel her skinny jeans off. The music downstairs waxed sultry; Minnie started to act out a strip and dance in front of me. She was opening her petals to see if I would come in.

Sweet. There's nothing quite like watching the freely flowing dance of a woman, witnessing her in her elemental way of being.

Captive became captivated.

There are two types of relationship, what we might call real-relationship and mind-relationship. When we are in real-relationship we are physically present with a person or whatever we are relating to. Real-relationship could have sexual or intimate propulsion. I was in real-sexual-relationship with Minnie at that time.

Relationships are special when I give them every bit of myself – in that moment. Whoever I am with deserves my fullness, my full undivided presence. When I am in real-relationship with another; total, sacred experience can arise.

Reader I hope I have *your* undivided attention right now.

When we are in mind-relationship we aren't physically present and the person or object has become a memory. For example, I am in mind-relationship with Minnie as I write. I relate to her by way of thought. It isn't sensory. Yet when I was with Minnie, I was real with her but in mind-relationship with Jane! Jane was just a thought. We give so much weight to relationships, yet most of the time they are only thoughts.

My teachers tell me that thoughts are not real.

Only real-relating is real.

The wave of a relationship moves as nature intends. A relationship could "end" but we might snatch an easy-fuck at some later date. Did the relationship really end? Does a relationship ever end? For example, there are many people who I have known, who I still relate to as a mind-relationship. They still have an effect on my psyche... So relationships continue, people still mean something to me. I wonder if they know that... Of course they do as they still have a mind-relationship with *me*!

Relationships come and go. That's the way all of nature works, relationships beginning, rising, falling and ending. Some relationships last a lifetime and others a juicy twenty minutes.

Minnie's dance had my total attention. She danced her lovely body and generous heart through several layers of religious upbringing and several outfits. I offered my appraisal and I made an impact. She got sexier by volunteering knicker changes to match her ensembles; I was happy to help her with that task. What was the sex god having me do at any expense? Eventually my interest in her couture started to diminish – so we settled on a toga. Ha, what a laugh. A celebration was in order. I wetted my finger with her saliva and touched into her where she yearned. She was a frigid frig, but an unspoken sexual tension between us started to resolve. She soon warmed.

Repression compression released.

We found a chair and she forcibly sat atop me. Her nipples daubed in my face. The party music changed from garage to a big rave groove; and we resynchronised. What debauchery. What consensual fun, sex for sex sake.

Vidi, Vici, Veni.

Intuitively I have always been able to feel if my lover was emotionally connected or detached to her sex. Minnie felt very detached that night. It was a snatched fuck. I liked her; I felt I had a lot to offer her. Together we could have created space where she could relax and become okay with her sex; but it would have taken far more time... But then she'd probably go and fall in love with me and want me all to herself.

Nothing need be owned in the midst of abundance. It was time to be in real-relationship with the lovely Lexi. Where was she?

I found her dancing in the lounge.

'Lexi, Lexi it's that song you love, you know the one where he says that life happens while we are planning other things.'

We sang along. Then burst out laughing sharing our joy of such wisdom. We totally lost ourselves in the dance for a good while.

Eventually the party bonfire became scintillating embers. We made our way to bed tiptoeing over straggler bodies and empty bottles.

'I don't trust you Ben.' We slid under the duvet. 'But then I don't need to trust you, because you are perfect for me right now.' We cuddled. 'I'm not going to be another one of your dazzled then disappointed women.' Smart girl?

I loved Lexi, but didn't have to sleep with her (every time). I had met Lexi several months earlier. She was one of those girls who I just *had* to ask out. After a riotous evening at a bonfire festival we returned to my digs. She took a fingered orgasm but she wouldn't let me fuck her, claiming her boyfriend back home really wouldn't approve. She was a lovely cuddler but selfish in bed. It was her outrageous intellect that I adored. We were good friends.

She fell asleep.

In my afterglow I laid there reflecting on my sexually excessive day. I had enjoyed the attention. I felt good about co-creating experiences where we experimented and connected with our bodies. I had given and received a lot of pleasure. I felt appreciated for my ability to do that. I felt needed. Life was innocently good.

But my heart was uncertain – it was uncertain where this fucking abundance was leading. My heart has always looked after me; it has always known everything about me.

Each was an ordinary girl, each capable of mood-swings, bitchiness and heartbreak. Each was also a goddess, pure love, looking for her prince. The fragrance of their womanly essence had attracted me to come closer. Each one had a bright flame glowing in the hearth of her heart and was ultimately marriageable – each was capable of loving me to wholeness for the rest of my days.

I wasn't ready to be loved *totally* by just *one* woman though. They were all too possessive, they wanted me to be only-theirs, they didn't want to share me. Each would try to tame me and have me to themselves.

Women are entrapping and constraining to a man. They easily confuse sexy fun with the possibility of something everlasting. It is Venus' way. I saw the pattern evolve – attraction, hit-it-off, have sex, love arises, lock-me-up, make me their own, possess me. No! Then it was broken hearts all round. So I subscribed to the overlooked strategy of "having Jane, my distant girlfriend". I protected myself from allowing a girl to get too close by having a Girlfriend and many girlfriends. Some of them knew that I was prone to sleeping around a bit. They reported that my manner was sexy and alluring to them; though Lexi wasn't too happy about it.

Jane also did her lock-up job; albeit long distance. I wasn't ready to be trapped by her either *and* I didn't want to hurt her. The result, I was more honest within casual relationships than with my real girlfriend. I had become cleaved from my authenticity.

I was in service to sex and I was of sexual service. Nay I must be churlish, I was out to fuck and be fucked and I loved it. I loved loving many women; it is the same today. The need to reconcile my behaviour with the established expectations of my culture was growing.

I was trying to make sense of the world. I was caught in the paradox of following instinct and trying to please others. Life was just happening to me, I wasn't consciously going out to make it happen. Back then I didn't even know there was a difference between being conscious or unconscious.

Where were the Masters back then? I needed sagely advice. I had big questions for them.

Where was the fucking manual?

Aren't We Gorgeous

Reader, I was just reflecting. Why am I writing this book? Do I wish to tell the world what a stud I am, what a liar I am or how many damaged shortcomings I have? Or perhaps it's a mid-life crisis; what a wonderful way to relive the flamboyance of my youth, one more time. Truth is, one morning I awoke with a compulsion to write and these words started to flow. Creative muse is palpably using me, tales and insights gushing forth, from whence they come I do not know. These words, written in awareness, are sexual energy transformed into service and for that reason my writing feels very much for purpose. Some people advance the knowledge of human-kind during their lives; they leave something behind that is useful to future generations. In sharing this tapestry I trust that some healing (however small) for all sons and daughters can take place. Perhaps one more woman shall be worshipped, one more man shall celebrate his sex and the Mother energy of all-life shall sparkle with evolution. **When we all have a loving relationship with our sex god our peoples shall be healed. Go honour your sexuality.**

I was twenty-three when I flew off with James for some world travels for a few years. Using my time to live my life.

'Hey James, I'm going down to the beach to get some air.'

'This jetlag has done me in, I'm gonna hit the hay mate. I'll see you in the morning.' We had only been in Tahiti for a day.

I wandered off down to the beach to take stock of the day. I found a felled palm to sit on. A sweet Polynesian breeze washed the av-gas off of me. I could hear small ripples slurping at the beach and the pffff of the big waves breaking far out on the reef. The stars were stunning.

I watched the silhouette of a woman approach slowly along the edge of the water.

'Avez-vous une cigarette?'

'Non Mademoiselle,' I replied struggling to invigorate my language-centres.

'Quel est votre nom? ... C'est beau ici, dans mon pays¿'

'Je m'appelle Ben, et oui, il est tres beau.' I chewed the words out amidst my surprise at her forthrightness.

'Puis-je m'asseoir avec vous?'

The palm trunk bowed with disapproval. We moved to the sand and chit-chatted in franglais for a good while. I couldn't believe my luck. I'd been in Tahiti less than a day and I'd just pulled a Tahitian woman, no wonder Gauguin liked it here! Rather too quickly for me, she had her hands down my pants. I let her of course. She seemed very forward, but it was okay. She had a feel around and was vocally turned on. She sucked on me for a while, and then proceeded to jerk me off, she knew what she was doing. I came and she gobbled with approval. I started to find my way into her clothes, she resisted at first. I persisted and she acquiesced. Her skirt was hitched up. My hand slipped into her knickers.

I found her erect cock.

'Argh,' I screamed and ran.

'Argh, come back,' she said.

In Polynesia there is a cultural phenomenon whereby a family that didn't have any female children might raise one of the boys as a girl. These transvestites are known as rae rae's.

Is our sexuality learned? I was once told that there are actually thirty-two genders of sexuality; go fathom. I wish somebody had forewarned that innocent lad about their existence and ways! I've known plenty of gay men over the years. I love the energy they bring to the world. I've never felt the need to sleep with them though.

We adopted a bar. It was a tiki-shack that had been hastily rebuilt from plywood after a severe south pacific tropical storm. The sandy floor, heavy tropical rain and island harmonies didn't stop a stand-out cowgirl from teaching us Europeans how to play pool – rather she taught us how to be skilfully beaten at pool. Kit's outrageous persona filled the bar. I spent the entire evening thinking James had scored nicely; such was her interest in him.

At closing time she took my arm tightly, it was an unwitting seduction.

'Hey big boy, you gonna take me home?' Brassy; was she a man?

'Me? I thought you and James were hitching up?'

'You big boy, you're the listening-type. I want you. I want a man who listens... and has a big rod.' Life is so fresh.

'Well, I guess if that's how it is I'll head back to our digs on my own. I'll see you both tomorrow, be good.' James bowed out gracefully and headed home alone. This parry dented our friendship more than I appreciated at the time.

Kit and I shared an abiding kiss, a kiss featuring suggestive subtle communications – my tongue playfully licked her lips as though I were between her legs. She approved. Nature facilitates the meetings of people with similar needs. Sexy people or people into sex can find each other amidst the masses. I am certain it's an energetic attraction – as alike essences draw unto themselves. Kit had met her match.

'Where are you staying sweetie?'

'Oh we're down at a dive shack down the road, it's a really cool place, friendly people with group feasts every...'

'Let's go back to my place, my dad got me a decent hotel as he didn't want me to be hangin' out in dangerous places.' Bathed in starlight we wandered back towards town.

'You wanna fuck me sweetie?'

'Harder than you know, Kit,' I asserted without kidding.

'Think you can handle me? I'm a cow girl after all, used to being taken good care of by my guy.' She smiled. Androgynous yes, but she wasn't a man.

'Harder than you know, Kit, how far is your hotel? Let's go get to know each other carnally.'

'Carnally, you some kind of smart ass, whas that mean?' She guided me down a sandy track that lead to her small chalet.

'Unfettered sexuality Kit. Harder than you know it Kit. I'll show you very soon.'

What a rare pleasure to meet a woman in her fullest power, aware and open hearted. She wasn't about to give away her body just so that she would be liked. I love a woman in her power. There isn't a word in the English language for a woman in her power.

There are two types of sexual confidence: inner confidence and outer confidence. Outer confidence might be learned or mimicked from others and would make use of our will to be a certain way in a certain situation. For example I might puff my chest up and be arrogant to appear confident (or appear like an asshole). Inner confidence is about ease and wellbeing in a situation, being comfortable in your own skin; simply being *yourself*. I am the most qualified person in the whole world to be me; nobody can be me, better than me. I had learned a great deal about the endless varieties of womankind during my lusty libertine years. In that moment with Kit I was paramount and in my essence. I loved my sex god. I was thoroughly confident being me and that ease was shining through. Kit had started our intimacy as if *she* was in charge, my presence and confidence had won her over. A woman loves her lover to be present. We were *both* in charge!

Stripping her, I peeled off layers of outlaw cool revealing a soft and svelte body. The maleness of her cow-girl persona became embodied in the heap of clothes on the floor. Like kids, we assumed unembarrassed nakedness together. I saw her beauty and the beauty within her; both in form and energy. Beauty can be seen in anyone when I cut through my obstacles to witnessing it.

I hastily commandeered some cushions and pushed her back, parting her long legs. Embedding my tongue into her orchid, I once again playfully licked her lips. Lingering cunnilingus; god I love to lick pussy. As I gave, she relaxed and the protective layers of her male disguise fell away. I reached for her hand and guided her to finger herself. Her goddess was revealed containing all the succulent forms of feminine nature. She was a delicious woman with a vast capacity to receive.

A man being a man is only a threat to a woman who is unhappy with herself. I entered her slowly and she made it clear that she savoured every inch of my manhood. We surrendered our confidence and lost ourselves into the rainbow of endless hours of electrical passion.

Her eyes dazed closed.

'Oh my god you are so doing it for me, oh my god Ben, oh my god.' Her armour fell to Earth in the amour.

We were like inseparable mating dragonflies. The more I gave the more she opened, the more she opened the more she could take me; we were very symbiotic together.

How different it was those days; several years earlier, love making was about "get it in her hard and quick". I had learned from many lovers that a woman must first be opened. Opening my woman had become an enjoyable art. She let me continue to grow into my sexuality.

'How do you want me baby?' she offered.

I smiled and put on some better, faster, harder music as a soundtrack.

'On top baby.' We perfectly delivered on the conjoined compulsions and urges that we were heir to. We only ever ask for what we think we deserve.

Kit went better, faster and harder. Crazy bronco woman.

'How do you want me baby?' I offered.

She loved licking my asshole. Butt cracks are sexy. There is no part of us that isn't sacred. Was it some childhood experience that had us dislike that part of our body?

We eventually collapsed together, imploded, exhausted, cherished, entwined and in a lovers knot.

I awoke; which is always a bonus. A south pacific dawn was imminent in the next hour or so. I took in the vista of her beautiful naked body and small nipples. Those were days of mythical stamina; I was still rock hard. Nobody is responsible for my sexual energy; I was loving myself and my sexual energy.

Sliding down between her legs; her ample lips reached towards me begging to be savoured. I laid there ingesting her, returning her from elixir. Encore.

We were at it again; fucking all night, I was sex incarnate for her.

Not every woman needed or wanted stamina though, some would cum within minutes of starting and would then be sated. They avoided the infinite joys that a skilled lover could give them; the hearth of their hearts remained closed. And others don't let themselves orgasm. Kit was different.

Kit knew how to orgasm. Her face died. She went. To where, I am not sure. Maybe she had a glimpse of heaven, an instant of bliss on the level of form (where it cannot be found).

But she couldn't dwell in her wholeness forever and would soon find herself once again in her body. Our orgasms were defining moments; our psychic connection became eternally fused. Fused in a way that would not be possible with a fake orgasm.

The orgasm is a place where we can experience the highest frequencies of experience possible; it is a sweet drug indeed. The paradox of orgasm is that it leaves a woman feeling full and a man feeling depleted, such is the flow of sexual essence. It wasn't uncommon for a lover to leap out of bed replenished while I would fall into a depleted rejuvenative sleep.

My teacher tells me that there is much for me to learn about male orgasm. She says that I should avoid ejaculating whenever I can. Sometimes I am guided to do otherwise as Source or my ego calls for my seed to be given to my woman. Women love to take your seed. Some will go out of their way to get it from you, even if you are practicing retention; they will test your resolve. Kit took as much as she could get.

We were not counting orgasms that night, but as the multi-orgasmic beings that we were, we lost count. We moved from placid waters to ocean tempest, from yin to yang energy throughout the night. Another peak arrived. I lay there with a heart beating like a Taiko drum – my breath journeying me through all time and space.

I eventually returned.

She was stroking the outline of my shoulders and then circling her finger lightly around the helix of my ear. She then ran her fingers through my long hair.

'I can hear your heart pounding sweetie.'

I noticed how beautiful I was. My body is all I have and it's truly beautiful.

It was a complete moment. I was suspended in an ephemeral glimpse of what was profoundly possible between a man and a woman.

If I committed to that woman, where could she take me?

'Aren't we gorgeous sweetie.'

I lay on her chest, most peaceful. Receiving her and attuning to various rhythms from Source; her breath, my breath, her heart, and our *Yin-ing* sex god.

'I'm a bit sore sweetie.' That creative friction again.

'Yeah, me too.' It was time for a break.

My world was dripping with colour and I was keenly aware of it.

I swayed with the steam dancing and curling off my tea into the fresh morning air. I reflected on the depth of our lovemaking and on my glimpse into a new possibility. I had sexed away even deeper layers of the feminine. It was as if our energies had made love. I had witnessed my desire to be intimate with something more than form. I thought I had found paradise everlasting.

Romantic and sexual union is a path to wholeness.

'I've got my man in Sydney that I have to go back to sweetie.'

'That's okay Kit, that's okay, we've had enough good times to last a year or two... When do you leave?'

'Friday.' Sadness rushed my cells.

Our breaths paused.

'We can still share more time together this week Kit, carnal times, assuming you'd like to of course.'

'Yes Ben, I like it carnal... I really love him though; you just need to remember that.'

After some introspection. 'No worries Kit, I've got my girlfriend back home too.'

Kit had a divine pussy and diviner energy, her temple required a daily pilgrimage. Our sweetest melody joyfully played for the next week. My worship of her allowed me further into the feminine essence, further than I had ventured before. When I visited her temple my attention moved deeply inside "us" and I became capable of noticing so many small things, physical and energetic. She let me spend hours laying in her womanly energy. I learnt that there is a difference between sex and intimacy.

We shared purest bonded intimacy and it inspired this sexual scripture.

Oh how I loved the sex god back then.

When I arrived on earth twenty three years ago, I had within me the potential to become all that I may be. It's as if the Universe provided the sunshine for me to grow towards and the sex god provided the creative juice to get there. We grow and bend towards the sunshine. I felt unified with the sex god and its causes and intentions; it was flowering in full sunlight.

My beautiful sex god had me tasting smelling eating looking and feeling Kit (there is no hierarchy to the senses). It penetrated her being in any way that it could find. It penetrated the Universe through me to find the wholeness and completing union it sought with its feminine aspect.

Me and my body were the experiencing instruments of a sacred and primal dance of Nature.

It was with Kit that I realised that a woman must be worshipped by a man for the deeper layers of her heart to open. Those deep layers couldn't be flippantly *given away* even if she tried, they must be worshipped open by a man. Sometimes foolish men will think they are getting into the wet panties of those deeper layers... But wet doesn't mean she is opening her heart. And some women may pretend or naively mimic an open heart in a manner that they have seen elsewhere.

The revelation of a woman's authentic love is unmistakeable. If he is a real man he will detect it and if she is a real woman, not stuck in media stories in her head, she will receive untold gifts from her own feminine elixir too. A worshipped woman unfurls the flower of her being. She blossoms and re-consumes her man in Love.

In the space of a week the deeper fragrances of Kit's heart were revealed. They washed over and through me. I admired her, respected her and deeply desired her. Her blossoming heart allowed strange magic to arise. I fell in love again; the after-glow tingling of which can still be felt today. Had we been blessed with more time together our coupling would have become infinite – notwithstanding my aversion to being trapped and of course the love of my life back in Canada.

'I must return to my man in Sydney now Ben. It was so important to me that we did this together. You have shown me so much; you have shown me what is possible between a man and a woman. I needed to do this once in my life to know the fairytale is true.'

Tears hung in the air. Lamenting how I was missing her already, my stomach tightened – but my heart opened.

Sometimes my body feels painful feelings.

She was chatting too much that day, broadcasting things unnecessarily. I just wanted her body, her energy. I put my fingers to her lips.

'You are so beautiful when your lips are closed.'

And so this yarn came to the end of its spool.

As the tapestry takes shape we see new threads woven with old threads, woven with golden threads and darkest threads. They are all interwoven upon the warp that is my soul and the weft that is my genetic, cultural and environmental conditioning. The weaving becomes the fabric of Nature arising into culture that is already present.

I received a letter that day from Jane. She told me that everything was set for my visit to Montreal in a few months time. I took a moment to reflect on how I had been behaving like a free man and had been living very inconsistently with being in a long term relationship. It was the time of my life. I knew I should return to Canada to see her but until then it was sex god business as usual.

We continued our travels onwards to New Zealand. James wasn't too happy with me as I had disappeared and left him to "his own travels". I'd eaten so much pussy that I got a serious throat infection and completely lost my voice.

He wasn't speaking to me, *and* I couldn't reply anyway.

Eros

I was full of sunshine. I took in the distant blue-sky-kissed
mountain ridges through watery eyes. The wind howled through
my core as I held my board steady on the lip of the snowy eyrie...
I was ready to shred. Ready for rapid descent, I looked down,
my adrenalin surged. I slid over the edge accelerating rapidly.
I squeezed the juice out of the mountain face. All that mattered
was this. I could only be present with this, utterly present. My
board skeeted across the broad slope; I was at the edge of comfort.
Hardening my edge, I scythed into the iced powder then hardened
further and control returned. It was so good it hurt. Similar
feelings can be felt at the edge of a retained orgasm. Cascades of
icy powder spewed up and shot me in frozen waves. Carving is
thrilling. Like orgasm it's an intimate dance with big nature. It is
utterly erotic.

Mythically Eros is the firstborn light from Source; it is
simultaneously the force of love and the creative urge of ever-
flowing nature. It is the way that Source enters into the physical
world, the way that it comes into being and orders all things. Eros
is the origin of experience and it embodies the experiencer. The
experiencer can choose to taste all manifest Eros erotically. It's as
if the erotic is a way of being totally in, and of, experiencing the
world. Eros is a divine motivation to taste the actuality of form
– it's rather like Source gleefully celebrating the latest new form
of itself. Your ego is a villain that stands between you and purest
being; it *is in the way* of becoming the erotic.

Anything in life can be erotic – everything in life *is* erotic.
Even right now Reader... Perhaps with the bubbles in your beer,
the unfurling buds on a great oak tree or with the warmth of your
hairy butt on the chair. When experienced erotically, all of life can
take you back to Oneness with itself – that is divine. It is Divine
Eros.

I rode crazy hard to the edge of the piste and landed on a
small plateau to be in an exhausted and sweaty wonder at it all.

'Wicked ride dude!' A smiling pink ski bunny yelled across to me.

'Woohoo!' I panted, it was the best reply I could muster. I was full of playful spirit. I shimmied my snowboard towards her and clumsily rode into her, wiping out. I was prone to losing control in tight places.

The ground started shaking. 'Was that an earthquake?'

That part of New Zealand was prone to earthquake activity.

'Whoa I think so... Freaky! There's nothing to fall on us out here.'

'Nothing except snowboarders.' She grinned.

A ski-patrol with a loud hailer asked us to clear the mountain.

'Rats, I guess that's it for today, better head down to find my mates. My name's Ben, by the way. It was lovely to share that earthquake with you. Are you here alone?'

'No there are twenty of us on a school ski trip. My name's Taylah, nice to meet you too.'

'Well, shall we?'

'Let's gooooo.'

'Woohoo.'

She skied, I boarded. We raced. She won.

'Nice work Taylah, byeee,' I shouted.

I saw James over by the ski racks and headed over his way, spraying him with a rooster tail as I came to a stop.

Reader, does it matter if this story is true? What if it is all fantasy, all a fiction? Is this unusual lexicon biographical or simply pulp? Simply pap to titillate, challenge and teach you while you ride the train, recline on your sun lounger or skive a day off 'cos you drank too much wine. How does truthfulness change your enjoyment or disdain, your growth or shut-down to my sex-is-sacred vibe? Aha Reader, I exercise my playful muscle. I do this in the name of healing intent and transmission of a teaching. This is a recount of my path, your path will be very different – some things that I've learned on my way will be useful for you. May all beings be peaceful.

Several hours later tough-guy Scott, manly man James and my good self headed out to play. We chose a bar; the only bar in town.

I like to spend time with men. In the company of men I share cutting wise-cracks and an occasional truths indirectly told. Man-talk is rarely deep as the rest of our life is deep, while we shoulder responsibility and keep our women safe.

I can't trust any man. I can't trust him with my woman, in business, as a religious leader or to be transparent with me. Men always have an ego strategy; they always have their own agenda. Their unhealthy male essence is greedy and Earth destroying. Men can't be trusted, as they do not trust themselves. They don't trust themselves to be themselves. They can be overpowered by pussy and then betray their tribe. Can I trust my own judgements about another man?

I could probably trust a man to save my life if I needed it though. I can trust a man to die for the safety of my peoples. I can trust him to come-on to my woman while I'm away or to watch my luggage while I take a pee.

Can I trust myself? Yes.

Can I trust the sex god?

I *can* trust Love.

'I'm going to take it easy tonight chaps as I don't want a hangover to get in the way of my last day of boarding.'

'Or get in the way of another night of that women worship stuff you keep going on about more like. They don't deserve it,' chimed Scott.

Scott was emotionally damaged. In our travels together he had shared stories from his youth; of how his adoptive mother was abusive and neglecting of him. Her cruelty probably resulted from the damaged men that she had encountered in her own life... And so the damage propagated.

I ordered some beers and a coke. I was declared a lightweight but I didn't care. We settled down to banter.

'So what are you planning to do with your life then James?' Scott enquired from the eyrie of having his life already sorted out.

'I really need to get out there to make some money. My dad says I should go into technology and the newspapers say that computers are going to be big ticket in the future.'

'Yeah, I've got some friends doing some computer stuff and they've been telling me I should get into them too – I think I'll stick to trading motorbikes with Indians though... hey, check out that girl over there, she'd look so good on the end of my cock!' Scott rasped.

'My dad told me that if you don't know what you want out of life, you'll probably work for someone who does know.' We all let that one sink in for a while. Most men are naive to the profound power in their male essence.

I preached further. 'You guys are missing something though, listen to you, you are talking about your lives from the standpoint of other people – your dad, the media, the vicar. What about *you*, what do you want to do? It isn't about needing, having or wanting to do something, for me it's got to be about *loving* to do something – and I'm the only one who can know what I would love to do! That's how I can be myself.'

'So what would you *love* to do then smartarse?'

A wise-arsed reply emerged. 'Women. Whadya think!?'

I eventually tire of the company of men. My need of a woman arises and I strike out on my own. Our intellectual conversation was clearly over... so we started pulling.

I became touchy-feely with a couple of local girls. Then I noticed Taylah watching me. She had me sussed, me thinks. I watched back at her heart melting demure. She was an ordinary girl. I noticed her lips. I noticed my erection. I noticed her hips, perhaps she was moist too.

'There he goes again. I can't stand all his worshipping women stuff. Why doesn't he act like a man? Yeah, in the time it takes him to seduce one woman, I could have had my DNA all over the tits of ten whores who know how to appreciate a real man.'

'Yeah but they wouldn't have loved you Scott, that's the difference,' I barked.

I wandered over to the bar.

'Three Steinlager's please...'

The bargirl was overwhelmed and smiling to survive, it took an age to get the drinks order. Taylah broke ranks and sidled up to me.

'Fancy a beer Taylah?'

'Steiny please, but what about your friends, they seem to really like you?'

'Make that four please... Oh it's ok, just a couple of local girls I've just met... and I've been getting dirty looks from the meatheads over there and besides... you are far prettier.'

'And faster,' she said blushing and pushing herself into me.

'Let's head over here where it's a bit quieter and get out of the rabble.' My pilgrimage to her treasure was underway.

I knew I would be flying to meet Jane in a few weeks, so my play-time would be ending soon. Without duplicity, I was up for one last fling to bid farewell to my libertine age.

Taylah was a home-girl blonde, quietly cautious and not exactly spoilt. She had a syrupy kiwi accent – she'd be welcome to read me bedtime stories any night of the week. Our chatter continued for an hour or so, sharing diverse conversations of class disgust, imperial pride and absent partners. Our connection developed. I enjoyed her innocence.

'Let's go for a walk, get some air...'

We negotiated our exit from the bar into the ozone-crisp mountain air. That penis of mine was up to his usual tricks, rock hard and stretched down the leg of my jeans – uncomfortable as my jockeys cut in painfully. It wasn't interested in offering soft dignity. I'm sure I left an impression on her when we hugged. Relief arrived when Taylah cracked some joke about it, allowing him just to be. Such is life.

Everybody hugs differently. Some hugs are strong and engaged while others have an empty, frail quality to them. Taylah's hugs were alive with energy. I am certain chemistry can be felt in a hug.

Watched by owls and mountain spirits, we walked for an hour along a lazy stream in a pine forest. I felt her delicate energy and imagined what she would look like naked. A tender kiss and a

the sex god | 89

lust rush ignited itself between us. Perhaps our crazed longing to be in love fuelled the idealisation of what might happen next. We couldn't wait to rip each other's clothes off.

'I'm getting cold,' Taylah said shivering.

'I would offer you my jacket Taylah, but I can think of a better way to keep warm.' I handed her my jacket. 'My camper van won't work as the chaps will be back later,' I plotted.

'And I've got three other girls in my dorm room. They'll be back later too.' After some easy deliberation we decided that a top-bunk at her dorms would be the luxury option. Always better to be shagging among other girls I thought.

'It's sub-tropical in here.' The bunk-bedded dorm room *was* the right choice.

'This one is mine up here, at least we'll be hidden.'

We climbed the small ladder made for elves and dived under the duvet. Cuddles arose. Her nipples were too sensitive so I ventured down between her legs. My finger discerned a cleft through the taught fabric of her knickers. Probing deeper I felt a small firm ridge. She slowly gyrated her hips as I held my finger in place. Pleasure washed across her face and permission was granted to go further.

Suddenly she became rigid and uncertain. A forlorn look appeared and her sass vaporised. Women are often savvy until they get to the bedroom; perhaps that is true for many men too, I wouldn't know. We had created openness and trust between us but our deep intimacy called us to be nakedly honest for each other; *to be ourselves*. No wonder it was frightening. Sex is rarely neutral, what we both did next would decide if our connection would wound or heal our sex god psyches.

'This is all very new for me Ben... it isn't like they said it would be in Cosmo.'

A virgin.

'It's okay Taylah. We don't have to do anything you don't want to.'

It's a girl's right to have complete control over her virginity. Only damaged men would deny her that.

I stroked her hair.

'Please don't be rough, my sister has warned me that some men can be rough... show me what to do.' Shyness washed over her. 'I don't feel good in my body, I worry I'm not attractive...' She was flushed. 'There's so much wrong with the way I look. My tits are too small, my lips are too big and my ass...'

Sometimes we aren't ready. Sometimes we can't bear to expose ourselves for fear of rejection. Our fashion-conditioned ego gets in the way. Even when we are being unconscious we can still feel how strong an ego wanting approval can be.

There are two ways to be with a woman. I could choose to be with her from a place of needy damaged masculine energy, or I could be with her as overflowing healthy masculine energy. The sex god could be both. Taylah was in luck.

I placed my finger on her lips.

'Shhhh sweetheart... You are kidding me aren't you? You *are* beautiful. You are perfect just as you are. You should love every curve of your body and of your mind.' Another sex-education encounter; how did I keep attracting those types of girl?

My demeanour changed; our quick-shag was upgraded.

'You know what Taylah, let me simply and gently worship you. Let's go at a pace that feels right for *you*.' Alcohol-free sex is always superior. Sexual subtleties surfaced. A poignant and emotive oeuvre followed allowing us to safely get into each other's energy. 'No's became 'Yes's. I gently explored her armpits and licked her musk. Sex is so consuming, it's easy to miss the beauty and sensitivities of sex. My nature was to be of gentle service to her, to show her the ways of caring- sexual-intimacy with a man.

Her knickers were off, her flower opened.

'Oh wow, you are so beautiful baby.'

Veils dropped away as she melted.

I placed my finger on her lips.

'Tell me what you feel you need right now. Communicate and give me feedback.'

A spark arose; it was held between us.

'Communicate with me in any way that feels right Taylah.'

She spoke through words, through touch, through her eyes, through her sheer intent. Her sweet touch of me intensified, she was at times curiously anatomical. Then her youthful energy surrounded us like being born again. Not sure who was embracing who. I slithered down her body sniffing and drawing her subtleties deep inside me. I sucked, tasted and flicked. Her legs quivered. She moaned and responded ecstatically when I rolled her hood back and focussed with precision. Great sex isn't formulaic; the act grows in real time. We were lost in the same temperature and we were found by the way our curvy edges touched. Diving deeper into intimacy, I held her tight and made her take intensity. I let her feel in control but I wasn't submissive. I was totally there for her at the level she needed. That level unhurriedly escalated as the flower of her heart trusted me.

Stultified.

We both froze as the dorm door crashed open and three girls tumbled in. They were noisy and drunk and were sharing lusty could-have-been stories about the men at the bar. We needed to avoid the hysteria that would follow if we were discovered.

Our shared juices felt cold. I could hear her heart, or was it mine. In deep stillness we swallowed shallow. There was a space between everything in that moment including our breaths and our thoughts – but not our beings. It was a long moment.

We were not discovered.

I yearned to take Taylah. I had worshipped sweetly and given much for my prize. I thought long and hard about what my next move should be.

Once I was certain the girls were asleep. I encouraged Taylah onto her side. She was uncomfortable with the presence of her roommates and closed off my efforts to enter her.

Eventually the sunrise came and she had relaxed again. Her yearn met mine and she finally took all of me. I was lying behind her. I expanded into her. Her back arched, splendidly. Hard and still, I didn't move. We flew together without any movement, we were so pent up. Our energies and seeds merged and an emotional freedom pulsed its way through us.

'Was that an Earthquake?' I whispered.

I awoke from a melted sleep and returned to this mysterious existence. My head was on her chest, I comforted myself with her heartbeat. I could sense a pleasurable glow of energy in my genitals. Taylah awoke slowly. The other girls were comatose.

'I was deeping so sleeply... are the others awake?' were her first words.

'They're all asleep. I should go now, are you ready to hit the slopes?' I whispered. 'Can I have that grapefruit?'

'Will I see you again?' she sleepily replied.

I delivered a kiss to her forehead.

'Thanks Ben, I had such a lovely time, when can I see you again?'

A storm was brewing that required a humane dispensation. Some chicanery was needed.

'It will have to be in a while as I'm leaving for Montreal soon.'

She held my face and stared into my eyes as we said goodbye. 'Oh please come and see me, send me a letter, I'd love to see you again, we are so good together.'

'Okay, I'll be in touch when my travels are over.'

Heart breaker.

Though I'm happy to hang out with men from time to time, I've always preferred my own company, or the company of women. I had left James and Scott at the bar, such was the brittleness of some male friendships. What is it with men? Maybe I see the ugly side of my lovely father in other men, and it repulses me? Or perhaps talking for hours about football, purposelessness or petrol just doesn't do it for me? There have been a few men that I've loved though, they were truly amazing friends and I could almost trust them.

I sat on a bench outside our camper van warming myself in the morning sunshine; I was voluptuous with smile. I peeled the grapefruit, first the rosy-skin and then the segments individually; juice flew everywhere. I thought I had life really sussed. From my joy I hatched a plan to fly back to Montreal to propose marriage to Jane. I'm not sure why exactly, my friends were marrying off and it seemed to be the done thing.

James and Scott emerged shoe-gazing from the camper van, puffy-eyed and desperate for coffee. Scott looked like a beaten up leather sofa, they had had a boy's night.

'Hey guys, how was your night? Did you get rid of all your DNA or shag any grannies, Scott?' I sheepishly enquired, for I knew they didn't pull.

'Oh, we just drank too much; there wasn't any vadge worth bringing down last night,' rasped beef-cake Scott.

I interpreted his comment to mean "there weren't any girls as emotionally retarded as he was, looking for abuse last night". Though some may say that my own "love 'em and leave 'em" manner needed some emotional evolution too.

'Oh, that's no good chaps.' With un-feigned surprise.

Scott was a good guy and huge fun to travel with. He had a crass way with women, which I was ashamed to associate with. That was my projection at least, when in the company of a woman he may well have turned into a big pussycat for all I knew. Judgement aside, Scott was yet another facet of male energy, the kind of male energy we might rely on to go fight a war and protect us. He was the untamed warrior man, in touch with his wilder side. I'm sure he thought I was a bit of a dandy. Over the years I recognised that I am a gentler man, in tune with my feminine side as a lover. I have a wild man but he is well under water. My strong feminine aspect allows me to notice what feels good in my body when somebody speaks. I am always observing nuances in a voice, how relaxed it is or if it's coming from a place of mental tension. I am constantly feeling what's mean in a room, what's closed in a room. I can embody presence but am tuned into my emotions.

I have learned that the healthy masculine is in fact a gentle loving energy. But men can live through any of their stronger archetypes in the service of their women.

A chunk of muscle really does it for some women. A bad boy with a thick cock; you know, to grunt and treat them badly (subjective I know). I guess with a bad boy at least they know

94 | the sex god

what they are getting. Together they may foster a closeness glued together by jealousy and disrespect. Perhaps they play out libido that transmutes sex into abject violence. But there may even be a healing opportunity in that kind of sexual play. Who knows they may even be faithful to each other!? I have met girls out looking for some rough and they didn't find me sexually attractive. I would have been gentle with them, worshipping them to bliss... and then I would leave them or cheat on them. Who am I kidding! Perhaps even you, dear goddess Reader are that type? Needing to masochistically take it; or maybe you just feel the need to be treated roughly sometimes? Why is that? Or perhaps you, dear god Reader are that emotionally retarded *Eamon Shoot* type of man. Unable to be of service to your woman as pure Love, a goddess. I trust that this story elucidates for you another way of being, another possibility. I realise that I may be coming across as sexually pious at this point, so I should own up. I too can have violent lust flowing through me as we shall witness later. Sex and violence energies come and go like waves throughout a lifetime. It is all Love though as there is only Love.

Taylah's energy was sweet and innocent. But a woman can be different every day. Sometimes a woman's emotions can be ugly, maybe uglier than a man's. A woman can be ugly. Men have an excuse, 'cos they are men and it is expected of them, but a woman? I'm not talking about an unfortunate, unloved, un-self-loved soul like a hag. I'm talking about the *hell hath no fury* type, bitch, bunny boiler; Kali[iii] incarnate ugly. Surely pure love shouldn't have to look that way. At once fragile and savage, the sometimes melodramatic excess of a woman can fast become angst for a man. Especially if he isn't a big enough man to handle her, to coral her and let her know she is still adored and safe.

But Taylah was a sweetie.

I saw Taylah on the slopes later that day; she was awkward amongst her friends. My hard-on returned, we had a silent giggle.

---

iii   Kali – A Hindu goddess who is considered the goddess of time and change. She is also a figure of death and annihilation.

We smiled an *adios* to each other.

Perhaps this journey isn't personal; perhaps I am just a passenger.

So Reader, the tapestry of sacred explicitness is building but it's too soon for a pattern to appear. It's all good stuff so far, but the dark and light threads in this weaving are starting to convene. As the tapestry is woven, overarching pictures and stories are being revealed. Perhaps by now there's a hint of a golden thread starting to form?

How could I be trusted? I was an owned-up liar! How could any woman trust me? Maybe, just maybe, they trusted me as their infinite-love saw something deeper in me, something that they could heal? Maybe they didn't need to trust me so long as I was there for *them*!?

Did my interest in sex grow dominant because I wasn't truthful with its true nature and pushed it underground? Was it all nature's balancing response? I had a simple motivation for all my youthful playing around... I loved the joy of the chase and the high I got from a successful seduction – it was all very in the moment. It was dope, not heroine. There was never any intent to hurt others. There was never any pre-meditated plan, life was just happening to me. But as always in life, there are consequences. The consequences of all this play were profoundly unintended.

Life was good in that golden age. But it was to be the end of an era, as my ways were about to foster their own set of dramatic dilemmas.

I was enjoying the precarious thrill of hovering at the edge of the adult world that I *thought* I understood.

Addiction – Purpose

Authentic

Reader, today I sit and write in a graveyard. I have come here to reflect on the statement that *you don't need a dress rehearsal to be who you are*. A raven lands atop a cold stone and checks me out. Then my awareness shifts to the hyphens between the dates on the gravestones that surround me. I ponder how each hyphen represents a lifetime of breathing through suffering – this is true for every peaceful cadaver six feet below me. Sex gods now departed, each one of them experienced love and hate, compassion and greed, and damage from unhealthy masculine energy. Someday I too shall have a hyphen to symbolise my lifetime. None of my search for meaning shall have mattered. But Reader, in that moment my search *did matter to me*. My mind wandered. I was alive and that was good! It was radically yummy. It was so good to be with the abundant richness of life. Timelessly changing aliveness is entirely different to death. We must embrace the eternal movement of life if our lives are to have meaning.

Reader, what if you and I agreed, right now, that there is nothing to be fathomed? How would our lives be different?

Being yourself is being authentic, authentic is sexy. Others notice you when you are passionate without expectation. Our authenticity is unique. The "ease" that we feel inside guides us to our own "uniqueness". Being yourself is about refusing to be bound by the conventions that society throws your way. Not falling into the destiny of a racial, cultural or family group. I'm not talking about being a self-absorbed jerk, I'm talking about rising above the rushing river torrent of humanity. A major part of who we are as individuals is the expression of our cultural heritage. The man that understands this can break away from it and stand alone.

My emotional complexities shaped who I had become so far. As an emotionally naked young man my reptilian core wanted to have sex, lots of sex. Having sex, often, with many lovers felt like a great way to live my life. That urge clearly went against the grain of what society (and Jane) expected of me. The pressure for commitment is considerable from a nubile woman, after all the quest for safety is in her nature. Deep down I was a progressive free-spirit, but I hadn't claimed dominion over myself yet. The unquestioned momentum amongst my peers was to go get married, have kids etc. Who was I at twenty-four to doubt that that should be my path too?

It is all Love.
Could I be Love?

Meat Hooks

Our apocalypse arrived. 'Are you going to tell me the truth about what you have been up to Ben?'

High on my world travels, I had arrived in Montreal a few hours earlier. After a warm embrace I noticed the bleakness in Jane's eyes. She seemed dry and clipped; there was a peculiar charge in the air as she straddled the axis of excited-to-see-you and a deepest-sense-of-betrayal.

'Are you going to tell me the truth about what you have been up to Ben?' Her thousand-yard stare said it all.

'What d'ya *mean*?' I tried denial – dumb-arsed man – the gravity of the situation was failing to chime with me. I had lost my smile.

She was growing irascible. 'Heather has told me everything... How many Ben?'

Everything! I thought. Fuck, did Heather even tell her about the flings we had shared too? Jane was a seething cauldron; two people will interpret an event in widely dissimilar ways.

'How many Ben?' Chunks of rage flew across the room. She was deeply wounded by the blunt sword of my infidelity. Her anger was her fire – there to keep her safe.

A woman always wants to hear the truth even if it's a truth that they don't want to hear.

Our opposing paradigms clashed as she packed a punch right through the marrow of my being. My only intention was to playfully give my love to the world; I didn't bargain for life serving me this wallop. I felt the feelings I last had as a seven year old little boy, impaled on a stake, in front of my father. I felt the feelings that I'd never wanted to experience again. All my clever efforts to avoid those feelings, alongside my efforts to protect Jane from "having to endure the heartbreak of dumping me" were now naked to her verbal axes.

I tried to be clever and stand my ground... for around thirty seconds. I feigned that I was unable to comprehend why she didn't see the same view of events that I did. She was hurt, angry and humiliated. I couldn't look her in the eye. How different it was to being infatuated with her. How the fairy tale had cheated her.

Reader, the consequences of your actions are inevitable. My skin crawls to recall that moment.

'You FUCKER, how could you do this to me?' She was livid and was having none of it. She had me on meat hooks.

Over the years Heather had been a loving confidante. She betrayed our confidence. She had told Jane *way too much*. Sisters were finally looking after each other. I wished that I had fucked Heather back at that college party. I know we would have been hot together. As I licked my wounds, I wished I could fuck Heather again, vengefully. I would have really given it to her. From malice, I wanted to use my warhead cock to stab her womb deeply. My damaged masculine sex god would be animal with her; violence would be in my sex. Perhaps she would have liked that – the unhealthy feminine essence in many women loves to be dominated and profanely wounded. Though I'm not proud of that sexual distortion it was there in me, as in every man. It was the same energy that revenges upon women the savagery of brothers in war. Sex rage is an ugly energy.

When I was done with Heather I would have crawled into her large bosom crying. I would have thanked her for being truthful and I would tell her that I loved her for it.

Can I trust a woman confidante?

I now know that I can trust her to show me the way back to Love.

A blistering broadside from Jane followed, far too violent for me to repeat.

I wasn't evolved enough to stay sweet and connected in my vulnerabilities back then. I was a wreckage of a man. Sex god, is that what you wanted? The sex god didn't care, as it would continue to use me to fix its needs whatever the outcome.

She stormed off leaving the door wide open. The only response I had was to escape the illusion and fall asleep; I thought she might have returned to dispatch me in my sleep.

I had a dream, where I died. I was killed by a bear.

Over the next few days Jane's predominant quiet was punctuated by violent outrage. She needed her space to integrate my untruths and work out what to do next. I remained sheepish for I needed to work out what to do next as well. I felt very alone. There wasn't anyone to speak to or wise men to seek counsel with, there weren't any masters in my life back then. The only thing I could focus on was putting one foot in front of the other, while my core festered under a shit heap of guilt and remorse. My silent scream told me that it was the end of an era.

Our aching hearts had been threshed and laid naked, ground to whiteness[iv]. When biblical dramas play out on the stage of youthful romance there is a dance of power. I believed that Jane had all the power. The healthy and obvious choice for both of us was to split up, or try some time apart or walk some other middle path.

Jane sensed that I was still interested in her and came up with a list of crucifying conditions for the continuance of our relationship. She bargained hard; for she became the embodiment of what she couldn't forgive. Those conditions amounted to "Ben you must lose your Self, do not be Ben". I sensed pressure to move me to a decision that I didn't want to make. Was she trying to control and manipulate me as a means of rewriting her own personal history and loss of control in childhood? Control is a false sense of safety.

In spite of being a self-indulgent so-and-so, perhaps I loved her more than I loved myself? I was prepared to give her respect, romance, communication, sex and consistency. Unwittingly, I was to give her power over me as part of the bargain. She liked that. It was the crushing of me. But no, maybe I am twisting and spinning it all too much. She was simply a woman desiring to love her man and to be loved herself.

Something, something, something deep inside that was testament to the forces that have shaped me, told me that I should

iv   K. Gibran – The Prophet, on Love

stay with her. She was the woman I loved; she was the woman that I wanted to marry. Marriage for me meant she was the woman that I planned to be with for the rest of my life. The ignorance of my youth; as I didn't know how long a lifetime was. I didn't know that humouring her would lead to resenting her.

The sex god was to be given to only one woman.

I turned the plant away from the sunlight
I proposed marriage.

The basis for a co-dependent relationship was sown; the relationship amounted to "He cheated on me, so to teach him a lesson, I shall marry him".

She accepted, with conditions.

We got married.

The Flower Blooms

I gave her my sunshine. She responded by unfurling her precious and incandescent petals; an unfurling that would become the completion of her flowering. A man can only witness that phenomenon if is wholly committed to his woman and sticks around. I saw the flowering in Jane.

In the full radiance of the flower of her love, a woman will steadfastly stand by your side. She will shine her beauty, her love, her wisdom and her intuition onto your own purpose. She will lovingly support you on your own life-journey. She will be on your side. She will bear your children and do *anything* for your children – even die for *your* children. She will drive two hundred miles to bring documents and office keys that your overburdened responsibilities had you leave behind.

As the worship of your one woman deepens, you get another step closer to the infinite love in her heart.

For seven years I wallowed only in her love.

Turning Point

Over the past thirty years I hadn't been constrained in exploring the world around me; I am compelled to avoid the mundane and mediocre. Sex with Jane, if it showed-up, had become ordinary. The high-octane sexy rampancy present in the springtime of our relationship was fizzling. Lost in our habitual programs, we had become mechanical, boring and repetitive.

What about humdrum dull sex Reader? You know, the kind of routine fucking we might reluctantly take part in when we are tired, perhaps with a belly full of cheap food. Sex is often ordinary. I have chosen not to fill this story with endless recounting of ordinary sex, as it wouldn't interest you. Sex doesn't have to be ordinary though. The formula for non-ordinary sex is openness and trusted communication. Jane and I had started to lose that.

The opposite of ordinary is extraordinary. Extraordinary sexual play is beyond technique. It requires *a lot* of practice, meticulously held between two lovers – who are prepared to schedule love-appointments, be spontaneous and laugh a lot. Special lovemaking can arise whenever we are committed to allowing it into our relationship. Jane and I had no such commitment. I had become a sexually frustrated man.

If another woman expressed interest towards me, the sex god would awaken. I had the propensity to tease or be very naughty; but there wasn't a glimmer of follow through. I was a committed husband and a good boy. The sex god format wasn't broke - it was taken off air, until a particular night out with some close friends...

We had been out for a celebration dinner. I had coiffed way too much champers. We returned home for some after dinner drinks. The four of us crashed through the front door with much debauched joy. Somehow things got sexy. Alcohol probably made the day... and spoiled the night. My last recollection prior to passing out was a slender naked Ellie fucking herself mental on my mediocre stiffy. Unlike my mythical-fornicator nights with Taylah or Kit, I gave an underwhelming performance. It was a shame to be with such a beautiful woman and then not remember it. But I didn't get in trouble that night as we were swapping, Jane was with Ellie's husband!

And then it was back to ordinary.

Reader, did you ever notice after a fuck or wank that there's a fizzing sensation of leftover energy? A remnant of charge that you didn't let go of or quite reach. A wank at a later time can be used to retrieve it. I use the breath and sounds to reach into it and spread it around my body. If I am able to enjoy noisy sex, there are never any leftovers. I was able to go back into salvage the glowing energy that Ellie left in my pelvis for a month at least.

In his early years a man explores the physical in sex and relationship. Physical is everything to the sex god. As a man grows older and his sense of self strengthens, his attention often turns to the psychological. Vulnerability can be exposed and explored. When a man embraces his vulnerability and becomes transparent with his feelings, he can free himself. Vulnerability is his power. When he pretends there is no vulnerability his soul becomes brittle. If a man can be vulnerable in the glow of womanly love he has an opportunity to evolve, awaken and grow up. Many men would rather be angry than vulnerable. I wasn't ready to look at the vulnerabilities in myself or my marriage.

Jane and I had thus far enjoyed a beautiful partnership that affirmed life and lead to great things. But the fruits of our togetherness were still bruised from the meltdown of my infidelity. Like many people I channelled my considerable creative energies towards my business instead of Jane. The misfortune was that we weren't emotionally aware or mature enough to identify the early stage malignancy that had crept between us. If we *had* known we probably wouldn't have known what to do about it in any case. Our love for each other was our marital glue during those years. We really did love each other.

So what of the institution of marriage? Perhaps marriage was an institution created to restrain opportune competition for nubile women by our forefathers? A few hundred years ago marriage became a formal arrangement with both religious and state entwining. Marriage as we know it today is part of the fabric of our culture; albeit a frayed part as today's marriage institutions are not able to contain our true Nature. Go back a thousand years and things were very different. Courtly-love institutions typically condoned non-physical love that would escalate emotionally rather than physically. Sex life was deferred to trysts (usually extramarital) that were created for fun. These days marriage can be an insane attempt to give life stability and structure. But we all have sex gods and the marriage container often cannot contain the needs of the sex gods. The propensity to marry, divorce and shag-around is a natural phenomenon that predates the state and religion. Primitive societies recognised the tension between marriage and the erotic, but my marriage refused to.

A modern marriage can be a beautiful partnership that affirms life and leads to great things. It can also be a cage that constrains growth and individual journeys. How do you be authentically-yourself within a marriage? I could feel that many of my sexual boundaries were inherited from my partner. But her boundaries *are not mine* as we are two separate people. Could our marriage fail because the sex god wasn't being sated? Do fairy tales instil a possibility that is rarely met? Were fairy tales all written by men to sugar coat the saccharin reality of living in a patriarchal culture?

In recent times I have heard of an ancient Druidic marriage ceremony known as a Hand Fasting. Some modern couples practice this ritual. The Hand Fasting marriage vows may be for "a year and a day", "a lifetime", "for all of eternity" or "for as long as love shall last." Smart people those druids. Whether the ceremony is legal or a private spiritual commitment is up to the couple, or multiple partners in the case of polyamorous relationships. I can relate to this form of marriage, it feels true to me. I can commit to my woman for this moment and the next, for the next year and a day; at which point we shall both see where we are and (hopefully) recommit. This structure allows both of us to be true to ourselves every-day without the hammer-weight of guilt and institution. The prospect of recommitting to my woman daily, with my open-heart as opposed to a mind-made promise-gone-stale feels alive, respectful and powerful. We could both keep reinventing the newness of the relationship. Maybe Jane would have been too insecure to un-marry and re-marry with a Hand Fast. I never did ask her.

When the right woman finds me, a woman who is capable of giving me "that feeling", then perhaps a Hand Fasting would be a vibrant way to be together. Angelica where are you?

So I was stuck. The overestimation of love and marriage led to disillusionment; her desire to possess me resulted in my wanting to escape. We were together but on a delicate plateau of control dramas and power struggles; mix in my apparent inability to express my emotions, and well, you can probably guess the rest.

An escape hatch appeared one perfect sunny day on a warm beach where the stones rattled in the surf. Relationships change when the sun shines. The relentless pace of the day had left Rene and I alone for a few hours. We were to reconnect with my wife and the others later; giving us ample time for some candid gossiping and sun-kissed lechery. The tempestuous but nuanced Rene was an attractive woman with an exotic continental accent. We had always enjoyed real friendship and had successfully harboured our secret desire for each other. Sitting and dialoguing about everything deeply was our forte, and on that sunny afternoon that is what we did. The attraction was palpable in spite of her air of unavailability.

We returned to the beach condo for a shower before dinner. She left the bathroom door ajar; I loved the way she misbehaved. I restrained myself on the floor outside as I marvelled at the cascading splashes of water. I indulged in the lure of her curves through the steamy glass. The woman I can't have has power over me. The divine feminine has power over men; if only women lived that.

She knew I was watching. We continued our fertile conversation above the spray. I could see her tight fit body; fit for display at any beach volleyball match, you could bounce quarters off her ass. Women like Rene are like an adventure. I wondered what it would be like to kiss her; would she be intrusive or agile, would her eyes be open or closed? I speculated that she would be hot in bed. I needed to have her.

Jane returned, the escape hatch closed.

The Revelation

I had slept as if an angel had sung me a lullaby. Beyond the duvet landscape I could see Maria's leotard, tangled tights and black dress strewn across the bedroom floor. Slowly turning my head so as not to wake her, I noticed her chest gently rising and falling. My gaze fixed on a couple of moles and then on some silky ringlets of hair at the nape of her neck. Thirteen hours earlier life had become interesting. Source had planned for me to learn something special about myself while Jane was away on a business trip. Life isn't all innocent.

We had been on a "lunch date" which was followed by copious flirting at a bar. Our connection escalated as we made our way along the seafront. We watched a blessing of dolphins play just beyond the wave-break. I felt beautiful as I watched her silk scarf shimmer in the wind. A deluge of rain that we had seen approaching over the horizon eventually brought our promenade to a close. We made tracks back to Maria's place and played a game of catching raindrops on our tongues to spirit the journey. A fresh relationship is so vital, so child like.

We arrived home sodden; we could have been drier if we weren't so wet. We cuddled and peeled each other out of our dripping clothes then leapt into bed to warm up. Her fragrance was heavens breath.

She kissed so well.

My teacher these days instructs me to consistently and confidently be in my male power if tested by a woman. She says I should align with my healthy masculine essence in order to know how to make choices. Had I known this back then I might have been faithful. But the sex god's irresistible urge to merge with the other polarity adamantly overwhelmed my marriage vows.

I failed or aligned.

I stroked her glowing olivine skin. I felt her open to me. We lay for a while staring into the mutual recognition in each other's souls. I saw great depth in her, she was an old soul. I saw beyond the beauty of her form, there was pain in there – I could feel that she was invested with bruised humanity.

Maria was a Spanish au pair. She had stylishly cut dark hair and big brown eyes. Her confected beauty was palpable beyond the perfection of her body – for her beauty could scare other women away.

Something was intensely wrong; and it was confirmed by the tears welling up in her dark eyes. There is so much more to sex than sex.

'I'm sorry Ben, I shouldn't cry, I don't want to spoil our day.' Mascara was drizzling down her cheeks.

I cheated on my wife for this! Perhaps it should have been me crying. Playing around was supposed to be fun.

She burrowed into my shoulder and I held her tight. I felt her heartbeat escalate and soon the tears became tsunami. I laid there just holding her as she cried for Spain. Intimacy only takes place in the present.

Composure returned. 'Please listen Ben, I need you to listen, just let me speak.' I stroked her soft hair.

'I can't let you touch me more Ben,' she stuttered. 'It hurt too much, it... it hurt my body, hurt my heart'

Unbeknownst, we had been brought together for a reason. She required me to be a bigger man than I realised I was. I held her and fixed into her eyes, feeling her pain. Her hesitation was a cue to go slower. My damaged masculine needed to be healthy. I dug for emotional literacy. I became present. I didn't move.

'Hurts your heart?'

Her eyes closed. She went quiet, absorbing the safety in my holding her.

'The men did it me, they did it to me, they took it away from me, my innocent.' She had witnessed the ugly ways of the damaged masculine.

There was a long pause. 'Which men?'

She started crying again, anger arose. I expanded her space as she pounded the pillows.

'He know what they were doing, that bastard.' Her anger moved towards me, but that was okay.

'Who?'

She stabilised. 'My Dad, he know what they were going to do. He should have stop them.' Her rage escalated. 'That bastard he should have done something, why did he let them do that to me? I was fifteen, for god sake I was only fifteen. Why? Why? Did he owe them something? He must have.' She sobbed.

Where was her mum in all this, did she just turn her head? Was she a silent abuser?

When two people make love they merge two psychological and energetic realities. My festering ego that thought "she could have waited for a better time to share her trauma" was arrested. I saw her beauty amplify as her hurt child seeped through and eroded the way things were supposed to have gone. I was bridling with testosterone, it would have been easy to spread her, fuck her and go home. But she opened my heart to a possibility beyond "a quick shag". I became enduringly fascinated by her and my disposition was only to move us towards a healthier state. I continued to lay there holding a space and listening without reaction; I was witnessing presence.

When I am in presence, energy flows from me towards whatever needs attention. I was present to the total truth of our moment. I was not overwhelmed or in denial. I was somehow a catalyst for her unexpected sharing; I became psychically and physically intrinsic. I was embodied to her unravelling. The alchemy possible at the confluence of sex, love and spirit is a miracle. The wounding possible at the confluence of sex, fear and ancestral damage is also a miracle.

After an eternity, Maria regained herself. 'Oh my Ben, I survived but I so sorry that you have to hear this to me.'

I kissed her gently on her forehead and resumed stroking her back. She proceeded to explain that three village men had taken her to a local wood and had taken it in turns to rape her over a period of several hours. The blindfold didn't make things easier.

She shared many cruel details that have no need of repeat; detail she only captured with adrenaline awareness.

Her friends, her sisters, had called her a whore. But in her culture she wasn't forced to her marry her rapist.

'Did you know who they were?'

'Yes.'

'Did you tell the police?'

'No, I too fright.'

It had taken her eleven years to share her trauma for the first time; and I was the speechless recipient.

Another eternity of blended stillness passed. An energetic intercourse took place in our communion. Abused female-essence was held.

'Your quiet says all the things that those men will never be strong enough to say. Thank you Ben.' Stillness passed.

A delicate smile appeared. The divine masculine is beautiful too.

'Undress me Ben.'

I obliged and slowly peeled off her remaining clothes including an exotic leotard that seemed so European to me. I tossed them playfully across the room. Chanel Number 5 aromas swelled into the air.

'Please touch me Ben.' Her declared boundaries changed. She closed her eyes.

I remained speechless, and nervously unsure of how to proceed. I ceded my responsibility and acquiesced to the intuitive actions that were flowing through me. Source had a purpose for the two of us that night, one that I didn't know I was capable of facilitating.

I stroked the length of her body taking in all her unique textures. My fingers toured all of her, tenderly caressing her inner thighs and loving the gaps between her toes. Occasionally Maria had sudden inhales or small shakes.

'You okay?' I whispered. 'Yes, it's working, it's good, go slowly, do more.'

Intimacy deepened.

Her breath hastened, she was sweating profusely.

She let out a 'Cooo... oooooh.... It's good.' I continued to move around her body with a touch that was dense with love; I was uniquely tender and yet penetrating.

Her sleeping beauty awakened.

'Please make love to me Ben, please.'

In one firm stroke, I pulled myself deep inside her, easily.

She started crying again, as I held her tight with a gossamer strength. I was motionless as I lay deep inside her. We bathed in the mixture of silence, respect and lightness. It was innocent sex, it was beautiful sex. The meaning of the communication is what was received. A transmission took place.

'They are forgive.'

I lay across her while watching the pulse on her neck. She had witnessed the same thing that I had – and it certainly made an impression on me. An occasional tear ran down her cheek. She smiled as she slept. I am not able to un-experience that moment. I had become a bigger man than I realised I was; I had engaged with my healthy masculine within.

Love only wants the best wellbeing for the other person.

Could double alchemy have been possible for Maria, could she have realised the innate power that she had as a woman. Men do stupid things just to get close to that power. When women collectively recognise that they are the holders of power they can assert their boundaries and change the world.

Sex shapes our lives, if we love our sexuality then the world may heal. When I transcend my conditioning and follow my intuitive flow, the flow of Source or Tao arising, then the extraordinary tends to happen. By following the guidance of my heart, beyond mind, love can just be and miracles can happen. Maria had called on me to sexually heal the unconsciousness of other brothers, to help her reclaim the strong softness of her divine feminine, her sexual right. I journeyed the waves of her pain and unconsciously witnessed profound feminine energies. I shared alchemy with her and through a gentle sexual union a healing took place. Sexual healing is possible through me – though the concept wasn't even in the outskirts of my mind back then. All men can be a healer when they leave their damaged masculine at the door.

Healing is an interesting word. Where do the psychic wounds come from that need to be healed, to be energetically neutralised? Reader, let's look at this. Some wounds result from direct experience within our own lives, perhaps from encounters with wounded-others. Many wounds are inflicted when we witness inconsistencies-with-Truth while growing up. Much of our conditioning stems from the parent/child relationship and ancestral inheritance. We allowed our parents to be experts who know. We didn't question them. We adopted their wounded conditioning. Our parents inherited their conditioning (wounds and all) from their parents, and so on stretching back through all of time. Anytime there was a wound or trauma in the lives of my forebears the energy of that incident would be passed on through the generations and then eventually onto me – the same goes for Maria, the rapists and you Reader. We are all the latest link in a long chain of ancestral pain, a complex chain of entanglements from the past. The day we are born, we become the next link in that chain.

All of humanity bears wounds, pain held within our global subconscious. Our patrician ancestors were ravaged by the needs of male egos, of warring peoples, horror, suppression, violence, pestilence and hunger. The belief that ours is the most gloriously sexual of ages, rooted in endless fun and rebellious novelty is widely held – but our ancestors also all had sex gods of their own. As a riposte it doesn't take too big an intellect to see that rape, abuse, subjugation and other vile ways of the sexual landscape will have been rife back through all history – and that their legacy of damage will have been amply passed onto us. Those ways are still rife.

Today, we live in a world where women are sedated and controlled; they are only allowed to be whores or mothers, or to behave like men.

I shed tears for that sad burden.

In every moment we have a choice. Our choice may allow some small part of our ancestral wounding to be healed; for our children and future generations. A few years back I went on a Yoga retreat in India. We would meditate at 6am, after which I would take a swim in a cool pool. We would then practice a couple of hours of Yoga before reconvening for morning Chai. One particular morning as I sipped through the steamy vapours of my oversweet cardamom tea I looked back at the pool. Ripples were still rolling around in the water, *two hours* after I had finished my swim. My actions had created those very ripples. The energy of my actions had left a vibration behind. My actions always leave behind an energetic effect and that effect radiates outwards into the All; nothing exists in isolation. Every choice we make has an effect that touches all the people around us. Always.

Yet how rarely we bring discernment and attention to our actions.

Every move our sex god makes has an effect on the people around us; especially if it results in a newborn. In a split second a choice that we make can cause lives to change immeasurably. The energy of that choice will then radiate outwards with considerable pace. Many of the choices we make are instant reactions. These choices still leave a ripple in the pool of life. The ripple affects people closest to us immediately and eventually billions of others. Now and in the future – most of whom we'll never meet. The effects of our choices mostly fall outside of our perception. The energetic waves, and tides, of our existence are created by our choices; every choice affects the cosmos in some way.

But the many choices that we make every day are our personal power, even the mundane choices. Choices you make today will affect the manifesting of some future possibility – just as the choices of all my ancestors were needed for my love affair with Jane to happen. So we believe that we have a choice, and that our choice triggers an effect. This principle makes us very powerful people; it allows us to change ourselves and the world around us. The deep imperative of an ancestral healing might be possible with a healthy choice. Somewhere within every one of us is a heart-conscience that somehow knows whether a choice contributes to the evolution of humanity, its illumination, or not. The choices that Maria and I made undoubtedly did. But I was cheating on Jane.

I have love for many women. Maria was a special woman; I am still in gratitude for what she taught me about myself. I almost promised her the moon. We became an illicit item for a few more weeks. She then went home to Spain and the ending of our relationship arose. Our Work was done.

Maria appears in my thoughts every now and then, as do other lovers. I wonder where they are now, what their lives are like. Do they ever wonder where I am? An energetic connection between us certainly still exists. Classical physics describes action at a distance as non-locality. It is a direct influence of one object on another distant object. Perhaps at a cellular level Maria and I are still entangled; from the quantum entanglement that arose during our love making. We had a lingering effect on each other and the Universe.

Reader, do you ever think about lovers from your past? If you could be with anyone right now, who and where would you choose?

My heart simultaneously held the emotions of pleasure and pain from an experience that I judged as both good and bad. Cultural traditions that I was born into split the world into light and dark, spirit and flesh. My teacher told me there is no light and dark (good or bad) in the Absolute. Light and dark are the workings of the egoic-mind; they don't actually exist. But I wasn't aware of that truth back then. She told me to transcend such mind-made concepts, as it *all just is*.

If only my marriage could accommodate such truths and the apparently unacceptable ways of the sex god.

We are all attached to our own idea of what is right or wrong, good or bad. Reader, what if the purpose of each soul is to be truly liberated, to evolve beyond *any* attachment, including attachment to rightness and wrongness?

I had become a cheat. I had "committed adultery". If only my wife and I could have re-scripted our old fashioned marriage vows that were tipped towards notions of fidelity and betrayal. If only we were evolved enough back then. I could have done without the headache in my heart.

Good As It Gets?

"Provoke, confront, elevate" were the words printed on my tea packaging this morning. Here goes...

The bluest sky was soon dappled with salmon pink and the mighty Pacific roared down below. Radiant nature always makes a moment special. The golden light in the maturing sunset had caught my wonder and so had the siren radiance of Penny. The presence of such a youthful feminine essence is nourishing for a man's soul. Her effervescence would be primally attractive to any man not caught in his head. My teacher tells me we should look from a distance at a young woman to savour her youthful essence... and then let her go on her way. But I didn't remember that grain of wisdom back then.

I was watching the sunlight dance on the bottom of the swimming pool. Penny bent over and reached across me to fetch her water; the tight buds of spring so full of promise. She then stood up tall with steaming Jacuzzi water raining down around her. She was the perfect alignment of maidenhood, beauty and blossom. If ancient alchemists could have bottled that essence, they would have; it may have been called *Aqua Creation Itself* and it would have been used as a salve for all of man's vicissitudes.

Men are susceptible to youth and beauty, whereas women are susceptible to status and security. I reflected for a moment back to my college shagging days with all those eighteen year olds. What I didn't realise back then was that one day, suddenly, I wouldn't get to sleep with eighteen year olds again. Perhaps I should have slept with more?

Reader, I make much ado about form, beauty and good looks, don't I? Like most of us, I am attached to form; it deserves a special mention. All of existence manifests as form – it appears. Surely our attachment to form and our sensory experience of form is in some fundamental way an attachment to life itself – or an aversion to death. Was my attraction to the potent life in Penny's form an exquisite strategy to avoid death? I am, I must confess, attached to the all that flows through all my senses. I love life!

My teacher says I should see a woman's soul, not just her body and she is right. Let it be said that beauty is present in the whole of a woman. Her body, her smile, her laughter, her spirit, her heart, her ever-changing way of being, her infinite capacity to love *and* her cruel shitty moods.

We returned to the hotel room to get ready for dinner.

'You're twenty, right?' Blossom about to burst forth.

'Twenty one now, my birthday was a few weeks back, remember?' Her eyes twinkled.

I smiled and took a savoured swig of my beer. I recalled my time in New York with Collette, how the polarity between us was exotic. It was the same age difference. Here I was in my mid-thirties and successful in business. I wondered if she found that attractive.

The white curtains billowed into the room as the humid breeze caressed us. Penny was a talker. She proceeded to tell me ALL about herself, her insecurities, her parents, her dreams, her boyfriend. She shared way too much about how she had always wanted a real man, how her boyfriend was sweet but clumsy in bed. And. And. The misguided angel arose in her.

'Actually...' She stopped. 'Oh I'm too embarrassed to say.' She collected herself from a giggle. 'Can you help me Ben, I so ache to know more, what it feels like to make real love with a man, what it feels like to be held tight and looked after... Would you show me, teach me?'

Sometimes life calls us out to the end of the branch to reach the sweetest fruit. Nature had put me in a tough place. What should I have done with the feelings in my genitals? Could the sex god steal away all sense of moderation and jettison my reason? Even by my standards (yes I do have some), Penny was dangerous territory. But what man would say "no" to her? A man with a healthy masculine aspect perhaps?

Reader, what do you think about this one? Your held-idea of how a man *should* behave, that is good or that is bad behaviour. Those very ideas can cause *you* suffering. So everything "I do to you" which exposes your attachments (suffering) is surely a blessing?

We had less than an hour before the others returned from town for the evening fiesta.

'Are you sure about this sweetheart?' I hesitated for a moment. 'We can only do this once; it'll be our special bond.' Life isn't a rehearsal.

'Yes, how lovely, yes, yes, let's, show me.'

We are responsible for our own pleasure. It is up to us to get to know what we want and then ask for it. Men are not responsible for a woman's pleasure. Not just in bed, but in all of life.

I took her hand inviting her to stand up.

An emotional bungee jump started as I inhaled her confection through a rush of desire. Desire had always been a natural part of my condition, perhaps arising from an inner sense of lack. When I give my desires attention, they grow. When I ignore my desires they disappear. The desiring sex god had my attention.

'This is our secret Penny. We need to be quick, I need you to submit and let me drive, okay?' The MTV was cut, allowing a fragrant Latin salsa groove from the poolside to waft into the room.

But how to proceed? A young woman doesn't know what she wants as she is on a new journey. Maybe she has a vague idea of what she wants from her own masturbatory exploration; but Penny didn't communicate her needs. Indeed sometimes a woman has an un-awakened yoni that requires an innocent or masterly opening. How can a man possibly know how to please her? Every woman is to be discovered, explored.

I embraced her with one arm from behind; her waif body melted in my strength. I inhaled her, she was lightly perfumed and had tequila on her breath; fragrance is so much of an experience.

Her body was shower-hot against me. A confident seduction started to flow through me. Trepidation became torrid passion, her robe fell to the floor. I looked over her shoulder down her chest admiring her small pale breasts, waiting. My free fingers glanced over one nipple and then pegged onto the other. She giggled at first, but her gently swaying wriggle told me that she loved her induction. I bit her shoulder tenderly and sniffed behind her ear – I felt her relax. My fingers toured her tan lines with a gossamer touch on her porcelain skin. Her eyes opened and we could see each other in the mirror. I slid her legs apart with my foot and then dropped a finger down into her dark pubes; so contrasted against her pale un-tanned skin. She tensed in anticipation of my ravage.

Her clit protruded itself. She was unusually sensitive. My finger penetrated her, shallow at first and then pop, it slipped in. No saliva was necessary. She collapsed into her own bliss, breathing fully and moaning simply. Turning her around, I picked her up and carried her over to the display table, her legs straddled my waist. A bronze sylph and an orchid fell to the floor. They were replaced by Penny who was now on the table against the wall. My thighs held her legs apart and our gaze locked together. Positions are like toys, we take to them, we play with them then we move on. It has always been a joy to freely allow the Tao to dance sex through us. To freely allow every arising position to be perfect. Oh the rejuvenative quality of sexual energy. Sex god you are a god.

Some lurid detail is appropriate here: There are many degrees of erection. It can be any of: retreat, recharge, nice-one, hard, stiff, good one and seriously STIFF. My cock is always changing. There aren't any particular rules to determine just how stiff my stiffy is. A mystical flow of yin-yang determines this. After all what use is a serious stiff in wee hours of the night? If you are a brother, you'll know the ones... like when you are woken up by your bladder-is-full-alarm needing to pee like a racehorse and... you've just been dreaming about combine harvesters or the like? C'mon Universe what are you playing at?

My cock was seriously STIFF. Penny looked down at me a little surprised. Girls have commented on how a hard cock can look so threatening, like a weapon.

Holding her firmly against the wall, I entered her, she was electric. I was fully touched by life. Moving slowly at first then working my way up to a hard deep thrusting fuck. Our gaze re-locked. She took all of me easily, I thought she'd need a subtler style but her fire had opened her. I stood up, lifting her off the table. She sat atop my shaft while I manhandled her up and down. Up and down. She was (too?) noisy, grabbing onto me, pulling my long hair. It was wild deep sex at its finest ever vintage. I didn't need to cum, instead she filled me with *her* essence.

We collapsed on the bed laughing and wallowing in our juices.

'I hear voices down the corridor, Jane is coming back!' It wasn't a cheap trick to create a bit of drama. I had the sweet fruit in my hands and the branch had snapped. Sadly we were jolted way-too-quickly out of our good-as-it-gets fucking.

Avoiding the cosmic significance of a domestic trauma, I charged through the connecting door into my own room.

The unsettling temporary pleasures of delusion, hey.

All was well.
We believed.

Sadly, youthful beauty disappears.

One day even Penny shall become a crone, the most feared and misunderstood feminine archetype. Perhaps women suffer more than men with the agony of growing old, probably as they fear abandonment. A woman-worshipping man needn't abandon her though as he is in love with her goddess-essence beyond form. It's her inner beauty that he sees and finds attractive; beauty that is often disguised by her issues, fears and anxieties. Women aren't simply bodies to have sex with. They are beautiful alive soft complexities with hard shells, wounds and neurosis. The whole woman must be loved in every moment; all that she is being and becoming is beauty incarnate.

Later that evening, by way of some whispered giggles, Penny kindly gave me the knickers she was wearing.

Reader, are you provoked, confronted and elevated?

Be Life

Reader, what was your reaction to my gorgeous piercing of passionate Penny? How was your sexual mind confronted as I penetrated her pout? If you've been cheated on yourself, you probably thought I was an asshole. If you've already cheated on your lover, then maybe you thought I was a hero. Or maybe it's your benevolent god that shapes your reaction; perhaps He would strike you down if you were to follow His life-creating energy as I did? The way that you react to experience is shaped by your life experiences, your conditioning and your beliefs.

What sexual beliefs guide you Reader?

How did you acquire the particular set of beliefs or prejudices that define how you relate to your own sexuality and the sexuality of others?

Let's take a closer look at beliefs.

A belief is a thought that you have given weight to. A thought is lighter than a belief and therefore easier on the psyche. We have a preconceived model of how reality *should* be, made of beliefs. Your own model may have been challenged by Penny's honest behaviour. Can you see that agitation arises within you when life doesn't match your model-of-life?

How are our beliefs formed? If we examine them closely, we can see that they come from other people. More often than not, beliefs are the opinions of others; opinions that we have given weight and meaning to. When we give (both positive and negative) beliefs weight, we may act on them even against our self interest. Beliefs shape our experience of life.

Sexual freedom can be created when our beliefs about sex are challenged; when the veils of the sexual mind are stripped naked. Be life, don't believe. Beliefs hold us away from the raw reality of life. How would things be different if you became life itself, devoid of beliefs? You may think it would be mayhem, debauchery, anarchy? But no, life itself is only Love, and Love only wants the best outcome. It is only beliefs that divide us.

Reader, take a look around you at the raw reality of your life, right now. What's real for you right now? What is around you? What beliefs do you have about your environment? How do those beliefs change your relationship to life? What feelings and sensations do you have down in your pelvis?

I write from an aware place. As I sit here free and open, in exquisite relationship to life, a novel phenomenon has arisen and I am compelled to share it with you... What's real for me just right now is that a honey bee has landed on my laptop. She is crawling all over these words. I can feel the interconnectedness of all life. Like all women she makes honey *and* she has a sting. No belief or cosmic meaning need be inferred. I delight at her visitation. Now literally memorialised and shared with you.

What's also real for me right now is that the Chakras (energy centres) in my pelvis feel open and empty. I haven't enjoyed any sex today, not with my beloved or myself. I preferred instead to channel my creative energy towards you through my writing. As my day draws to a close I feel sexually depleted. Men you will know the feeling of having too many orgasms; that empty feeling, that woozy "G n T" feeling. Women won't know that feeling as they usually feel full and completed after sex. Perhaps I have given my manhood to all who encounter this writing today. Or was it to Penny!?

Affair

If everybody felt "sexy" the world would be a better place. But when two lovers come together their sexuality carries psychosis, demons and ghosts from the past. We each have an energetic imprint of various sexual maladies that we may have encountered. You know the form Reader:

She's frightened of getting out of control
Feeling inadequate
He's the right partner but he's violent in bed
She's shy
She's a sex addict
She's had abortions
She's numb and disconnected from her sex
Sex is for making babies
He's uncomfortable
She can't orgasm
He's stuck with the wrong person
She's stuck with a person with different energy
He abuses
He's not allowing himself to enjoy sex
She's dominant, I'm dominant
He's got an STI
She was abused
She's a forty year old virgin
She feels too old
Can't get it up
No sex this year
She feels dirty if she lets go during sex
Ethical Slut
Sex god
Compulsions that overpower their wills
He is scared of the power of his sexuality
Premature Ejaculator
Mistakes and remorse

Masters and free people
Religions
Cultural conditioning
Repression
What's hot (Brazilian), what's not (bush).
Not enough partners
Too many partners
Media influence
And on and on and on...

The list could fill this whole book. You can double the trouble when two people are involved and cube it if there are three.

My own sexual maladies had started to appear during those years. I had lost my way in my marriage. Loving a woman for one night or a few years was achievable but worshipping her for a lifetime felt beyond me. I had withdrawn from our ordinary lovemaking; we occasionally made love in our sleep. I had started to prefer my extra-ordinary fantasies about older women over the real thing.

I was loving in interesting times. Amidst the hurly burly of the business conference in Miami, I saw a familiar face. It was Rene; last seen in a steamy shower. I loved her perfume. We arranged a meet at a funky deco hotel over in South Beach.

Monogamy doesn't rescue you from the terror of attractions.

I was always able to be honest with Rene, we could talk forever. A woman like Rene is good for a man. I always felt she was on my side even though she usually proffered rebellious points of view to challenge my ways of thinking. She slowly introduced me to new paradigms and ways of looking at the world. I loved Rene. Could I trust a female confidante?

'Things haven't been going too well with Jane lately. I'm walking on eggshells all the time... We went to see a therapist the other day.'

'What did you learn?'

'I realised that I'm able to look after Jane and keep her very safe. That's what she wants from me. But I can't say what *I want and need*, I'm fearful of being ruthlessly honest with Jane. I feel trapped Rene.'

'Couples have time to go to therapy but no time to connect with each other hey Ben.' Couples spend thousands on a wedding and very little on maintaining the clash of their two wounded childhoods.

'Ha-ha. Ain't that the truth.'

'But seriously it's great you are doing therapy together. You are so overdue for therapy Ben!'

'You can talk!' She was a bruised peach with plenty of baggage.

'Was the therapist any good?'

'Yes, I think so. It was my first time talking so openly about sex and intimacy with another woman? Wow, I could say everything. Therapy is cool!' Therapy required vulnerability.

'Are you committed to your marriage with Jane, Ben?'

'Commitment, interesting word that... with commitment you are either in or out aren't you, Rene.'

'Well are you?'

'Yes I feel committed to my marriage, I love Jane and I want to make it work. But I find making it work so challenging. Maybe by having some fun a few months back I was able to let off some pressure. In some bizarre way my fling allowed me to stay committed to her.'

Much is made these days of men's commitment phobia – which could be translated as "If I commit to this woman she is the last woman I will ever be able to shag without guilt." No wonder small men run a mile. I have never been a commitment-phobe. But I did need to modify the small print of what I was committed to! I couldn't find a way to renegotiate our deal though, Jane was intransigent.

'How can you be so committed to feeling caged and trapped Ben, you sound like a hostage?'

'Hostage! That's a good one, that's exactly what it feels like...'

'That's what you sound like... Why don't you just leave?'

'*Leave?*'

'Do you really not know what to do Ben?'

I knew what to do but I didn't have the courage to do it.

'I'm not sure it's about leaving, I just don't know how to be monogamous.'

We laughed nervously.

With seventy percent of men having affairs, surely the institution of marriage is broken? If sex could be openly discussed then cheating might not happen in the first place. It takes women to play their part in that broken institution too.

Perhaps she was about to play her part? She drew deep on her cigarette.

'When I was with the therapist, I spoke of my love for Jane and the simultaneous yearning for my old life and way of being. Funny thing was, she pulled so many stories out of me about my relationship to sex. I told her about the healing of Maria and my other dalliances.'

'Very brave!'

'But it did get ridiculous Rene. I am ashamed to own up to this, but... I started to think the therapist was cute! She kept asking me the deepest probing questions. I got very wet!'

'Naughty, naughty.'

'Do therapists get turned on Rene, you should know?'

'They're human.'

'She seemed enamoured by my having a gift that was locked away. She certainly encouraged me to give my gift to Jane, for so long as I felt that I was being true to myself... She made a big thing about being true to yourself, about marching to the beat of your own drum.' That was very new thinking for me back then.

I am sure there was a lot that the counsellor said that I wasn't ready to hear. You only "get it" when you are ready. You can only "get it" if you are really engaged. While I was working hard to reignite my marriage, the sex god had other ideas. He was wondering if the therapist would be a neurotic fuck or not.

My counsellor became a secret lover in my fantasies. Listening to some of her sixties free-love stories I bet she'd scream like a night vixen. But no, seriously, I desired her but didn't need her. I didn't need to fuck her just then as her work with us was truly invaluable.

Desire is a fascinating causal force. Every desire comes with its own obstacle? They always travel together, don't they? Desire always requires effort doesn't it. It would have taken much effort to get my counsellor into bed. The desire had many obstacles to overcome – my embarrassment, her morals, a suitable venue, an alibi and her little lacy knickers to name a few. Some things show up in life that we don't desire. They require no effort on our part! You don't desire what you already have.

I gave my life and soul to my marriage in the early days; I *was* determined to make Jane my only wife. Fundamentally, I just didn't feel as though my love was being received – there was too much abject wounding between us. I wished with every cell in my body that the counsellor could have found a way to clear our growing blockages, got us sexed up again and then paved a way for us to be together forever.

'I like this music, shall we go back indoors.'

We hugged for a while. She was purring. Then Rene energised and said 'Hey let's go to the beach. We always have fun at the beach, I feel like running around for a bit.'

'Great!'

Television and the media show us how things are "supposed" to play out in our culture. There's no question that the cultural stories I had fed my mind made our heat somehow okay, expected even.

We found ourselves at the beach, bathing in the rhythm of the waves and laughing through the spray of the surf. Rene had fiery energy that night. Her considerable intellect and perfect lines gave the sex god much to lust over. Why are women attracted to married men with status or wealth? A large part of arousal is the result of meaning projected onto a situation. The mind is a significant sexual organ after all. (Perhaps the sex god is all in my mind?) The minds of both men and women love newness. Rene was new and Eros was at a high vibration. Her smile evolved with wickedness.

'Not sure I should be here Rene.' I was momentarily uncomfortable with an attack of Jane guilt.

She wasn't deterred. Can a woman always beckon a man to his doom? It never ceases to amaze me how determined a woman can be when she is about to get a man. It was pussy power and she had one; she needed it filled. So much tarring about men thinking with their dicks, but it always takes two. That wasn't a lame statement to make my transgression *her* fault, it was simply the truth.

Was it *really* necessary to put all my loving attention into one woman? She kissed me a complicit kiss with closed eyes. Full, tender lips, such sweetness delivered. The subtle fires of love were stoked. I colluded with the sorcery of her heart. I have always been able to love more than one woman at once. I have love for many.

I remember as a child I used to go outdoors and play all day, and into the night. Life was only ever adventure.

'Let's go in the ocean, I need to cool down a bit. We shouldn't be doing this' It was her turn to change course.

Life is change. Being fully alive is being with the constant changes of life with ease; without expectation.

A beach-police patrol car drove by with glaring search lights illuminating the beach saying "the tax payers of this county do not welcome you here". Their targets were partakers in dark activities, dealers, kissing Latinos and illicit encounters. In the umbra we shed our clothes and charged into the surf where we were found-out by the floodlights from the beach mansions ashore. I couldn't take my eyes off of her body, her pert tits and gorgeous curves. I'd seen them all before of course but last time they were veneered by a swimsuit. Did she have any idea how men look at her? We played like kid dolphins until the patrol car returned. Then it was back to the lifeguard hut to pretend we were simply sharing a cuddle (not yet banned on the beach). The cuddle matured. It was embalmed in ten years of mutual pent-up energy. Men use affection to get sex. My fingers felt into the elastic softness of her plump lips and I started rolling the fullness of her clit. It was exhilarating. Sex gods were joyous. We both knew we were in dangerous territory; but we ignored our comments to that effect. Women use sex to get affection. Danger amplified the electric polarity between us.

I sniffed my fingers.

I had to taste her. I bent her over and gorged on her hairy salty cunt. Then she sucked the last embers of doubt out of me. I became my truest nature.

A woman doesn't usually say what she wants, so a man must guess. Flicking the head of my cock across her clit, I sometimes penetrated her soft dark hole. It was like waving some string in front of a cat to get it to play. Every woman is different, which can be confusing for a man. The same woman can be different each time, which is also confusing for a man.

'No, no it's too much.' Some of us aren't able to accept pleasure.

'Fuck me Ben, FUCK ME.'

I rutted her.

Purposely she tore the condom. She wanted my seed.

I'm not sure she enjoyed it. Did she do it for me? It was a *very* quick fuck. There was a lot of baggage.

'Just cum, quick just cum in me.' That was easy.

She wasn't an orgasmic woman, her stuff was in the way. Perhaps she just wanted to get it over and done with.

The patrol car drove by closer this time, it was time to make tracks.

How many women can you fall in love with at once? Every woman is special to me while I am with them. But I can love many women, all at once. An ongoing affair was a possibility between Rene and I. It seemed to be the done-thing back then.

A few days later a letter arrived...

"Dear Ben, we are not supposed to be together. I cannot open to you while you choose to cheat on your wife. I gave you what I thought you wanted. I wasn't having the fun that you thought I was having. Now I feel bad inside..."

All I ever wanted was to love and worship her and maybe find more than a fleeting glimpse of bliss through her. I believed there was much sexual healing possible between us. I wanted to adore every part of her. I loved her. I needed more and more, but she wasn't game on, the secrets of her heart declared "please don't pull any more petals off of me, please don't".

I hated her perfume; it made my heart ache.

I never realised back then that Rene had Kali embodied within her. That she could be a ball buster.

Our affair came to a halt but something wasn't completed between us, it felt left-open. Experiences not fully lived, any moments and emotions not fully felt, become unconscious patterns in need of completion. I have noticed in every relationship, indeed every life experience, that there is a notion of completion or incompletion. Experiences complete when emotions are resolved. Some relationships last a fleeting second and are complete (like holding a door open for a pretty girl). Some relationships last several years before they complete (like making a few million with a business partner and having them screw you over), and still others last a lifetime and don't complete (like my relationship with Jane). Maybe all incompletion deposits karma in the soul?

Our psyches grow from the relationships that we choose or encounter throughout life. The personal-self eventually becomes the sum-total of all these relationships. Sex allows us to enter the deepest realms of our lover's soul without conscious barriers. Sexual relations of any duration indelibly deepen our bonding and psychic cording. Good sex or bad sex deepens it further (subjective I know as it is always just what it is). We carry the results of these cordings with us in our personality for the rest of our days.

At my core I had a heart longing to live in the fullness of relationship; where was Angelica on my thirty second birthday? It would be several years until I played again and twice that before she would find me.

Exacerbated Masturbated

I love to self pleasure.

Frankly, there is nothing original or shocking in my confession as almost everybody masturbates. The behaviour is in fact a healthy and inclusive aspect of our human sexuality. Self pleasure is where we learn about our own sexual response. A woman should worship her clit and a man his cock; what sensory blessings can they bring us in this lonely experience of life. But why are we so secretive about such a pleasurable behaviour; it's rather like talking about death! Maybe masturbation is threatening because our partner is usually excluded or because we find it challenging to translate our self-sex into sex with our partner?

I love to self pleasure using fantasy. I may enjoy recreational fantasy when I'm lover-less; just naked-me and my wayward sex god. In fantasy all kinds of dirtiness might arise, dark Eros, light Eros, giving Eros. Wanking certainly got me through the parched-desert years of my marriage to Jane. I remained a good-boy by choosing a fantasy over succumbing to girls who were only a phone call away. Self pleasuring was safer and better. One day I realised that I preferred the freedom control and raw dirt of my fantasies over making love to Jane. If she got the hots, I was usually already spent. Our marriage continued with so much to be happy about; our sex and love making did not.

There are so many genres of the fantasy art-form. One day I may be with a noble older woman, another day it could be a waitress girl or a yummy mummy I saw on a bus.

Sex is always around us. Reader, keep an eye on your own sex god today. Notice how many people you desire to sleep with today!

A fantasy can be used in so many ways: to provide relief, a moment to feel good, an escape, to take revenge, recreation, no-mojo-today-with-this-lover, to revisit old lovers, to rev-it-up, to cum quickly, to make-her-look-like-a-great-lover, anticipate future lovers, to research possibilities, be unhealthy, to get through a sympathy fuck, be sadistic, be loving, be dirtier than you could imagine, a girl of your wife, explore masochism, to be with your wife, beside your sleeping wife, to name a few... and they are all yummy. A fantasy can be more potent than the real thing and doesn't cause a headache in the heart.

Fantasies arise that have no apparent relationship to love. But all is Love.

Reader, you've had fantasies so you'll understand my viewpoint. Let me summarise. In a fantasy I can fuck anybody, anyway I like, with the subtlest control over the extraction of my orgasmic nectar. For example, a fantasy might involve a debauched and dominating doing of a woman I know well, like my sexy mother in law. Indulging my senses in fabulously raunchy detail, I could be as molestingly-curious or pleasurably-penetrative with her as was my preference. And my fantasy would be utterly safe; no diseases, blindness or kittens killed. To top it all if the fantasy wasn't shaping up horny enough, I could swap partners at whim. I could invite others along or switch and make use of an old "reliable" fantasy. Try doing that in the flesh sex god!

Thankfully most desires a man may feel are not actioned.

A vintage fantasy may arise from time to time. It can be revisited from many angles and intensities. I can systematically go a little further, a little raunchier with each re-run; rather akin to a mini-series. I am a connoisseur of the practice. Reader, do you have any guaranteed to make-you-cum fantasises?

Sometimes a wank is potently worth it but often the outcum is usually mediocre. Many jerk-offs are simply medication or neurological release. Giving me a moment of relief from the world and a great feeling; those ones usually give rise to flat wet-fish-orgasms. Then there's nothing left to give to my beloved.

What about using fantasy in lovemaking? It's very old-school to use fantasy to reach for your orgasm during love making. In fantasy you are so in-your-mind that you miss the beautiful energy exchanges taking place with your lover. You miss the sensory escalation that is there to be savoured in full presence. Do you know what out-of-your-head-and-in-your-body sex is like?

When you are lost in your mind you start to fuck your *idea* of your lover rather than your real lover. Perhaps your idea of her has become jaded or familiar, even though life is new in every moment. Or perhaps you are thinking about how crappy you feel at work spending all day pretending to be somebody else. Habitually you start to reach for your little-death and to stoke things up you make use of your trusty old "reliable" fantasy to heave your dribble into the world.

Some women aren't too comfortable about getting themselves off. Others are cool to masturbate *and* to talk about it. In deep intimacy some will even let you watch. Watching a woman masturbate is a very special way to learn about her ways. Women can have fucking horny fantasies!

What about sharing fantasies? In spite of our uniqueness, we often have similar fantasies. Fantasies are a joy to share. Somehow a sexual healing is available when intimate fantasies are shared with your lover; as another small echelon of shadow is made light. Angelica and I shared a fantasy about the pretty woman who sold us a couch just today.

Sharing a fantasy within lovemaking can be way-juicy too. Several years back I tried to get Jane in on the act, but my wrigglingly horny fantasies simply made her upset. If you are a married man and you were *perchance* to have a fantasy, should it only be about your wife? What if she had that expectation of you? Somewhere in the small print of my marriage vows was a line that read: "and don't have any fantasies about anyone but me." Was I supposed to spend the rest of my life either abstaining from fantasy or only fantasising about Jane?

Our thoughts precede our reality; so perhaps we should be careful with our fantasies! Did the cosmic-people who wrote about *The Secret* consider that fantasies may have the quality of manifestation within them? What have my fantasies with thousands of porn girls, all the lovers I haven't mentioned in this book, the thirty thousand wanks with teachers, waitresses, in-laws, assistants, the girl on the tube, at the office, at the check in and on the plane and on and on manifested? What reality did all those thoughts create? We shall see.

One of my Tantra masters condones masturbation but warns against spurting my precious energy. She encourages me to retain my semen and to use my lifted and expanded sexual energies for creative transformation. If you are disciplined and using awareness in your spurting practice, great discoveries can be made about the alcoves of the psyche.

Recently I have been experimenting with some esoteric sexual practices. I make use of a fantasy while conserving my semen or experimenting with the ever intensifying pleasures available by avoiding ejaculating all over the place. By using a subtle breath control in cohorts with an escalating fantasy I can lift energy up, up, up through my core to flow into the most exquisite experiences of feature-length cosmic bliss. It is rare that an in-the-flesh lover is sensitive enough to feel my sexual energy and give me such a long orgasmic journey.

Though such women do exist beyond myth, I have met them.

As I get to know the nature of my sex-organ-mind many more questions appear requiring deeper enquiry. Can you have a fantasy without mind, without thoughts? A sensory fantasy perhaps? Is there a thinker of thoughts? How much of the sex god is mind? Does the sex god live behind mind? It certainly lives without mind. Are fantasies real? What is the difference between a fantasy by yourself and a fantasy with your lover? Is there any difference between sensory reality and mind reality? Is anticipation and desire the same as fantasy? You know, the thoughts that you may have during a date or during foreplay. Surely those thoughts are fantasy too.

I love to self pleasure without fantasies. Being sexy is the opposite of being sexual. Being sexy is for somebody else's pleasure. What about your own pleasure Reader? You can be sexual while with a lover, or in solitude. Have you ever made love to yourself with self-pleasure?

There is another little known dimension to self-touching, self-arousal and masturbation that is worthy of mention. We don't need a partner to be sexual beings as *nobody else* is responsible for our sexual energy. Highly evolved self-pleasurer's can enjoy whole body orgasms by focussing on their senses alone. When we are capable of giving love to ourselves and being utterly at ease with our own sex *then* we are able to be profoundly sensual with others.

My teacher has taught that self-pleasure without fantasy but with full engagement with inner masculine and feminine is a gift of human potential that few people get to experience.

Fantasy is only ever a lame approximation of the juiciness of being thoroughly in your body with your lover. Life isn't a lonely journey. When we are in fantasy we are missing life itself as all thought replaces real experience.

Since we are all stuck in our thoughts isn't all of life a fantasy?

And yet some people do not masturbate.
They have never self pleasured.

Go fuck yourself.

Flow

I have always been a flirt, I love being a playful flirt. I have always found women attractive and I'm usually aware of any reciprocal interest. In this book I am writing about some successful sex god encounters. Obviously I am not writing about the girls that I *didn't* get to sleep with. Or the drunken shags, quickies or foreplays that didn't go anywhere. It would be a fat book but it wouldn't be nearly as interesting. Most girls weren't attracted to me, nor I to them. Most sexually driven men will agree it is a numbers game. I was often rejected. Rejection is the way of the world, rejection is everywhere. The honey bee and butterfly choose which flowers to sip from and reject the others; we too exercise choice and rejection as we go about our day. It's okay, it's natural. Let's get over rejection. How many people did you pass today and not speak to? How many people did you pass and not make love to? In every encounter, brought about by Source, the sex god or otherwise, there is always a chance that one or the other will bail. As intimacy deepens between two people, one or the other can choose not to continue. Being attractive and not rejected is a rather delicious outcome though.

I had a drink with a Korean client after a business meeting. She shared that she had thought about fucking me during our meeting. It surprised me that women are letches too. Attraction becomes friendship becomes romance becomes a play thing for the sex god. Men often have fantasies about women and vice versa. Is there some sort of pact? We don't act on those fantasies do we? Has everyone simply agreed to ignore the feelings in their genitalia otherwise we would surely all jump each other! Could thoughts precede reality?

I was craving Jane's attention and approval and the sexual schism between us continued. If we had talked about our behaviours we might have robbed them of their destructive power by bringing them into the open. Sex god energy unreleased between us had to go somewhere. We were learned people who knew why infidelity happens so we shouldn't have had to be victims of it. Why wasn't my wife my fullness? Masters of loving-relationship hadn't yet taught me that she could be. She was certainly a sexually active woman, why couldn't I see that? Perhaps I saw her as an object of my own self-betrayal. How could I be sexually attracted to the woman who I had allowed to close me down? Why was I more interested in the possibility of sleeping with other women? Perhaps it isn't therapeutic to ask all these *whys*. What had gone wrong between us?

At that time in my life I really needed the fucking manual.

Reader, do you remember that I said every relationship is unique. Relationship deserves our full undivided attention and presence. When we are in relationship to another there is a subtle dynamic worthy of mention. Every person we meet is a mirror reflecting ourselves back to us. Jane was my mirror. We bump into ourselves through our relationships. In relationship we co-create circumstances accompanied by behaviours. Every circumstance is an opportunity to learn about ourselves through our interactions, an opportunity to grow. By growing we have more to give our partner and those around us. Lovers (and wives) are especially strong reflections of our selves. They are mirrors who show us where we do not love ourselves. The more intimate our relationship, the more we may learn about ourselves. Assuming we are awake and choosing to look.

I too am a mirror for *you* Reader. In reading this story you will bump into your edges. We have co-created this moment together. All that I share is an opportunity for you to reflect on various parts of yourself. Including your denied parts; parts that are without your love. Perhaps I can help *you* grow, to respect and expand into your own healthy sex god? Perhaps I can help you transcend the sex god and move towards peace. Peace is your birthright. That would be a gift of creative change, a gift from Source itself.

Indian wisdom traditions speak of the Leela, the great play of life. Leela is a way of describing the Cosmos and all reality as the outcome of creative playfulness by the divine Source. The Leela was surely playing with me the day that I met Jenny and Carlotta. I felt as though I was playfully laying on a luxurious raft staring at the blue skies above while heavenly bodies stroked my soul. I was in the flow of the river of life...

The last day of the seminar transformed into a dinner for sixteen in a trendy neo-Italian eatery down by the water. As our sharing of food came to a close, five of us flowed back to Jenny's flat. I had noticed Jenny on the first day of the conference and per my reptilian programming, I did check her out. Nice arse, tight for her age, pretty smile and an attractive vivacious manner. I had entertained what it would be like to sleep with her. Many a man would have such thoughts as they appear whenever the free fragrance of a woman's essence is scented. In fact I entertained that fucking idea with Carlotta and most of the other women at the gathering. Could thoughts precede reality?

Jenny's flat was simple and movie-industry stylish. She warmed essential oils and put on some chilled music. I have always been titillated by a progressive intellect and the company of women. I love the way that women relate from feelings rather than fact. Anna soon declared she had to get home as she had an early shoot. It was getting late and I attempted an exodus... but I was persuaded to stay when Jenny lobbed a sultry look towards me and announced that it was time to open a vintage '83 Margaux[v] that she had picked up in Cannes. A short while later the other guy decided to leave us, for some reason he was uncomfortable. Three of us remained, Jenny, Carlotta and my good-boy self.

There I was surrounded by womanly essence. I harmonised my mood with them and our little party started in earnest. Perhaps it was time to lean beyond my edge as a rather beautiful motif was about to be woven into my tapestry. If I had *tried* to make

---

v   1983 is a classic Margaux vintage that exhibits a rich, complex and mature bouquet. As it develops on the palate, the impression remains of great power with firm tannins without any hardness. All of life can be erotically savoured with our senses.

that evening happen it would have been scuttled by my grasping desires.

As I reclined into the natural flow of life, magic showed up.

The three of us had very long hair and somehow the androgyny of our hair bonded us. Hair was central to our play together – draping hair in each other's faces, kisses and whispers lost in hair, fingers probing, swaying hair, it was feminine elixir. We had all become very sensual and my inner-feminine was being loved. Jenny and I became tactile much to the delight of Carlotta who assumed the voyeuristic role of helping us along.

I am a polyamorous creature. It is in my nature to have plenty for several. I did think momentarily about my wife who was visiting her parents back in Montreal. I could feel my love for her. I chewed on my guilt for a while. Monogamy didn't feel natural to me. Lifelong monogamy didn't feel realistic, what were my chances of keeping our sex spark alive? It would require that I deny the true nature of my sex god? So it was a case of deny or lie? Lie won. Then I bumped into my marriage vows which were taken verbatim from a momentarily adopted Christian church amidst the prevailing messages and customs of my culture. Already a sinner I was to be fearful of the judgement day if I didn't adhere to them. But my vows were a leaky vessel for the sex god. They couldn't contain my true nature. So... the sex god took over with hedonist delight. I became nature.

Nature has no morals it is perfectly natural. But we mustn't take "no morals" to its fullest extent. I don't condone non-consensual sex. Reader, if you are looking for an eventual descent into the subterfuge of rape, extreme S&M and the exploitation of children in this book then you're at the wrong show. Thankfully my sex god is gentler than some.

'You girls keep warm together, I've gotta go take a pee.' ...I heard plotting and giggles taking place downstairs.

'My turn!' Jenny went to the loo.

'Ya know what, I met a photographer the other day who asked me if I would be interested in taking part in a photo-shoot for a book he was planning to publish – he said he was creating a tastefully sexy photo study that explored the similarities between a girls lips and her pussy lips.' Her lips were deliciously full.

'What a lovely thought, I have often wondered that myself,' I came on, though I can confirm that there is no correlation. 'What a great idea, what a great way to find out. Become a photographer and document it, some guys have a cheek don't they.' I paused.

'How about your lips Carly, is it true?' Sometimes in sex I am the initiator and sometimes I'm the follower.

'Ohhhh that *would* be telling wouldn't it.' She had a cheeky grin.

We lingered too long in a thieved kiss. It was halted by Jenny's return. What was I doing? I was a married man. The evening progressed and the soiree ignited.

'You've both made me want to go!' Carlotta went to the loo.

In an act of self-less generosity, Jenny got a taste of me.

'Let's do this all slowly,' she whispered.

Zorba smiled on us and a bond of mutual trust formed. Where there's trust there can be intimacy. We had all night so slow was good. I've never really been a sexual robot (though I can feel that my relationship to the sex god does feel programmed and robotic!). Slow sex was just fine; slowly is holy. Living life slowly amplifies sensory aliveness. Try it Reader, right now, do something slowly that you would normally do fast. Savour a long cold beer, watch and absorb every detail of a football match or sniff your husband all over.

Few men get to experience lovemaking with more than one woman. The experience is most unlike that portrayed by the porno industry. Often a ménage-a-trois will involve women who adore each other. The Sapphic arises in a three. When that good fortune shows up and we can contain our excitement; by being present, self-less, slow, free and serene, then we can *witness* the uttermost pleasures of Sapphic adoration. Like the dancing fluorescent curtains of the northern lights, two women loving each other is peak life-nectar to behold. My teacher tells me that a woman has an inexhaustible supply of yin[vi] sexual energy to wash over

vi   Yin – femininity, slow, soft, yielding, diffuse, passive; water, moon.

her man. When two or more women are present, yin is doubly stimulated creating a deeply saturated field of sexual essence. The field has a doubly potent charge beyond that which can be created by one woman. (She tells me this isn't true when two men are present as their yang[vii] energy would amplify and would work against itself.) Once I move beyond lust I'm certain that a Sapphic gathering has magical powers, great beauty and high potential for a man. It has high potential for the girls too. A life-loving and potent power can be harvested there that can be taken back into all of life. Magical power that isn't available to the monogamist.

Multiple ultimately-compassionate female energies in the bedroom make a tasty recipe. There are so many flavours of sex that could result from that recipe. Sex-play is temporal and dependent on myriad untold influences. That night could have been down 'n dirty, bondaged or raunchily fast. Or it could even have ended up in a big stroppy fight.

'Anyone want a joint?' Carlotta asked, looking for accomplices. 'But don't tell anyone as I'll lose my law licence.' She worked in high places at the Crown Court.

'No thanks sweetheart, not my scene,' I declined, Jenny took a hit.

'That's cute, he doesn't do drugs! Well hope you don't mind us, will you... You two just carry on getting it on, and I'll watch you.' She alpha'd me and took a hit from a well loaded spliff.

'Go on Ben strip her and really give it to her, here I'll help you.' Carlotta proceeded to unbutton her.

Out of our slowness appeared Jenny's unusually teaty nipples. While sipping on one and rolling the other between two fingers, Jenny started to wriggle and die. A special quality to lovemaking can arise when breasts are lovingly included, especially if your lover sees herself as a pure expression of the feminine.

Jenny was soon very naked. Like a Leo, she was at ease displaying every last bit of gaping self. Carlotta and I shared our

---

vii   Yang – masculinity, fast, hard, solid, focused, hot, dry, aggressive; fire, Sun.

delight at her curves. Indulging myself I inhaled deeply from her wet armpits. Our consensual giving and receiving rhythms intensified. Their sparkling nature was revealed.

'Oh Sister!' Carlotta slithered down. She went down on Jenny with wanton devour. I watched... for a long time.

'I want cock, give me some cock.' The inevitable arrived.

'Come join us Ben, we are ready for you now.' Our lust and tenderness started to intermingle. Moving around behind Carlotta, I pulled her knickers to her knees. I was curious to see if she matched her pout. I had two very different pussies before me.

Pussies have personalities, they are so like characters! Big lips, little lips, loose, tight, hard, soft, puckered, sprawling, pink, meaty. Yes men, we love them all. (And as for cocks... Somebody else will have to write the book about thick dicks, long schlongs and wee willies and all their personalities.)

'Go on Ben, give it to her, she wants it really hard, she told me so a little while back.'

I pulled my jeans off freeing my stiffy. Jenny pulled her knees up to her shoulders, opening, opening; she liked it that way. I plunged myself into her, I should have been more gentle. Carlotta continued to egg her on. She started spanking me to fuck Jenny harder. In those young buck days I was able to deliver long and hard if required. Jenny was delirious and panting for more. Our giving and receiving rhythm gave way to a yin and yang rhythm of strong male energy comingling with her submitted womanly beauty.

We moved together towards a peak.

'Don't cum in me,' she managed to get out in between arghs.

'Yeah I want some of that too,' Carlotta asserted, pulling me off of Jenny.

I was lying between them. They both set to work on a feeding frenzy on my cock. It became a wanking game. I loved each of them more than the other one.

'Come on, I want it.' Carlotta pushed Jenny away for a while before coming back for more herself. They playfully scrapped over the imminent arrival of my seed. I would have feared for the life of my genitals if I wasn't so seriously out of control. I eventually came. They shared face masks and self congratulatory pleasures.

'I didn't get enough, shall we see if he'll do it again? You okay with that big boy?' Jenny declared. The defiance of what my biology was capable of began – they were good and I was hornier than I had been for years. Jenny took me again, Carlotta became the voyeur. Exhausted, Jenny fell asleep...

'My turn now honey.'

She needed seducing, but it didn't take long before she was splendid. As if working herself up, she started strutting around the room sharing her strong almost-male energy.

'Shall I do you now Carly? Hey? You want it? You feel very wet, from all that watching you've been doing, you naughty woman.' I took in a long inhale of my fingers. Rich complex and mature, like sweet molasses. 'Mmmmm.' Latin spices. 'I need more of that.' I pushed her back.

'Okay, okay, are you safe? No diseases.'

'I'm clean baby.'

'Okay, okay, don't touch my nipples, they're very sensitive, and stop. Hold on. I need to be in charge... on top of you. And do not touch my breasts... Could you keep your hands above your head so I can relax? I need to trust you.'

Have you ever lived in LA and dated? She rolled me over and I held my hands high. My cock prized her puckered pussy.

'You sure you're safe?' She took her time to shimmer my cock into her compact pussy; firm but without any hardness. A slow performance of piercing intensity followed; her pussy gripping the base of my shaft. There was so much male energy in her that her movements made it feel as though her cock was fucking me. I became her. We penetrated each other so deeply we became each other.

Oh the joys of more than one woman.

I preferred Carly's pussy. Never compare lovers, as we are all unique. If you have to compare then compare *yourself* today with how you were with your lover last time. Never compare yourself with others but against yourself. You know yourself too well. Have you grown, have you opened, are you a more finessed lover? Knowing who you are now, where you came from and where you are going is a key to life.

The morning arrived. 'Where are my knickers Ben, I need them.'

I just so love it when women go knicker-less. Just knowing that they aren't wearing any while being around other people, is a high-voltage horny pill. Though I love knickers in all their species too! Sexy couture and lingerie somehow allows a woman to step into her feminine confidence and then auspiciously present her curves and beauty to her lover. But a vanilla pair of white knickers would be gorgeous too. And in a rare girl-next-door moment, a scraggly old pair she was wearing because she was lazy and didn't expect to get a man that day would work a treat as well! They're all good – but then these are the words of a man with a knicker fetish. Knickers were like symbols that allowed me to feel close to my lover, her smell, her juices and her shape.

'Oh, no you don't!' She snatched them back amidst much laughter.

Those were fun times, we all knew the score. We were playing, nobody was needy or looking for anything longer term. But on reflection, a seed of neediness was sown in me by those two lovers.

I wanted more.

Where would I be without the story of "wanting more"? Does that story make my life go better? For so long as I have an ego, I shall want "more". The seeds of addiction were sown right there. A hole in me was to grow and be filled by demons. I was on the hook.

We always have a choice don't we.

When the Tao lands in your lap in the form of two gorgeous women, what should I have done? Said "No thanks"?

If a man doesn't find an outlet for his sexual energy an inner anger may result; that anger could become violent. Some men substitute violence for their suppressed sex god. Instead, I chose infidelity.

We always have a choice don't we, or is life flowing through me?

Or perhaps the only choice I really have is where I put my attention?

Gods

The Sun rose again. Thank you. It's up to me now. So this day,
I shall continue to weave this shimmering sex god tapestry.
A tapestry woven from sacred and animal threads poignantly
recording what happened when some sexual stardust met light... So
where to start?

The sex god and my sexuality is not the most interesting
thing about me, but it is what *this* story is about. As I write I have
just realised that all the other gods were peaceful. There are so
many gods: Gods of love, fathering, house-holding, power, chance,
harvest, wisdom, war, justice and prophecy to name a few. But
it was Aphrodite and Eros that had taken over the heavens of my
being.

We could observe that there are two primary forces present
in life. The force of Creation that brings All into existence. And
the force of entropy, a destructive force that reduces all structured
existence to noise (it shall transform your lover back to dust for
example). The sex god appears to have both of these forceful
qualities. It seeks to create nothing less than new life, wholeness,
a healing, or a fucking good time. It is also capable of destruction;
destroying families, friendships, trust and well-functioning people.
My sex god flowed through an unhealthy masculine aspect
within me. It would remain unhealthy until my neurology was re-
parented or reprogrammed. Healing is possible when I am loved
unconditionally; especially by myself. We would all have a healthy
masculine aspect if all the men in our lives (fathers, brothers, sons,
lovers, trusted men) also had healthy masculine aspects – if those
men had been raised to know that sex is beautiful and natural.
**Surely no shame is necessary towards the energy that created
all life and all the Cosmos?**
Unhealthy masculine energy abounds around us. Reader,
shouldn't we all question our sexual conditioning?

The sex god was usually docile. But the presence of the divine feminine, a woman, would make the sex god adamant. Reader, the sex god has had me do the ridiculous, reckless and irresponsible as it flexed its pumped-up muscles. I longed to bring the sex god to order; to calm the emotional storm it was creating but its adamance couldn't be ignored. A deeply seated impulse in the human species is to make order out of disorder.

What did the sex god want? What it wanted I didn't need; its motives felt ulterior. It wanted more of what I needed less of. It wasn't open to repression, it had immense power. My attempts to dominate it were naive – in fact my attempts to dominate it resulted in *it* dominating me!

My teacher concurred, gods must be respected. She told me that they can be coaxed like a genie into an alchemical container by using our will. Mastery of our will is the key to our liberation and personal power. But she also warned that the sex god has many exquisite strategies to overcome even the strongest of wills. When we use our will to control life we can become self-torturing, particularly if we use self discipline and brute-effort. No matter how much we use it we are often subject to unconscious factors as our will isn't omnipotent. The leadership of the will becomes suspicious. Said another way, *what we resist persists*.

I had started to feel like a warrior wrestling an opponent. A warrior has qualities like courage, determination, focus, clarity and an unflappable zest for life. I am a Spiritual Warrior. In Eastern martial arts an opponent is disarmed by not-resisting him. By not pushing against him and with nothing to push against, your opponent has no power over you. Whatever bothers you only has power over you if you resist it and struggle against it. The moment you *fully allow* or accept the phenomenon, it begins to subside. A martial art approach was needed to first align with the sex god and then to unwittingly annul it to impotence. That martial art would require considerable will, a will that gave direction without imposition. I wasn't sure I had that will.

Though I was determined to find it (sic).

Am I programmed to go find completion through sex, to find intense intimacy and transparency? What would happen if

I became the sex god, integrated it into my whole, listened to it unflinchingly? We shall see later.

My teachers tell me that the sex god will become unimportant to me someday, it shall whither. But until then my seed shall be sown, unless my evolution as a human has me know better.

I have waxed lyrical to provide a more erudite understanding of my sex god phenomenon – it is the title of the book after all! But perhaps I could simplify the whole thing and say that the sex god is simply the birthing energy of the cosmos. It is creation itself initiating and propagating all life! Nothing more.

Fucking is too easily imbued with meaning that we choose to place on it; there is always a context for passion. That context changes over time. I wonder if any of the girls within these pages would sleep with me today!?

What if we men avoided manipulative behaviours that sought orgasm?

How would life be different if I took orgasm out of my experience?

If I didn't have sex, would I die?

My teacher says that perhaps a period of celibacy would have allowed me to see the truest nature of the sex god. To recognise that I was indeed bigger than it. So I tried celibacy for a while.

It drove me crazy.

Receiving

Kristen had a great ass.

Several more years of tormented marriage had passed. I was yearning for spaciousness in the forgotten corners of my heart where I kept the things about myself that I was hiding. I started searching for answers in various spiritual wisdom traditions. I read books about Tantra and High Sex. I learned of the healing powers of mind-less lovemaking. I dreamt that someday I would find a tantric lover to accompany me on such an evolved journey; I wished to become a worshipper of women and a master of the arts of love. I knew that Jane wasn't the one. Angelica wasn't anywhere to be seen. Perhaps it was Kristen, who was about to once again pass through my experience...

Kristen was a former employee; so stylish garb was appropriate. We hadn't seen each other for a few years, and there was a lot to catch up on. We had a strong connection, heavily invested with a common spiritual view of the world.

I have always been a penetrator of life. My creative and business journey had made me "successful". My success was confirmed by comparing business-cock-sizes with other men at various dinner parties. Some women found "successful" attractive; which proved problematic to my efforts to be a good-boy. Over the years as a businessman, I had declined numerous opportunities to have flings, affairs and quick shags with various young-things that had worked for me. I had always separated church and state as it were. Of course I indulged in a fantasy or two, but *I* was a married man and I wasn't into breaking the rules for some dull sex. I didn't expect that my evening with Kristen would be any different.

I was zinged from a particularly strong yoga session. I arrived early. I noticed several billboards outside the restaurant that were using sex to try and sell me something. Kristen soon entranced shining brightly in a small summer dress; she was fashionably late. She was blond with peach-fuzz skin, the pearl on her necklace gave her a notional innocence; she was wearing more makeup than usual. Kristen was a sun flower, a joyful soul. She had a big heart. I suppose I was a bit of a philanderer, but just because a pretty girl walks into the room it didn't mean I had to sleep with her.

'I'll have the pumpkin-sage ravioli too, that sounds good.'

'So Kris, have you found your man yet?'

She flushed sensitively. 'No not since Stephan back home in Switzerland... I've had a few false starts with some commitment-phobes, but none that have gone anywhere. I have the view that people are either drains or radiators. Too many of the guys I've met lately are purposeless, they've no money, they seem lost in this world. Drains ya know. I'm not sure it's my job to sort life out for them... *and as for the sex* they have a lot of growing up to do. You'd be amazed how many of them lack basic skills! I think they're looking for a mother half the time not a lover... It makes a girl want to freeze her eggs!'

What is a damsel like who is no longer distressed?

I glossed over her mention of sex. 'Yeah, so many men are lost or caught in the to-do list of life. It's a feature our times... Ya know what Kris, the thing all those guys are missing is simply being themselves, they're too busy doing the media sponsored thing.'

'Yeah, that's it they're all trying to be somebody else. You've hit it, they're not authentic. They had good hearts but they were so self-absorbed, misguided.'

'Floundering in mediocrity.'

'So no, no man yet.' She sighed. 'But I'd really love to find my man, fall in love and settle down. I'd love to have children too... us girls have to keep one eye on the biological clock too Ben.' The childless woman has plenty of time to prey on other women's husbands though.

'Biological clock, ha, c'mon Kris you have ten maybe fifteen years before you need to worry about that, plenty of time!'

Women often talk about their biological need to go have children. What about us men, we have a biological need too; to go spread our seed! It's in our DNA and in the interests of genetics.

'I just need a man, okay!' she declared with a glare.

'But what if you were choosing to be alone in life Kris? What if you're avoiding deep relationships? Perhaps you love your freedom too much or maybe you don't want to get hurt again? After all if you're alone nobody can leave you!'

A pause arose. What was I avoiding by having sex with so many women?

Our food arrived; gorgeous aromas.

The sex god arrived.

My biological clock chimed that it was time to make tracks. We decided to short-cut through the park back to the station. As we passed a flower stand heavily fragrant with all manner of exotic colours, she sought connection by holding my arm.

Women *are* divinely powerful for they hold the crucible of creation. Women have something a man needs; they could rule the world with their pussy (or love) if they chose. I guess a few thousand years ago men knew that. They set about neutralising the power of the divine feminine, the goddess earth mother, with a clever cultural structure called patriarchal religion. What better way to overpower your mother-ruler than to create and convince her that she is worthless and that a bigger ruler than her exists!? A few remnants of matriarchy perhaps continue; did men really choose to be the disposable sex? And a culture where you could only have sex with one woman after marriage surely wasn't designed by men?

Men can usually resist pussy power but not every time. Our stroll matured into adventure when we realised we'd been locked in the park. Source had some plans for Kristen and I.

'Let's skip back through the park to the far end Ben.' I love youth.

'*Skip*?... I can't skip, I'm not sure that grown men skip Kris.'

'Oh c'mon, of course you can, where's your playfulness with life?'

'Okay, here goes...' We skipped and laughed and skipped and laughed. Skipping was so free. My playful spirit was awoken.

'Thanks for that, I thought the skip in me was gone forever.'

Seeking some respite we stopped to consider our options. We were soon kissing and her vagenda consumed us; maybe she was attracted to my open first-chakra, hanging between my knees. London became silent.

'The moon is pretty tonight.'

'Mezzaluna... Oh Kris, you feel gorgeous.' The low-back on her summer dress beckoned me to kiss my way up her spine. She was scented with an unusual fragrance, bergamot and lemon notes were easily recognisable. Another marriage vow failure was imminent.

'Ooh you're making my hair stand on end.'

A park bench waited close by. She slumped across my lap and melted in my arms. Her pheromones seduced me. I saw her petals fall away as her essence enshrouded me. Oh Universe did I have to make a choice, again?

'Kris... my mind is telling me no, but your body is telling me yes.'

'It's okay honey, we've known about our affection for each other for a long time. Where is your playfulness with life Ben?... I'm just attracting into my life what I want to have!' The selfish sexual behaviours prevalent in my college days persisted into adulthood.

'Ha-ha, got me... But I'm married Kris... with children.' She was silent and after a pause she kissed me so gently, her hand fawned across my face. The frisson challenged me.

"Click" and my top trouser button was undone. She slid her hands onto my navel stroking me. How could that moment be mud?

'Your hair is so soft, I like that.'

Another tender kiss, I was being seduced – what a joy. I hadn't felt attractive for some time; she was awakening something far beyond a dopamine reward. I leapt once again into the great unknown of sex. Many a man needs sex, it changes his day.

How threatening the single woman is to the married couple. A sex starved single woman is dangerous energy to stir into a relationship that has sexually faltered. She needed it and had nothing to lose, I needed it and had everything to lose. I wonder at the willingness of a woman to betray her sisterhood. Is her betrayal driven by her own unhealthy masculine or damaged feminine energy within? Or were we nature; diversity-seeking Darwin-genetics in action? What kind of man would turn down such an available woman? What kind of man would pass up on his sex god desire to service her? A joyously satiated, unconditionally loved, un-needing and committed man of course.

The single woman is dime-a-dozen these days. It's a feature of a culture where women try to marry when they are older and men don't want to commit. I could be conventionally sexist and suggest that the situation would improve if women married when they were young because that's when they are most attractive to men, and men married late, because that's when they are most attractive to women. Women would trade on youth and beauty and men would trade on wealth and status. Maybe there would be fewer single women around?

The other side of the problem is that there aren't enough quality men around, ask any single woman! Not enough manly men, not enough baggage-less men. But there are plenty of sexually repressed men. Every combination is out there.

A rush of lust consumed me. I explored her and she didn't resist.

'I'm not sure we should do this Ben.' Her breath deepened. 'Sex is always profound for me; it has meaning in a loving relationship – outside of that it makes me feel vulnerable and open to getting hurt.'

I aroused her and she didn't resist. A man is valued by the feelings he causes in her.

'...But then sometimes the right lover comes along who can show me a new little part of myself; that part becomes worthy of exploration.'

The kiss that followed said it all. Sex shapes our lives.

'Where shall we go? Do you have to get back?' The last trains had already left. I vacillated for a while. The sex god arose like a hungered serpent ready to strike and ingest. Eros had to get creative to make our fuck possible.

'Why don't we go back to my place, it's just a quick cab ride away.' I'd never done that before, taken a girl to my marital home. It was a mistake to breach that frontier – the sex god was eroding all frontiers.

'What about your family?'

'They're out of town tonight, in Montreal, so we'll be fine.'

What was I like? How could I be authentic while lying to others? I was being authentic with Kristen, yet leaving out a significant part of the truth with Jane. Why couldn't I give my sex god to Jane?

I had bought into the illusion that marriage would last forever. But a caged wild animal is eventually beaten. I didn't want to hurt or hurt others. But I didn't want to feel trapped anymore. Jane had convinced me that "feeling trapped" was okay, it's just how marriage is. But she also made it clear that "not wanting to feel trapped" wasn't allowed.

Reader, I am sitting here writing, allowing words from beyond to flow through me. As I write, Angelica has just entered the room, slender, topless and in a flowing skirt. She is dancing a feminine flow through the room. Whilst *I* am about to share a graphic and juicy account of an affair with a former lover; such is life. I absolutely must pause to be with Angelica's dark beauty... A dancing woman is a riveting distraction. When she dances, I cannot write a thing. The mysterious flow of life continues.

I lit a couple of beeswax candles, grabbed some large cushions and we settled into a big goose-down couch. Her top was soon off. She was surprisingly flat-chested, though her bra had advertised otherwise; acorn-hard nipples were on full beam. I love flat chests, perhaps I'm the only man that does.

'Hey, you're all shaved up.' She looked gorgeous, the mind loves variety.

'It's the fashion these days Ben. But I love to be that way, I think it looks good. I wouldn't dream being with a man with my big hairy muff! It makes me feel so feminine, and so young. Do you like it?' She did seem far younger than her already young years.

the sex god | 159

Fashions change, but hairlessness is perhaps another damaged distortion that women have bought into courtesy of the porn industry.

'Like it? I love it, come and lay down.' She laid back. I could feel that she needed to be slowly relaxed and opened.

'Finger me again Ben, I like fingers.' We are in our power when we ask for what we need.

'More fingers....' Stretched.

She moaned so nicely she could have been faking it. Many women fake it; the pressure to please their man is enormous. How stupid can Don Juan be if he doesn't suspect it? Perhaps she would think "what a dumb-ass man I was for not realising it"?

Much time passed.

My mind wandered. I felt more determined to re-commit to Jane and make my marriage work. If I could change myself, my relationship would change. My marriage must work at any cost, even myself. Could this illicit encounter be healing for all concerned?

Then I returned to real-relating.

Kris had a sweet fragrance. The sense of smell is so primal, so attractive; hopefully not repulsive. Her fragrance was carnally attractive and it reminded me of Aija from Finland all those years ago.

Though vulnerable, I was strong. It was time to fuck her.

'Take it easy Ben, I haven't done this for a while.' She surfaced with gorgeously rouged cheeks.

'How long since you last had some of the other Kristen?'

'Not since Stephan a few years back.'

How could such a pretty girl be without sex for two years? How did she do it? Her sex god must be well tamed, or maybe she had lost touch with her sex. Maybe she had a Rabbit.

'What about you Ben? When was the last time you were with another woman... other than your wife?'

She had me nailed. I had been in control of my sex god and determined to make the monogamous requirements of my marriage work.

'Oh, it's been a good while.' I sighed.

Raunch arose.

We got ourselves together. She was tight; I felt clamped. Her cheeks were hot against my face. I thought she was going to pass out.

She wasn't so interested in receiving; she had very male energy. Many women play out their cultural conditioning to give to the world rather than receive. Surely a woman's true nature is to be receptive.

Kristen really preferred giving. We found a teasing rhythm on a furry rug. I let her learn about me. She started to wank me, rather too furiously, but I let her anyway. I let her be free with me; I was done to. She loved, I mean loved, to suck cock. I love having my cock sucked, especially when I know it will be for a long time. Her hand reached up to squeeze my nipples. Never before had a girl played with my nipples! Aliveness attained through sensory pleasure is surely happiness.

Reader, I must reminisce once more as I feel into all the kinetic sensations of that cock-sucked nipple-squeezed moment. I get wet just recalling it, how weird you are Nature... Aroused in this moment recalling my arousal of another moment! And this moment is being remembered too. Memory is such a mysterious thing isn't it. This capacity to recall life, supposedly had in "other than this moment". How the trace of memory records mind, feelings and all other sensory facets of reality. We are all five-senses and a story of the past.

I had waited an age to cum, my retention tension finally released as she orchestrated me with great skill. She gobbled cum off my cock as her sex god needed. She was a very giving lover. We then laid together swapping energy for hours. There was so much of it to share.

I wonder what that experience was like for her.

I had been taught that my sex god wasn't an okay part of me. Did I then spend a lifetime looking for women to tell me "Ben your sex is good"? I was starting to hear them.

In spite of the insight that I had had between Kris' legs that I should recommit to Jane, the afterglow of our fling left me feeling different. I did not feel guilty. I had crossed a watershed. It was now possible for me to cheat without guilt.

But as I watched the raw energies of my spirit, I could feel a hole in my soul. Some part of me had been lost and a hole was left in its place. Or perhaps it was still in me but I wasn't conscious of it? Whatever, I felt deficient. My actions were becoming driven by lack and neediness. The sex god was conquering new territory within me; it was merging itself into a gaping hole in my wholesomeness.

The destabilising feelings that I experienced strengthened my desire to have more sex with more girls; and to honour my sex god.

I continued to be Pan living my nature in an unnatural world. Sex wasn't my stupidity. There is nothing wrong with sex at all. It was the lying that was my stupidity.

Kristen called me the next day. She had lost her necklace at my house.

Safe Sex

When sunlight is focussed through a magnifying glass it intensifies and makes heat. The sex god was intensifying and Jane and I were in a romantic wilderness. Romantic love lasts for about a year and is replaced by a more stable form of love that we might call companionate love. We had been together for twenty years. Love was no longer a verb. I had been busting my ass at work for too long. I rarely felt appreciated; I think that's all I wanted really. All any man wants is to be appreciated. I felt betrayed by my wife and a hostage in my marriage. I had realised that I wasn't being true to myself but there was so much other great stuff in our lives that it didn't matter. But without worship, the flower of Jane's heart had started to patina, the fragrance of her infinite-love was calcifying. Our marriage could break apart because of this.

When I am a "small-man" my capacity to handle the full-on and ever-changing emotions, tests and love of a woman becomes greatly diminished. Perhaps I could handle them for a night, a few weeks or even years, but weathering them for decades was an overwhelming challenge. Fact is when a man isn't being true to himself, is lazy, or isn't big-enough for his woman, his relationship will degrade. Both parties will go elsewhere for sex.

A letter arrived from Kristen.

Dear Ben, Our time together a few weeks ago was special. There was so much electricity between us. I am sorry I couldn't give you what you needed. Perhaps we could meet again and spend more time together going deeper. xx

Lust is Eros wrapped in grasping. I found some Kristen-lookalike porn and started to get excited about spending more time with her. Like millions of other well-functioning men, I had turned to pornography. I was wanking myself stupid.

I loved porn as it allowed me to *safely* channel my still-considerable sexual energy out of my body – and into an empty spurt. I hated porn as I couldn't sniff her, worship her or probe the beauty of her being. I couldn't feel her essence bathing my wounded masculine to wholeness.

The women of porn are cleansed of all their problems and devoid of their testing neuroses; rather like buying irradiated meat in the supermarket in clean little packages without a sign of the industrialised chum behind the scenes. Shooting-up on porn allowed me to savour female energies without all the emotions.

Some men don't have access to sex; they may be wrinkling, wretched or alone. In those cases copious conceptual copulation with porn can be a healing salve. Yes Reader, porn stars with their minimal emotional engagement are in fact healers.

It's amazing the lengths we will go to look at sex, or maybe flee from looking at it. These days too many men, women and children are venturing into the wonderfully addictive world of online porn. Men who are seasoned porn users will be familiar with the empty-bollock ache that results from the perpetual fixes that are available.

Porn lodges a dehumanised view of women into a man's psyche. It teaches men that sex is all looks and performance; that it isn't a sensory experience. Feelings, imagination and "more pleasure than you can stand" have been sidelined and a man's ability to be intimate with a woman are threatened. The billion-dollar porn business doesn't show men what a woman actually desires. Did you ever see the words "worship her" on a porno site? Brothers she doesn't want abuse. She desires to be worshiped by her lover such that her heart may flower open. Only then can she smother her man in healing love.

The pedlars of online pornography are fuelling the debilitating furnace of addiction for many men. Tragically they are providing a hideously flawed education to men on the subject of how *not* to make love to a woman. Men rub away hours of their lives looking for harder, dirtier women. A hard woman is nice every now and then, but you know what, there's nothing in the Universe quite like a soft loving all-embracing real woman.

Women learn that they must remain sexually alluring objects to be valued. Perhaps the "goddess" is an objectification as well? As a counterpoint though, some women like pornography, they say it's fun and sexy; and that it can be used to raunch up an evening with a lover. It is possible to have a healthy relationship to it. In recreational doses porn has its place on the smorgasbord of life.

Could the non-consensual domination in porn be sacred? It isn't separate from Source after all.

The pornification of our culture is out of control. Men, young-men, even children, are unwittingly taking part in a sexual dumbing-down that is propagating the unhealthy-masculine of a generation. Perhaps all is well though as women will be able to resume their matriarchal power when all us men eventually become useless wankpiles. They shall reassume their rightful ownership of all the power in the Universe, the power to create life itself. The Earth will be saved.

A few days later I revisited the "so juicy sweet" lookalike images of Kristen, but like the circus-that-left-town, they had lost their potency. Occasionally I would find hi-res images of sugar-pie that were erotic to the core. Then like Gollum I would save them... "We wants it, we needs it, must have", never to look at them again. Such is human sexuality.

Unheeded porn rots your soul and you know it. I thought I was paying hush-money to the sex god when in fact I was pumping him up on steroids. The world of pornography is a dark place to hang out. It is private and shameful for most. It caters to any sexual fetish; taboos fall away. There is only one way to go with porn and that is down to dungeon darkness – sadomasochism, shit, pain, donkies, torture, non-consensual abuse and the unspeakable.

Maybe porn wasn't such a good way to save a marriage after all. Fuelled by the infinite possibility of porn, lust for the real thing only ever increased, the oxytocin-hits left me needing more. Curiosity turned to grasping and grasping became an unhealthy addictive nature. I was like a rat hitting a button to get my reward. Addiction can arise whenever we are in "destination consciousness", gotta get it consciousness. I became addicted to porn. Sex god what did you do to me?

The term "addiction" neatly labels a whole set of sex god behaviours that had me compulsively engage in sexy activities, despite harmful consequences to my health, mental state, or social life. My teacher says that addiction is used to silence the painful cries of feelings and unfulfilled needs. Addiction is what we do to avoid feeling our feelings. Can we safely say that every man who succumbs to its addictive grips is hiding pain of a damaged masculine essence? Perhaps due to his unfulfilled needs or because he has been trying for a lifetime to be other than himself.

In every moment we choose communion or separation. We always have a choice to commune with our feelings – or separate from them. A feeling is always preceded by a thought, and has its roots in the past. Avoidance of feelings gives them power over us and impedes loving communication. If we are to heal we must listen to our feelings. Have I been avoiding feeling feelings my whole life? Did you ever do that Reader?

Wanking held me in a numb power-sapped stupor. I used pleasure to feed a sense of lack. How could I shake it? I knew that I needed to face the sex god someday. The sex god was my *prima materia*[viii] the biggest opportunity my soul had for transformation. A sex god that feasts on porn could only be annihilated by a formidable inner warrior – **or the love of a very special woman.**

I knew then that it wasn't Kristen; but I was looking forwards to fucking with her again. Angelica where were you at the eve of the Millennium?

The Universe needed to provide me a crossroads where I could choose between facing the unknown or the safety and comfort of all that I had come to trust.

---

viii   The primary material that forms the basis of an alchemical transformation.

Chaste Chase

The material world which is experienced through our senses appears to be solid. Our senses can be pleasured by wealth, possessions, drugs, women and adulation of all kinds. Sensory pleasure is a dominant motivational force in life. When our senses aren't getting pleasures, we say we have problems. Problems are only ever problems in our minds. I had problems.

'What's wrong with you tonight Jane?'

'Nothing.' Jane had problems too. I was left to guess what she meant. If something was wrong perhaps she should have just told me.

My re-commitment to Jane had fizzled again. I'd had enough of porn. I'd had enough of being taken for granted. I needed to be held, touched, and found attractive. I needed to be loved and to give my love wholly. I needed to come home to the warm embrace of female energy, not indifference. I was tired of transactional love. I needed the real thing. God only knows why I wasn't evolved enough for that "real thing" to be Jane.

I had problems. I needed change. There are three types of change: an in-the-moment change, relief or fix, a context change, or a pervasive change that results from insight and understanding. I needed pervasive change.

I looked at myself in the mirror. I couldn't see my true face, only the mask that I was showing to the world. Who was I afraid of being? What amazing man was I denying to the world?

The next morning while wallowing in a sunrise surge of testosterone, I chose to keep myself small, I chose an in-the-moment change. I would go get some relief. Through facile escapism I could avoid real change, I could go get a fix and then get back to normal life. It was to be a harmless dalliance and nobody needed to know.

Morals are the domain of beliefs and the mind but within nature there is the ability to feel if an action has a quality of rightness or wrongness. My decision felt right. I was powerful and attractive and I could have what I wanted – I was used to choosing.

I always wanted to sleep with a Japanese girl or a beautiful Indian girl. The transpersonal and mysterious sex god had me do it; I chose an Indian one.

The sex god propelled me with its cosmic wind and a plan was hatched. It was during the early days of the Internet. Websites at that time were mostly unsophisticated billboards used by pioneer users. I found a website specialising in Indian brides, men and women looking for marriage. I composed a punchy email and sent it to ten random women who had listings on the website. It read something like:

Hiya, Pardon my intrusion. I am a 38yo married white man of good pedigree. I have always wanted to sleep with an Indian woman. If you have ever wanted to sleep with a man such as myself, please get in touch. If the chemistry is right I am sure we can share loving times together. X

I needed to transform the sex god else it might embody itself within my physical form.

Reader, I am writing this book to shine light on the sex god. Let's explore why it felt okay to go get some Indian pussy. To learn more, I decided to have some retrospective dialogue with the sex god in a meditation. The dialogue went something like this... Ardent sex god, what do you want from me? Are you my purpose, my soul in action? Are you my master? Are you an unhealthy, debilitating, destructive master? What am I supposed to do with the instinctual impulses that inform my life? You feel as though you exist autonomously beyond my sense of self. You have cleverly subsumed me for your own use. Are you stuckness on my path to wholeness – are you moving, evolving? Or are you a demonic and wrathful entity moving through me, using me to your own end? Are you blocked, disturbed or just unusually strong? Does everybody have a sex god like you? Perhaps you are trying to have fun? Perhaps you are a healthy sex god? Perhaps you are purposeful, embracing and blissful? Sex god, I need clarity. I know you are an aspect of me, but you are NOT me. *Where did my will go?* Sex god did you subsume and control my will as well? There was such dis-ease within. Are you antithetical to my spiritual path?

I awaited answers.

I became aware of the origin of the dissonance churned up by the sex god. I had a realisation. This is really worth sharing as it's another Big One.

Nature always seeks balance within its infinite systems, we call this phenomenon homeostasis. Nature *cannot* be unbalanced. There is a fundamental movement towards a balanced state in our world, at all times. This movement cannot be avoided. A bruised psyche or childhood wound will create movement away from a state, *even if* it is Nature's desired homeostatic state. **Nature vibrates to balance my world and my wound works against it.**

Reader, are you still tracking with me? My psyche is battling nature. There lies the fundamental pain that keeps me from peace.

For example, if there's a fire, I wouldn't put my hand in it – even if the fire would create healed balance. Nature requires that I love my sex god. Nature seeks peace and balance but my sex god, wounded by ancestors, culture, parents and unhealthy masculine role-models avoids peace and balance. My behaviours ensured that I was screwed until I healed.

But the good news is that Nature is omnipresent and would eventually solve this imbalance. Perhaps by having me heal, encounter deepest love and write? A worshipped woman could heal me.

Over the next week I received some replies to my emails:

- *You are a lecherous man, how dare you contact me.*
- *Maybe, but you sound a bit too old for me.*
- *I am a respectable woman, are you insane to contact me.*

And then a week later another reply arrived:

I'm interested. I have always wanted to sleep with a white guy, and the fact you are married and your upfront honesty

makes me feel safe. Give me a call so I can see if you are a
real man for me.

We're all unique aren't we? Love it. One woman's poison
was another's nectar. A forty percent response rate was good by
any direct-mail standards. So I was at it again... Wahoo! It felt
good.

Perhaps she was a guide from beyond.

We arranged a recce one warm evening to check each other
out. Her photograph had short-changed her. She had loose hung
hair and a simple middle parting; she was an enthralling beauty.

Most people recognise beauty without quite knowing why.
But beauty is everywhere. Reader, take a moment to breath in
the beauty all around you right now; reflections, light dances,
fragrances, sounds, the miracle of all the cells in your fingertips
perfectly, effortlessly functioning; the Miracle. See your world as
magic. Nectar is everywhere if we look. And it's all missed when I
do some porn.

We walked together arm in arm. Jas was placid and genial;
she was hard tail. A well educated woman, she worked as a lawyer
in the city. We focussed on connection rather than titillation. Only
occasionally did I wonder if she would grunt like a porno girl.

'So Jas, why haven't you found a man yet, you're so
beautiful.' I caught myself staring at her lips.

'My parents, they want to set me up with a husband,
arranged marriage you know, but I'm not interested. So we have
fallen out. But I don't have time to go find myself one! It's the long
hours you know. I work way too hard. The partners, you know,
they never let you go home until a job is properly done.'

Young women, and men, become entangled in the epidemic
of busyness in the city. They're stuck being constantly in motion.
They get squeezed until they become corporate, frozen and grey.
Indeed Jas' enslavement was doubly wretched as social climbing
had been bred into her. With so many conflicting messages, who
are women supposed to be? Perhaps the only way a woman can
feel safe on this planet is to behave like a man.

'What do you do all that hard work for Jas, wouldn't it be easier to live simply?'

'Well, it makes me feel better about myself you know. I don't often like myself. My work makes me feel good... worthy even... But the office is very male-oriented; I often wear colourful lingerie beneath my drab grey clothes just to remind me that I'm a woman!'

She had a point. She was a woman reclaiming her power *and* her command over her own sexual needs. A woman who becomes her powerful self could rule the World.

She was cute too; I couldn't wait to get in her knickers.

We strolled past a pond, the home of some copulating dragon flies. I was caught by the lights shimmering on the black opal surface of the water. I looked up. The billion-galaxied night sky made me feel so small. Jas disappeared as nature's Eros caught me.

'What are you looking at Ben, holes in the air or something?'

'Oh, the light on the water, look at it Jas, its staccato dance.'

'I didn't see that before.'

'It's so profound how it all works, it is all so perfect. I love it Jas... What do you love?'

'Oh, I'm a down to earth girl really. Simple loves, you know. Good food, good company, fine fabrics, yes I love beautiful fabrics. I love the feel of the weave, the textures, the colours. I love tapestries. So much work goes into making a beautiful fabric you know. A weaver might work for a lifetime to perfect his specialism.' She threw her silken shawl over her shoulders to demonstrate. My attention was grabbed by the incandescent play of light in her shawl, it reminded me of the possibilities available to me in my own life-tapestry.

'Okay, so we have shared our loves, what about cares. What do you really care about Ben?'

Caring is a very subtle energy, caring allows us to just be, just be who we really are. My answer arose, shadowed by some resistance to share it.

'I really care about unloved women. Women who deny their physical, their sex god, who have been made to believe they aren't attractive by their loser of a man or by the media industry or the porn industry.' (I splutter as I write, hardly a chat up line on a date Ben!)

Where did that blurt come from? Was I serious? Reader, do you remember Scott back in New Zealand? He was a "manly man". Well his stories of how he treated girls were abhorrent to me. It's true. I really did care about giving my love to unloved women.

We live in an age where men are confused about how to be in the world. Decades of feminism have asked men to get in touch with their emotions. Women have become men, hard arsed ball busters. Yet they still want a man to make them feel safe. Many men have become weeny, aspiring porn-stars. We are all stirred up, there's no wonder our male and female essences are so rattled, denied and unhealthy. But I was certain that I couldn't bear to see a woman of any beauty feeling unloved. (What about Jane!?)

'You are such a letch Ben, you know, I can't tell if you are for real!' Her eyes softened. 'Enough talking, it's getting late. Kiss me, I need you to kiss me.'

We shared a lingering kiss. You can feel your lover's armour in a kiss, you can feel if they are afraid of getting close. There wasn't any fear in Jas' kiss. She was a provocateur, the chemistry was hot.

'I needed to do that. I needed to know what it's like to kiss you. If we kiss well, you know, perhaps we will be magical together in bed. And god knows I need you to be good in bed Ben, I haven't had any for eighteen months. I don't want to be disappointed.'

'Oh Jas, you won't be disappointed, I assure you.'

Perhaps I didn't really want to pursue her, perhaps I just wanted her to hold me.

Everything is either a cry for love or an expression of love, there is only Love. A liaison was arranged for our fucking performance at her house in a week's time. She was to take a day off work. She preferred to meet during the daytime, it made her feel safer.

She came to the door wearing a short silk kimono. The tense frisson between us was probably observable from adjacent solar systems. It was easier to tightly embrace her than make nervous small talk. Her flat was decorated with light filled colours and textures... I didn't notice them. The Tao took over and we were at it.

Her mystery was soon naked. Then seriousness showed up.

'Ben stop, I just need to feel more comfortable. Do you think I should get labia surgery Ben, don't you think they're too big?' She was rather voluptuous.

'Oh no no no, Jas you are beautiful just as you are. Don't even think about it, most men would think you are god's gift. Keep yourself well away from surgeons. I find your lips very sexy Jas.' These days the American porn industry sets a standard for how a woman "should" look. Designer vagina media makes noble women look multiple orificed, homogenised and fifteen.

'... and what about my floppy tits.'

I glared at her and smothered her with a down pillow. Our intimacy reappeared and I started to play her like an instrument.

I soon lost myself in the elixir of slowly exploring every crease of her exotic body with all my senses – touch, taste, smell, listening, opening, feeling, looking. Yet during the whole seduction, she didn't make *any* move towards me.

'I would love to see you play with your clit Jas' she did as she was asked. Talking to her turned her on. Her self-love really turned me on. I appreciated her and encouraged her.

Though her utter submission was enjoyable, I waited for a cue to fuck her. A few hours passed and I was still fully clothed while she was goddess-naked. The absence of feedback and sex-play cues had me in a holding pattern of respect, awaiting her readiness. I was aching, bursting, dripping.

Over the years I've found myself in what might be called soft-play many times. If lovers agree upfront that no penetration is needed, then soft-play can be a magical experience. But I knew Jas needed it, it was required of me. But still no signals came. Together we ravished in what was my longest seduction ever. The romantic limitations of marriage couldn't be that wired, sexy and groin aching.

Finally she broke.

'Ben, what are you doing, I need you to fuck me you know, you've had me naked for hours. Give it to me won't you.' All she wanted was a hard fuck, forget the worship. We laughed hard, the tension dissipated. 'I'm used to my man driving you know, I am used to a man forcing himself on me, taking what he wants then leaving me. That's how it is for me. I'm used to a quick hard shag Ben.'

She asked for it.

My style changed. I held her tight; her size 6-ness was easy to constrain even though she was a wild one. We were soon on the brink of a miraculous moment when the sex god had had enough – my six hour stiffy became a withering recharge.

Men often lack energy. They have nothing left to give their woman. Energy-lack is endemic in our culture. Men lose energy when they wank too much, when they spend their lives without purpose or when they aren't being themselves. So much for "Jas you won't be disappointed"! I become acutely aware of my body whenever it fails me. I felt like a failed man. My ego refused to hear her okay-ness with the whole situation.

'See you again soon,' she said as I hi-tailed it out of there.

I wasn't enough of a man to see her again and put things right.

And so my life-tapestry continued to be woven. Dark and light threads convened purposefully. Woven images were starting to appear embroidered with golden threads. The sex god had dissolved further moral and commitment frontiers in my marriage. Programming that wasn't consistent with a long term marriage had been re-awakened.

But in spite of the darkness creeping along behind me, it all felt good. I was relieved to be more like myself. I liked playing around. I decided to remain open for the next opportunity.

Perhaps the sex god is simply the deepest held belief that something is missing and that a woman can give that to me.

Giving

I had arrived late at a small party in a fancier part of town. You know the type, yummy mummies, neighbours and social posturing. The gathering was well oiled with cheap champagne and the world was being put to rights.

'If you make it cushy or make it easy for him he won't take responsibility for himself. He'll use your generosity and still be doing drugs behind your back.' They were talking about a friend who had declared his addiction to drugs.

After a while the remaining guests departed and I was left with the two hostesses. Some clichés soon nosed into my reptile mind exploiting the obvious potential of two older divorced ladies and a game-on man. I sensed their energy brighten. We were soon talking about post-divorce freedom and unworthy ex's. They were battle-hardened divorcees with a fairly simplistic view of all men. Nonetheless, I had been chewing the consequences of divorcing Jane, so I was interested in their views. My mind wandered as I contemplated the sovereignty of the individual – some nascent thoughts appeared. My marriage really was too bad to stay and too good to leave. What would my life be like if I divorced Jane?

When a woman is interested she shows it through her eyes and pheromones. They both came on to me. The sex god scrambled, it's rather like saying "walk" to a sleeping dog! Was I able to create sexed up-ness out of any mundane scene?

Women can be so wise, so powerful, so intuitive and yet next to a man they become mango jelly. I didn't fancy faux-blonde Mary - she just wasn't my type. I chose Linda, an Italian woman in her late fifties, possibly sixty. Her good looks hadn't yet vanished. She was mischievous, fun and opinionated. She looked after herself, in a noble no-plastic kind of way. Women agonise over getting older but I have often found mature women attractive. The fragrance of her feminine hearth washed over me.

'So Linda, when was the last time you had some?' Leaning beyond my edge perhaps, but I had become a confident so-and-so.

I found her mother-energy alluring. She looked a little taken aback by my flirty forthrightness, but soon settled into our banter.

'Oh it's been years.' She was over ripe. The mundane scene fast became lyrical.

'Tell him Linda, I'll bet it's been ten years since that abusive ass of a husband of yours was finally booted out,' Mary chimed in laughing.

'How many years?'

'Oh... I suppose around eleven years'

'*Eleven* years. That's just not right, not for a lovely woman like you.' I was rediscovering my dare. Mary shifted jealously.

'I do hope you've compensated with self pleasures though.'

There were tears as she wasn't used to such an honest affront. Tears of laughter! 'I can't believe I'm having this conversation...' Gasping for air. 'Yes, I have been known to do a little self pleasure now and again.'

'Now and again you sex starved whore, tell him how much you need the real thing. It's *all* you ever talk about! A good orgasm with this young'n 'll calm you down Linda, it'll set you up for another week at least.'

'Yes Lin, did you know that back in Victorian times they used to forcibly masturbate women to calm them down[ix]? Especially when they got a bit neurotic, wank them off then they'd be manageable again.... Can you imagine having that as your job, a neurotic-woman-masturbator?' Perhaps I could have done volunteer work for such an institution.

Linda looked embarrassed. 'Yes, I can feel how that would work!'

'Is it true Lin? Want some real man do you?' Implicit coercion?

'Well yes that would be nice, but I think I'm a bit past it, sadly men don't look at me like they used to... Well it's not just that, I'm picky with men. I would have had some real-man by now, but all the men around have beer bellies full of baggage, there are

---

ix   C19th women were given genital massage by medical doctors to treat hysteria. Maybe our ancestors had lost the knowledge of how to bring a woman to orgasm at home; maybe they thought it wasn't desirable for her?

a lot of damaged goods out there. The married ones wouldn't look at an older woman like me, and the single ones are all abusive and crazy. I need to feel safe if I'm going to be with a man. I'm done with abusive men.'

'Yeah that ass was no good for you Linda, but he's gone now... Are you going to give her a treatment Ben? Some women just need a good wank or better still a good fuck.' Mary had a plan.

Linda continued. 'And besides, I feel unattractive, I don't feel good about myself, I'm overweight, too hairy... not good enough, moody and I'm not doing what I really want to do in life.'

'God Linda, you really sound as though you need a good wank.'

'I think she looks hot for her age, don't you Mary? And to top it all you have a lovely personality too. I can't believe a man would be so abusive towards you.'

'Yeah Linda, listen to him, it's what I've been saying to you for the last five years. You need to get yer ass out there and go get yourself a man.' Mary moved closer to me and was getting touchier. I didn't reciprocate.

'What about this man, Lin,' I taunted. 'I'd do ya.' I was being self-regarding but deep inside I felt as though I had a gift for Linda (far more of a gift than my stiff cock).

I watched what my sex god was up to. He desired Linda. He desired to adore her and make her feel like the attractive sexual woman that she was. I felt deeper into the desire – it was a desire to make myself complete through another person.

'Oh you guys really are taking this too far. I just popped round for a quick glass of champagne with my friend. I didn't know she planned to set me up!'

'Hey, I'm stayin outta this. He is cute though. Legs a bit long n gangly for my taste tho, nice firm tummy. Whadya think Linda? Let's check his ass out.'

The brothel was on fire, should I have stayed or ran? There was no debate. I became a sex god for them. I stood up and bent over.

'Go on have a good feel Linda... Feel between his legs as well, see how well he's hung!' There was much laughter. What a hoot. Linda had a feel around, somewhere between shy and curious.

'Let me feel too.' Mary took some with a firmer hand. 'Whoa, his woody is coming up nicely.'

'You guys, really.'

I wanted some. 'Your turn Linda. Come on, bend over.'

'Oh this is going a bit too far.' Faux outrage.

'Go on Lin, you're getting all stoked up, go on show him yer ass.' She stood up and bent over.

'Go on hitch yer skirt up a bit. Turn the man on will ya.'

I felt her ass-curves slowly and returned her courage by feeling the plump between her legs. Her face said it all. Life was flowing, sex was flowing. I was not pushing the river.

'Nice job Linda, thank you.'

'Stop it you guys.' She sat back down into her discomfort.

'Okeeee, looks like we've got a fun time on our hands. It's a lovely warm night, why don't I fix a few special pool cocktails, then we can go play in the pool together.'

In the space of twenty minutes that neighbourly soirée had transgressed from polite to debauched. We undressed for the pool, no swimmies were necessary. Redemption was imminent. I looked at Linda. I appreciated her tad withered yet noble body. I reflected on how she had said earlier that she felt unattractive. I could see all her beauty. I could feel the flickering flame of her womanly essence. Was I being a healer again?

'Wait Linda, before you get into the pool I just want to feel you. May I?' Loose, pleated, rich. She was wildly hairy; there was no time for grooming as she had not been expecting a man that night. She drove me crazy with desire.

'Okay... Ha. Hhhhhhhhh.' Sweet.

'Mmmmm, she's seriously wet Mary, I think she's hornier than she's letting on.' I took a hit of her musk.

'Yeah me too,' Mary broadcasted.

I climbed the pool steps. They were like excited school girls awaiting a 99 at the ice cream van. Very erect, I slipped into the pool. I was embraced by their laughter and jiggling saggy tits. If I were a tit man I would have slipped into heaven.

Amidst the games there were rising degrees of permission between us; all intimacy requires permission. In any intimate space permissions can build. Permission requires an awareness of the subtle communications that flow between lovers. Permission is crucial in any space where safety and trust are pre-requisite. At that point in the evening Linda had permission, Mary didn't.

Mary approached me, she was a family friend. I didn't need to sleep with her and unusually I (the sex god) wasn't up for a threesome. Our bodies were swaying together and I became aware that Mary was gripping the base of my cock. She needed consent to wank me. A boundary was being crossed; there was a NO in me trying to get expressed. My boundaries weren't declared; they were being subjectively inferred. In sexual relationship there is always a giver and a receiver, someone doing and someone being done to. In the absence of consent Mary wasn't giving she was taking. Linda looked on yearningly as Mary continued to help herself, wanking me up super stiff. Sexual politics are subtle.

I remained absent as she squatted and shoved my bone up into her pussy. She held me tight, she was larger than me. She fucked herself off on me. I wasn't consenting, I was raped but without resistance. It was sex without intimacy. She couldn't give back what she had borrowed.

She knew what she had done and soon disappeared off to bed.

'You two enjoy yourselves and I'll put my headphones on so I don't hear her scream when she gets that thing up inside her. G'night!'

You cannot un-fuck.

Permission is a key to intimacy. I had no hard feelings towards her; I just wish she had asked. A bad feeling is still held in my psyche over that affair. It gave me a sub-miniscule insight as to how a woman may feel at the receiving end of a hungry man behaving unhealthily towards her. A few years later I behaved non-consensually with a special friend. Consensual sex is a prerequisite of the flow of healthy masculine energy – else we may all become fragments in an uncaring Universe.

Good for Linda, for pulling a guy twenty years her youth. We retreated to a bedroom as water based sex really wasn't our thing.

'Shall we start again Lin?'

'Okay, that would be nice.'

She shared that she was jaded by how men had treated her in the past. How could I be more generous to her? How could our play be more than the rumble-rumble-jackpot she used to have?

'How about a massage Lin?'

I dried her off and gave her an oily massage. I wasn't sure if I was giving or taking. She gave me clear instructions on where to work and where to touch. Sex chemistry shows up in many roles, as a fiery Latin-lover, a powerful magnate, a rock star or a Son for example. Sometimes dominance and submission arrives, lovemaking is always different when we are not caught in humdrum. That night an alluring mother-fucking energy appeared between us. Linda became a Mother and I became a Son.

She needed me to be a softened Son, not a wild one – I liked that. I wanted to make it special for her. We slowed it all down. She submitted to being explored and compromised – she seemed to like that. Her maturity was worshipped through every sense. It was my pleasure to give to her. There were so many energies between us. She tried to give to me, but that night I wouldn't let her.

She tried to choke on my cock, I let her.

She had pulled a younger one and there was nothing to prove. I wanted her to feel like a sexual woman again, to feel attractive. I wanted her to see how much she was turning me on. I wanted her to once more reclaim her divine feminine. It was to be a noble fuck. I wanted to be a mother fucker. It wasn't decrepit heaving ugliness; it was wanton mother-son polarity. My teacher has since shared that that behaviour comes from my soul; it is my core wanting to return to Source, to where it came from.

I operated at the confluence of lust, giving and curiosity with her body.

'You are making me feel so special, thank you Ben, thank you for making me feel safe... and adequate.' Why is it that we need *another* person to make us feel a certain way, where did we learn that?

'My pleasure Linda, just let me give you what you feel you need. Ask for anything.' There was no real guilt or remorse, just pure play. Sometimes a woman doesn't know what she wants, it must be discovered.

Reader, how well do you know *your* sexual self? Do you know exactly what you want? Have you ever asked yourself that?

I took my time looking and tasting her – our softness morphed to safety. Sexual healing requires the special energy of a safe man. Only then can a woman open to herself again.

She reengaged with her sex essence and was soon begging for the deep and hard. We worked closely together, bringing her up. Unlike my naughty older-woman connection with Barbra twenty years ago, I had become experienced, confident and in charge. The sex god was in good form and I was letting it get inside what it needed.

'Get on your knees Linda.' I wanted her musk. I wanted to look at her older-womanness.

I chose to plant my seed deep inside her.

Her orgasm never arrived.

Maybe I wasn't a healer; maybe it was me who needed healing?

She lay still for a while, possibly shedding a tear.

'You are a fine gentleman and an even finer lover Ben. You have given me so much. I shall treasure our time together, but I think my body has changed... I couldn't find my sexual charge like I used to.'

'Oh let me come see you again sometime and work with you to find it. I would love to give you that gift.'

'That would be nice Ben, but I am sorry. I think my poetry has finished.'

Going Home

Mother Fucker. My teacher tells me that my life shouldn't be an open book and that I should leave a few chapters completely closed. I must not be all day with no night, some part of me should be a complete mystery. Only rarely should I allow somebody to enter my Self. That is what love is.

From love I have opened many of my chapters, with a healing intention for all peoples. But there are still many chapters that I shall only share with my intimate lovers and still others that shall remain only-mine.

This auspicious chapter is about going back home. Most people would choose to keep this one closed; they would keep a thick protective membrane between their fiction and their truth on this one. There is value in my sharing it with you though as life asks me to outgrow my old containers. So I shall go bareback for you.

L'Origine du Monde[x], I come from this, I am the same as all of this. Man is born of woman. All men come from the divine feminine.

Reader, do you recall my horny encounter with young Penny down in Mexico. Did you think it was real or was it just a fantasy? An elaborate and imaginative scenario, in which, any man might love to find himself? Does it matter to you whether it, or indeed this whole story, was a true experience or just a fantasy? I play with you!

Penny embodied blossoming goddess beauty and was like dancing bright sunlight on a turquoise lagoon, innocent, perfect, terribly actually, vibrant, serious and giggling grown up. She smelt like dew blessed freesias just birthing from their buds. I was her older man, her appreciated manhood. Well, this chapter isn't about

---

x   L'Origine du Monde (The origin of the world) is a painting by Gustave Courbet in 1866. It is a close-up view of the genitals and abdomen of a naked woman, lying on a bed with legs spread.

Penny, it's about my infatuation for her *mother*, Catherine... who once looked like Penny.

Fantasies often arise from our conditioning and inhibitions. They are repressed energy trying to be free. I'm sure this fantasy came from my soul. She lived in a wisteria manse. In a librarian sort of way, she was so proper; her fragrance filled the room like a fine old lily. Her glowing motherhood had matured like a fine wine; she would look special at a gallery opening, you know the sort. Like Mrs. Honey, Barbs and Linda, I wanted to seduce her with my delicate strength. I wanted to reflect her female nobility back to her. It wouldn't be a sympathy fuck. No. I wanted to be close to her, to hold her, worship every little wrinkle, her dark bobbed hair, her big clit. Our sexual union would proclaim the full beauty of life. I would make her feel like all the shimmering purples of the rainbow. I would proclaim her grace then dive naked into the womb of her soul.

All any man really wants is to be engulfed by the womb of rhythmic warmth of the Mother archetype.

I've shared some stories of encounters with older women and the special sexuality they radiate. I have noticed through much of my lifetime that I have been attracted to the occasional older woman; especially one who looks after herself.

To be clear, I have no wish to sleep with my own mother.

The psycho-therapies tell me it is because of Oedipus and the oedipal complex that is present at the core man. I am told that the complex arises from an intense mother attraction coupled with a distant father figure in childhood. Nobody has explained the theorem to me in a way that I can fully grasp. I needed to suss the origin of this mother fucking energy, so I undertook my own explorations using Tantra and meditation.

As a meditator, I am highly trained in the art of witnessing the ever changing subtle phenomenon of the human mind and condition. And in recent years I have been journeying down an intensifying tantric pathway. Tantra is "practice". The tradition teaches many practices from which we can learn about the truest knowable nature of ourselves and the Universe. It is a path to wholeness that enables us to be physical beings without being owned, defined or limited by form. It also involves us in rich and utterly juicy sexual experiences that are beyond our wildest wet dreams! The path requires substantial and dedicated practice.

In a Tantra retreat a few years ago, a layer-cake of teachings prepared me for a series of meditations that resulted in revelations of many subtle truths. **Deep within us all is a yearning to be in union with the safe and nourishing Oneness present in the womb of our mother.** We were complete and at home in Source before we were born. The desire to return to the radiantly loving mother energy deep within the feminine is also a desire to physically climb back inside her. Within our mother we can be safe and whole once again, free of vulnerability. We wouldn't ever again know the experience of isolation. In that place I would be loved and be Love. Away from that place I have the illusion that I am not Love.

My desire to give my love to the mother energy was an expression of wanting to love where I came from. Such that I might repose there and be so blended with her that there is no question of division or abandonment. It was clear to me that my primal wound, that of the original separation from my mother, had cleaved an abyss through the core of my being that I was to carry for a lifetime.

The archetypal mother energy can be witnessed in and through every woman. I am able to make love to all women through any woman as they are the divine feminine manifest.

And woman yearns to reconnect to man.

I was with a girl a few years ago who loved cock in her mouth, in her vagina, in her arse. She wanted them all at once, she wanted to be multiply penetrated by men, to be filled by manhood in all her portals. That was her nature, that was Nature; sacred profanity. The divine feminine wants man to come back inside, to return home.

She also loved to gag and choke on my cock deep down her throat, she held my cock inside her throat for longer than felt reasonable. Not only did she want me inside, she wanted to die (almost) with me inside.

I loved her when she did that; somehow we felt complete.

All is change.

I have just been discussing triple-penetration of a lovely lusty woman from Croatia and now I shall talk about trees. Reader, I look around the room in this ancient barn where I sit and write. There is a forty-foot beam of Elm above my head. This barn was built in 1760 and the beam bears the scars of being used previously in other structures. I pause for a moment and can feel stillness here. I can feel all of Nature, all of Mother energy surrounding me, in me through me.

All is that Mother energy.

Perhaps a threesome with Penny and Catherine would annihilate me into the womb of Source and Sauce and then suspend me in an awakened lifetime of cosmic oneness?

They may both be frigid and prude for all I know.

Angst

I was searching for orgasms more divine than the last one. There was a gulf between my emotions and my way of life. Reader, we have journeyed together from my being a young man full of spunk and innocent urges, and through my married life with its many joys and uncertainties. I have shared a few dalliances that had me explore the physical realm as well as those that explored psychological vulnerability. On this journey, you have witnessed the ways of the horribly compulsive sex god as both healer, and naughty boy. As I grew older there were destructive forces meshing together; they were most addictive in nature. I was becoming a shape that wasn't mine.

I am not one to spend my life at the surface of myself, but I can get pretty twisted with efforts to understand myself. I didn't know the beauty of life while I was being so self-indulgent, so up my own arse. As I evolved, those destructive forces were accompanied by spiritual insights that pointed to peaceful possibilities and freedom. I now realise that in some fundamental way, I was really seeking freedom back then. Not freedom from life's responsibilities though. I'm talking about inner liberation from the lifelong grist mill of sex-grasping and sex god aversion.

All a man really wants is freedom. Freedom arrives when we love ourselves totally.

I could have become my healthy masculine if I had known about it. After all, my male essence when behaving healthily was a saint, a sacred teacher, a healer and a lion's roar for Man.

There wasn't a wilderness of the heart either, I was still in love with Jane; but her love wasn't pacifying my storms. Pressure from Jane to be a certain way had made me stiff to life. I wasn't in love with myself or the sex god; my conflicted state was soul destroying.

The dark night of my soul needn't have been so black.

I was disposed to dreaming about new ways of being in this world. If I chose and was chosen by <u>one</u> woman then I wouldn't need to push my love everywhere. I would be able to, but wouldn't need to. Maybe the Universe could make me aware of that one woman that I could commit to. Where was she – out there somewhere? She would need to love all of me unconditionally, sex god and all. Together we would create and share a common intention. We would share dreams, fantasies, philosophy, interests, lovers, Truth-seeking *and* our juicy bodies. We would love and channel the sex god in service of our relationship and we would allow it to take us both home to wholeness.

I knew it wasn't Jane, she couldn't play her part anymore, not in this lifetime. Her heart was closing and I wasn't worshipping. My lies and damaged ways would be seen by her as another betrayal of biblical proportions. If my infidelity could have been openly discussed back then maybe our marriage could have healed and become stronger. Marriage is a container for a loving relationship. If love departs should the container be preserved at any cost? Rather than "could this marriage be saved" we should have focussed on "could this love be saved".

So for a new woman to enter my life I would need to leave my long-term marriage with Jane. The loss of our relationship would feel terrible. Years ago when I was on meat hooks in Oz I feared loss enough to abandon myself; in order to keep things stable. I used to smile when I was sad and pretend to like decisions that appalled me. The loss of my marriage wouldn't be cataclysmic if it healed my heart and soul though. If my heart and soul healed, I could be a better father. I knew that if I continued in my marriage I *would* lose my heart and soul; that would be Jane's tragedy, not to mention my own. We were at an impasse that prevented either of us really living.

Abandoning myself in an effort to keep someone else happy was a behaviour I needed to unlearn. I needed resolve to live my own truth so that my heart could return to peace.

There was a real battle of paradox going on back then. On one side was a Jungian-festival of childhood-wounding all playing out in the adult world. On the other side was my path, my karma, my DNA, the wave of stardust and light that I Am.

I could feel that someday I would run out of moves, and the arrogance that *I think I am in control* would become surrender, trust and thanksgiving.

I could have tried to change Jane. But changing myself was a challenge, how on earth could I change her. So one day I thought I would explore the middle road. I suggested to Jane that we could redefine our marriage. Maybe we could separate but live together; maybe we could have an open relationship for a while or experiment with swinging.

'NO.'

The Buddha has taught that *there is no external refuge.*
Honesty starts with self-honesty.
I just needed to stop lying and get truthful.

Need

I wasn't the kind of dog you could leave on the porch. Jane had
become my best friend rather than my lover and sex had become
something to be enjoyed outside of our marriage container.
The itch for variety and a real horny woman continued to be an
imposing one.

Variety is important for a man (and many a woman). I didn't
expect to eat the same dinner every night, and asking me to eat the
same woman every night felt like a tall order. In my marriage I
adopted a rhythm whereby I would go all soft and gooey for a few
months; I would be unquestionably committed to Jane and numb to
my numbness. Then a friend's naughty smile or the broad hips of
an older woman would captivate me. Their female essence would
work its ensnaring magic, the sex god would awaken and before I
knew it I was playing around again. What I had to have had me.

I avoided acting out *mostly,* but the sex god loved a chase.
It loved subterfuge, intensity and the danger of getting caught. It
conjured cunning plans to make debauchery happen and had me
jerk-off in anticipation of an illicit shag. I wrestled with it and it
with me.

In some way the sweeping palette of emotional and sensory
experiences in my life helped me feel whole. Deep in my heart I
knew that someday I would have a life partner whom I could share
the sex god with but until she showed up I continued to be a bit of
a player.

The sex god had become my curse; it could always get the
better of me, of course it would. Again, my need for a woman
welled up from deep within. I wasn't out looking for a goddess. I
needed a saviour and whore; paradoxically a woman can be both.
The consequences didn't matter.

When you reside in your sex you become attractive to others.
They sense you. If thought preceded reality then my thoughts were
surely manifesting the many arising opportunities! Finding lovers

was easy. It was as if my truest-self was vibrating at a frequency that would attract sexual encounters. I was attracting life-lessons that showed me that I was dying inside my marriage and dying inside myself.

One day I found myself on a cruise ship. It was a business cruise full of mawkish excess. At the gala banquet a delegate from another company sat down opposite me. Our eyes promptly grasped each other. An opportunity was availing itself; the mischievous god of desire shimmered. We made appropriate conversation alongside the other guests for the next few hours. With girl-next-door looks, she was elegantly polite with an occasional brassiness. I agreed with her point of view and made a point of disagreeing with the others. As the dinner came to completion we parted company.

Real-relationship can only take place in the present moment. In that moment my wife was in the past for sure. She would surely be in my future too. But in that moment, she didn't exist for me. Where in reality is our past and future? Reader, have you ever experienced anything outside of the present moment?

An hour or so later in the club, I saw Sabita sitting with colleagues, she beckoned me to join them. Amidst the jollies surrounding us we somehow became engrossed in a severe conversation.

'How can a woman recover from never having a stable man in her life Ben? I gave them sex and they still ran away. How is a woman supposed to get over abandonment issues when she has been abandoned by every man she has ever loved?'

She had been betrayed by the ancient contract whereby a woman gives sex so that she won't be abandoned. She had tolerated "good-as-it-gets" in the hope of getting some love and security. But perhaps we are at the dawn of an age where women should say "No" to sex and let their man run away? Perhaps this is the way that the divine feminine could regain power by having complete dominion over who is allowed in her womb. Always. Her clear boundary would require that men heal their damaged relationship to their sex. They would need to find a truer way of relating to women if they were to get any.

If we men could devotedly worship our woman she would love us more than we could imagine. Most of us stop short of being that total though. When our woman shows us her wobbles it's easier to run away. No man really desires to abandon a woman. It isn't in our truest nature, yet for some reason we do it.

'Could you be perpetually recreating emotional challenges from your childhood Sabita? ... And attracting men to keep reflecting those wounds back to you? ...' She didn't really want me to be her shrink and fix her, she just wanted me to listen to her.

She interrupted. 'I think my dad wanted me aborted, he wanted to abandon me before I was born. Then he left when I was nine. What part do I have in creating all this misery? What part? I wasn't emotionally unavailable to any man. I just want to love.'

She was fed up with damaged-male bullshit.

I was saddened at the ways of the unhealthy-male in my brothers. I needed to offer salving words that may touch her. 'Love yourself Sabita, it's time to be yourself, to love yourself. In this moment no one else is to blame.' I'm not sure she wanted to hear my wisdoms. Being abandoned was her story.

The dialogue stopped, we both fell silent and hugged each other. Much was communicated between us. Neither of us was in the right space to get to the bottom of her wounds that night.

Engrossed, we hadn't noticed that the others had dispersed.

'I'm sorry Ben to dump on you... You're so cute.' We kissed.

Oh how the fluid ways of female energies change through every moment.

Source knows when lessons are needed. It shoves the gift into your world and you take it. A wave shows up and you either ride it or wipe out.

'Shall we at least make tonight a great night Sabita, I won't abandon you tonight, even if we have to abandon ship!' I had decided to ride the wave.

She softened. 'If we spend this night together Ben. I'll probably cry a lot and may end up asking you to just hold me.'

I was happy to be a man for her.

Our energies radically changed, melancholy became mirth.

'Shall we get a drink?' Our emptiness needed numbing.

'And a good shag.' We needn't feel so alone that night.

"Jack D" showed up. Was I really moving towards transcendence?

Our sex gods showed up. A night of having our fucked-up needs met was imminent.

Our banter lightened and deepened. Somehow noisy sex became the topic of choice.

'What about sounds, Sabita, are you noisy in bed?' I letched.

She knew where I was going. 'Oh, yeah, I love to scream, I just love letting go. Embarrassing for my fella sometimes, but what the heck, I just love it.' She was shy and yet so forward talking about sex. In spite of her stuff she was easy and free around the subject. The sex gods had been match making again. I wanted her little honey, I was hooked.

'I slept with a girl a few years back who made all kinds of zoological sounds. I loved it, it so turned me on. She was so free. Where do girls learn to do that?'

'You don't learn how to be noisy Ben. You learn how to be quiet!'

Wow what an amazing woman, was she some kind of sex sage?

'What about you Ben, are you noisy?' I went quiet.

Reader, as I write I have become aware of a strange disassociation between the thirty-something and the mature version of myself. I remember in my youth being terminally embarrassed about making sounds. These days I am aware of the transcendental freedom present when we use our true voice in any situation. We become who we really are when we don't edit the truest expression of who we are.

We often edit our expression so that we don't upset (or deafen) others. Freedom in your throat is a prerequisite for being yourself. Recently my teacher has been teaching me about the use of sound in love making, instructing me to be free around the fifth chakra. When we have free sounds we have free breath. I have been putting her teachings into expressive practice with my beloved Angelica. I have experienced unbridled breath, unbridled sound. It's like having a flamethrower that reaches beyond the soul; sounds are volcanically expelled up through my core. There's so much energy in sound, so much freedom to be had in uncontrolled breath. This is true for every little sound; utterances of love, whispers of dirty desire, and all the ineffable grunts, coos and arghs that desire emits. Sounds are all energetic flows from Source, pure Nature. Free sounds are primal communications, animal interchanges; the mind needn't suppress them. Relatively speaking though, back then I wasn't such a vocal fucker.

'Ah, that would be telling Sabita. Perhaps you can find out tonight?' We were knowingly raising and cultivating our attraction for each other. I kissed her, gently rolling her head and muzzling through her hair – smelling the sex behind her ears.

We soon found ourselves outside on a first class deck, the moonlit ocean stretched to the black horizon. The ship had a good steam on; it was leaving a white cauldron of wake across the bay. We embraced there in the jet stream of ozone. Like a climbing creeper she clung to me, her black party dress fully billowing. I am certain the wind makes you crazy.

'Ben, I promised myself I wasn't going to do this anymore.' Her mischievous smile said it all.

I kissed her more deeply. Then gently rolled her clammy pussy through her lacy panties.

'But one last time will be okay.' Oh how the fluid ways of female energies change through every moment.

Thus far there weren't any tears, just a joyful submission. Maybe what she really needed was to feel needed, attractive and powerful for a moment, for those were my needs too. Her submission induced the fiery Latin lover in me; she made it clear that was what she needed. It wasn't a gig for a slow worshipping Romeo.

In spite of our best efforts, the exposed oceangoing deck was no place to make love. So we decanted to her tiny cabin. We were about to express our emotions rather than resolve them;

we were polar opposites brought together by Source to fulfil holes and needs for each other. Yin and yang, fiery-aggressive and submissive-taken. I felt powerful as I held her from behind; hitching up her dress and forcing my hand down between her legs. She buckled forwards, submitting. She was a groaner, how I love the animal sounds made by an uninhibited woman. I found my grunt as I consumed her. It was primal passion, no six hour foreplay or fucking manual needed.

With savage tenderness, I pushed her back onto the bed. I spread her and took an education of her anatomy; enough to fill my need. I ponderously ate her like fleshy mango, her legs went rigid. She pointed her toes and screamed – loudly. She jolted without breath and then gasped for air.

I wasn't of the school of "give her one first and then take your own". Orgasm isn't the objective of sex. Many men are appalling in bed; ask a woman who has had several partners.

She recovered slightly and sat up. 'Mmmmm so good, you've done that before haven't you?'

'A few times... ' I grinned. 'Wow... I nearly drowned down there you gorgeous juicy thing...'

I could feel that she was in her power.

She succumbed to her knees leaning against the bed. I lifted her dress up, exposing her. I was ravenous for her nice hips, nice ass. How could I give if I wasn't full?

I wanted more.

'Spread your buttocks.' Our trust had been established.

'What did you say, spread them?'

'Do it now, and just hold for a while.'

Consensually she was forced to obey. She was a sexually open woman. She spread herself, agape and compromised while I watched. I loved to look. Our energy intensified.

I petted the sap from her heavy lips up into the sphincter of her coffee skinned cleft. She was done-to but loving it. I penetrated her asshole with a rhythm that respected her needs. Needs that were clearly expressed by the way she writhed her body into my finger tip.

'Ohhh hh no,' she groaned.

We worked together like flints.

'You like my little Asian cunt don't you.'

'Yes, yes, little, I love your cun.. tight cunt.'

'Use it baby, use me, take what you need, I know you need it. I need you to use my little cunt... Oh you abuse me so well, make me so horny, make me so wet, take me take me baby.'

Megawatts of sex god electric coursed through me. I was fearful of experiencing so much pleasure. Like a small man, I thought about the Titanic to desensitize and cool down.

Then the feral entered our lovemaking. I spanked her tight buttocks delivering a sting. Sound amplified our love making. She was taking me to the dark side of Venus.

'Yes, yes, ow, that hurt... yessssss. I'm such a naughty girl.' She enjoyed herself more thoroughly than she was used to.

Reader did you ever have desires to do or be done in that way? Are there even a few cells within you that seek to meet with Eros in such a probingly confrontational way? Does your own sex god seek to touch *your* lover so crudely? Does it yearn to receive such open play, such freely abandoned sacred play?

Judgements that arise are conditioned mirrors. They hold us away from peace. Peace that is available through unconditional okay-ness of what actualises as a sexual human. Denial of what is – is un-peaceful.

Slapping dark meaning onto her spread buttocks holds darkness within you. Light can enter the dark crevices of your mind, if you accept life exactly as it is.

I fucked her hard.

Was I discharging all my stress and negative emotions into her womb? Surely that wasn't any way to treat a woman.

Her pussy was fervid and drew me in, clamped me in. She begged me for hardness. Sparks from our flintiness ignited and became fire as my unhealthy masculine met hers. I was greedy – she was needy.

I fucked her up the arse. Hard.

'No, no,' she groaned.

I fucked her and emptied.

Hard.

She fucked me.
Hard.
Cold fusion. It was too much.
Thankfully.

Our wake was strewn with consuming consummation and hollow emptiness. I was engulfed by a confronting paradox of awful and joyous feelings. What had Sabita got from our raunchy time together? What did her feminine essence, that seeks only to love, receive from our relationship? Where had the beautiful sex god gone? The one that connected transformed and healed. Were we healing each other?
Sabita and I eventually parted company.
Hard.
I had her jasmine odour panties in my pocket.

In blindly obeying the forceful compulsions of the sex god a darkness within was strengthening. My teacher would say it was all *for purpose* and Source had plans.

It's never enough though is it? Something inside *always* wants more. That fix was an opportunity to fill mutual needs and holes. Its effect was short lived though as something within was searching for a lasting satisfaction. It was the needs and holes that wanted more!
Can you relate to that Reader? What *is* that bit of us that thinks "something is missing"? It's only an idea, a purchased idea, a believed in idea.
Oh Lordy, let me suspend my beliefs and attachments for a second, a month or a fucking eternity.

When I returned home from the cruise I spent an afternoon in the sunshine and blue-sky breeze digging potatoes. I clenched the soil with bare hands; it grounded my spirit. My energetic body yearned for the centred chalice of the Earth.

Damaged

I read the news today. News media is the fearful-mind of society. Headlines are often about sex and the sexually deviant way of the world; bank chiefs and hotel maids, raped forests, government ministers into fetish parties, abused reefs, business moguls taking extreme sex with call girls, and the exploitation of toxic fish. **The damaged masculine makes the news.** Where is God in it all? Everywhere.

But then I guess we aren't governed by leaders willing to take a vow of celibacy are we. Not like the church, where celibacy vows might allow the powerful to be more *in touch* with their subjects; perhaps dipping a finger in the anus of a young lad or practicing celibacy with the youthful genitals of a parishioner's daughter? God is there somewhere. Mud is everywhere.

I read stories about men acting without permission, playing out their unhealthy-masculinity. Paedophiles driven underground, erections of highest buildings, rapists called to account and inflating oil company share prices.

I once knew of a barrister into S&M, and you may remember my meeting with a lawyer who was into dope and hard fucking. Perhaps their day-job had them sitting in court passing judgement over all these religious, corporate and secular sexual miscreants?

I read about a young fellow with woes claiming he was going to sue his father for not using a condom at his conception.

I read of reactions to the sexual repression brought about by our conditioned society.

I read too of a generation that is pillaging Mother Earth.

Maybe our whole generation needs healing? If our peoples were healed it would save us having to keep locking them up.

What you resist persists.

A sex god aligned with an unhealthy-masculine persists.

Sex gods that live through healthy essences can save the world.

If we love each other we can love the Earth.

Burning Brightly

I was in my forties and living back in England. My teacher had spoken of there being three energetic cups in any relationship; my cup, the other person's cup and a relationship cup. If my cup was overflowing, I could pour energy into the relationship cup. If my cup was depleted, I would take from the relationship cup. Jane's basis for relationship was "I have chosen you, now you must meet my needs." Our cups were empty. I yearned for deepest union and yet I couldn't even look into her eyes.

Did Jane suspect or know about my infidelities? Many women willingly take on such suffering. We still had love, but it was our marriage that needed saving. We continued to explore various therapies to try to save it. My core was still wounded from the last time I was exposed as a philanderer. Even though I wanted to, I was unlikely to come clean.

As I made efforts to tackle my cup-depletion, my spiritual journey gained momentum. Light was entering through my wounds. Authenticity birthed itself as layers and roles fell away. To be free, all of me needed to stand powerfully-vulnerable in the light: shamed little boy, spiritual seeker, addict, lover, healer, husband and all. Being a spiritual Ben wasn't about being "nice", it was about being complete. I had Work to do; though I wasn't sure where to find answers.

Diana and I had both become entangled in our respective dramas. Perhaps we became best friends as we could both complain to each other. We were beautifully clear mirrors for each other at a crucial time. Light can be held between two mirrors.

Diana was neither whore nor flower, but both all at once. She had a big-heart and a highly loquacious nature. She dressed her charisma in fine flowing couture and even finer lingerie. In spite of her temptressness we nurtured an unconsummated friendship over several years. We shared many secrets together. I was able to share my innermost poverty with her; could I trust a woman confidant?

One particularly warm summer night we were meeting for a date. She arrived in a blaze of jiggling breasts and sartorially confident gym garb. Source moves in infinitely articulate ways, doesn't she? Her femaleness was archetypal. I loved her, her form, her spirit.

'Do I notice a certain horniness about your visage or is it just me?'

'No, not horny just yet, I've just finished a fantastic yoga class, brilliant teacher, you really should try him out.' She was sweating and sporting a toned muscley abdomen.

'Champagne?' She always chose the exuberant alternative.

We explored women's issues of the day, isolation, harassment, discrimination, time pressures and support networks. We discussed sex, children, ex's, relationship schism, sad men, growing up, making lots of money, who's not getting it... and then eventually back to sex again.

'Oh Diana, I'd so love to make love to you tonight.'

'No. I'm done with sex Ben, done with men, after that last useless excuse for a man. I'm done, done.' She had recently exited a toxic relationship that had gone on way too long.

'No Diana, we would be different, I want to slowly worship you, explore you, caress you, serve you, make you cum, make you feel like the sexiest woman in London... then do forbidden things to you and make you cum again. Slow sex... And besides I haven't had any lately, perhaps once in the past six months, I'm pretty desperate.'

'Honey, if you are counting how many times you've had sex lately there's something wrong...' She sipped her Champagne. 'And besides if I *were* to fuck you it would be so hot, very quick and hard, none of your slow worshippy stuff, I've fancied you for far too long... But I'm off men Ben. Done, done.'

'Can I steal your knickers again instead?' Much laughter ignited.

'Ben, what have you been up to lately?'

'Well I've been throwing myself at all kinds of workshops and therapies... Trying to make some sense of myself and the questionable life choices I've made. I've been trying to discern social influences from who I really am. Trying to find how to self actualise, how to be me. You know the stuff, I'm always rabbiting on about it.'

'Love is a mystery to many people Ben because they don't take time out to understand their own heart, their own feelings. It's so good that you're really looking inside now, you're overdue for that.'

Reader, perhaps my continued exploration of psychology was keeping me inauthentic and asleep? The word-therapies can reveal a wound, and then talk about it, then talk about the talked-about; and on. My tapestry could become burled and pilled if I spent more time with workshops and therapists. Word therapies can consume a lifetime if you aren't on guard. When we ask questions about the corner in which we find ourselves, it is therapeutic to look at the question we ask. To ascertain if the question takes us *towards truth*; or *away from truth* into an ever deeper meta-understanding of concepts and words.

'I did a workshop last month that explored in detail how our guilt hides our gift. I haven't been able to grasp and integrate that one yet.'

'Ben what if your purpose *is* to be a sexual man, what if your sex god was your vehicle of giving to the world, of making a difference, what if? Just imagine, you'd have girls queuing up to get fixed, they're all going mad out there with those loser men. Mad, mad.'

I caught my reflection in an ornate mirror; I gazed deeply into my eyes. I heard what she had said. Could my wound contain my genius? Was my buried purpose being revealed by my addictive nature? What if my soul purpose was to be a sexually open healer? Was I here on Earth to fuck and to heal? It was the Lotus bud.

'Just be open to the idea Ben, see where it takes you... Another option is that you just have loads more sex – *that* would be a great cure for sex addiction, don't you think?'

The evening was young. It was good to swap stories of our conquests, both mediocre and pinnacle. We discussed the paradox of her new-found freedom and her sadness of her long term marriage now lost. We conferred on whether I should stay hostage in my marriage; it was apparent that it would be healthier for all concerned if I departed. I had witnessed Diana's considerable pain and incorrigible growth through her own divorce. I felt damned within but damned without.

Divorce is such an individual and wretched journey, especially for children. The exquisite sensitivity of children allows them to detect every crack in a relationship; they also detect the sadness born of inauthenticity in both parents. The gentle hearts of children do not weather a divorce well, though they are adaptable, they aren't resilient. I have witnessed damaged people in many workshops who traced their original wounds back to having an absent father. I was about to precipitate another generation of abandoned wounding. **For fucks sake God**, what was I supposed to do?

'Diana, if I'm to follow your lead and leave my marriage, my wife, my children; I need to leave it in a way that honours all the greatness that we had together. Because there's been so much....
I would have so much regret if I leave. I'm not sure my marriage has really failed. But it has caused me to become so inauthentic – and that isn't good. I guess that is failure though! It isn't healthy to preserve a failed partnership.'

I wished I'd been honest about the sex god twenty five years ago. My mind was tortured and my heart was bleeding. I knew that I'd allowed myself to get caught up in my wife's ambition. I was lost in my head, lost in the mincing of trying to work it all out.

Stay or go? Ambivalence pervaded me.

But the sex god was licking his lips in the corner of my psyche.

'My house is burning Diana. I'm bombarded with dos and don'ts while bumping into my old patterns... It's so good to be free with you.' Though I was authentic with Diana, being True Ben, simultaneously I was being inauthentic to my wife. I had already left my marriage.

'God listen to you Ben, fear of being yourself, fear of loss, fear of relationship jeopardy, fear... mind if I have another cigarette?' She lit up another one. '...Fear based love; your mind is in the blender. If your relationship with Jane is all good, then stay, otherwise get over it and move on and find another good woman.' I loved it when she kicked ass.

My marriage couldn't continue with an unloved sex god within our communion. I had "tried" to get brave and communicate to Jane what was going on. I never really hit the mark though as I wasn't a brave enough man to say it how it was. Was I hoping my diluted-words, my beating around the bush would have some sort of homeopathic effect on her? I was fearful of being honest with myself and more fearful of her response to my truth. Would she leave me if I revealed what the sex god had been up to? I had dug a very deep hole for myself.

I needed to take responsibility for myself, to love myself; a woman can love a man who loves himself. But frankly there was an unconscious refusal on my part to face and move through my pain. Could I really be okay with dying inside my own house? I was defeated.

The contradiction that the sex god was in fact my true purpose lingered on in me for several months.

I have always liked the subterfuge of a dangerous liaison. I enjoyed experimenting with more exotic expressions of my sexuality, dressing up in lingerie, arse licking, being dominated. Such is human sexuality. Was I playing with such intense sensations simply to give myself a sense of "Yes, I exist, it isn't all empty; I have control over giving myself good feelings, my life is happening"!?

For me, intensity felt better than numbing. Others may choose to numb themselves to an "emptiness-avoiding-dullness" with alcohol.

I knew that there is only light, but the darkness felt attractive. I had a great deal of light and goodness elsewhere in my life, maybe I needed darkness to balance the light. Perhaps I wanted to be found out, so that my sex god and I could go to the Emergency Ward.

Dangerous liaison was overdue. I was finished with Diana's torrent of therapese. I really needed to get physical with her. We stood in embrace; her feminine was embracing. The feminine is activated by love, and the masculine is activated by sex.

'Diana, I need to be inside you.' My masculine sought to penetrate.

'No Ben, I'm done with men and I feel from that large bump in your groin that *you* are very much a man.'

The Champagne had made our edges go soft and dreamy. I was wet; the sex god was ready to worship.

'Do you have any photos of when you were younger? I would have loved to have slept with you when you were twenty two.'

I sometimes wondered what it would be like to be with a lover when she was younger? To then make love to her through time, see her grow, see her change. The idea germinated, I realised that I have actually done that with my wife! We had been together for many years. Perhaps I could have seen her gentle ageing as the variety that I needed. An opportunity missed, to have seen my wife as *new* in every moment.

'No you wouldn't, I was a nervous young woman back then, I really hadn't discovered myself, I wasn't at ease with my sex back then. You'd have run a mile.' We laughed.

'It's really hard for me to be with you and not hold you in some way Diana... there is some huge energetic attraction, such that I just want to be in contact with you when I see you.'

'Ben, perhaps we should have more secrets together.' A woman's sexual energy originates in her heart.

I was burning brightly.

Over several years we had done *everything* except actually fucked each other senseless. I had expected that night to be much the same, deep conversation, deep touch, flirty, seductive. Stop!

We made it into bed with mutual promises of not taking things further, but the sex gods had other plans...

She whispered her desires to me.
Her feminine was moving from heart to sex.
Separate dancers, one dance.
Much subterfuge, but no violence. Profundity.
My masculine moved from sex to heart. What completion.
'Ben, you've no idea what a gift you've been for me. I really thought I was done with sex after my nightmare with that bad news of a man.'

Good orgasms had opened our love potential; if we had bad one's our love would have been constrained. My sex god had done it again. She too was a gift for me. Nature works in mysterious ways.

I laid there looking at her and reflecting on our cosmic entanglement. We were apart in the traditional sense of relationship, yet deeply bonded in the spiritual sense. We were testament that a man could love more than one woman and have many soul mates.

Her reflection was my shadow coloured in.

'Well we made it happen...' What comes now has gone tomorrow.

'Don't you feel guilty Ben?..'

'No I feel sad.'

Did I need to fight with these images of God? Is God not the very source of light that gives rise to all images of God?

'How long does it last?'

'I'm okay if you are okay.'

'I'm okay.'

'I have several friends that need you Ben.' She laughed. 'Could I loan you out to them? Go and give them a good fucking or maybe a gentle adoring.'

The idea was alluring, we laughed some more, but I think she was serious.

'You should write a book about sex,' she said. 'In finding your truth you must teach others.'

Chiron returns.

Tantra

Jane and I used to love each other. We then got to the point where all we did was scream at each other; it was a horrible way to be. It wasn't just us though; there's so much craziness in the world. We're all processing generations of un-integrated imprinting.

I had the feeling that I'd been left alone to struggle on this bizarre chunk of lost-in-space rock. What was this life all about? What do you want of me? Left here to perish or thrive; left here to seek love and warmth from others. God, what do you fucking want from me? Perhaps you left me here to find my way back to home to Source? Pah! The yoke of life.

Simultaneously I realised that being here on Earth is a nectar filled miracle that I can joyously witness. The fact that I am already home "for I am Source" could be felt within that deepest paradox.

Tantra is always about piercing the paradoxes that show up in life – being expansive with all that is. For example, I may well be practicing a sacred ritual in my barn and a tractor full of stinking cow-shit is left chugging outside my window. Animal and sacred all coexists at once.

I could taste a joy that was deeply subdued in me. I was ready to find depth in myself beyond the psychological. The sex god had led me onto the road that would take me home. I had committed to walking a spiritual path with all its challenges.

Spirituality isn't only about ascension and being in the ethers, the Work of a student of Truth requires you to connect profoundly with your body.

Spirituality for me has often simply been a walk in nature. Nature is the divine mother; I have always wanted to make love to her.

One day I went for a long walk deep in the woods where I was free of the "good opinions" of other people. I bathed and healed in the perpetual birth, change and death of nature. I realised I had become very good at hiding from myself; that needed to change. The sex god was living me. I sat and contemplated the possibility that the sex god was my purpose, my gift. If I could honour the sex god, it would transform. The sex god could serve me. What if I freed the impotent taboos and constraints on my sexual energy and helped others to channel it freely and to truly understand its wonder. My body and my sex are beautiful after all. What if I openly expressed my enthusiasm for sex? Sex needn't be wrapped in lies. Wow. If it is my gift then it would be a significant turning point in my life. If it wasn't then what else could my value rest on, what would be left?

I opened to guidance.

Flowers grow through cracks in tarmac.

A teacher, a Tantra Master contacted me. She said she had been sent to teach me about the yoga of love.

'You know, the biggest error in reasoning you have probably made up until now, was hoping things would get better tomorrow, next year or in five years. I can help you.' She was high octane. 'Ben, to access more of who you are and who you can become, you must learn some fundamental lessons in life. The first lesson is that our sex is ours.' She was a Guru, a mirror of where I was stuck. Needless to say I fancied the pants off her.

Tantra was exactly what I needed. We only usually hear about Tantra in a sexual context. Yet the Tantric wisdom tradition is an ancient path of practice that supports the unfolding of our potential towards *the truest knowable nature* of ourselves and the Universe. Tantra is healing and expansive, it is highly relevant and applicable to all aspects of our lives. Tantra embraces all phenomena of life as stepping stones to the expansion of consciousness. A central teaching of the tantric path is an ancient text known as *Vijnana Bhairava Tantra*.[xi] Only a handful of the practices in that scripture relate to sex. Though sex is all.

---

xi   Vigyan Bhairav Tantra discourses on over a hundred meditation techniques (practices) in the form of a dialogue between Shiva and his wife that can be used for realizing the True Self.

Over the next few months I bathed in a profanely sacred discourse about sex, love, energy and Truth. We used breath work, energy awareness and meditation practices. I realised that I am a being that exists on all levels, mind, body, heart and spirit; I am sweetly whole.

Tantra per se isn't spiritual, it's a radically down to earth path very much rooted in the body on all its levels. In fact it isn't a path at all; it's a way of life. It's a way that teaches you to say "YES" to all of life. That "YES" creates the possibility to meet almost anything that is encountered in life with understanding and acceptance. Opening to what is. Freedom.

It became clear to me that if I didn't understand my past then I would keep repeating myself in the future. The teacher exposed paradoxes within myself and showed me how to be at ease with them. Together we explored what it's like to simultaneously be joyous and sad, animal and spiritual, consciousness and energy, the sex god and True Ben. Peace can be found in the paradox. We meditated together. We talked dirty. She taught me about truth, honesty and honour of the Self. She revealed the stuck-patterns I was playing out that held me away from fulfilment. She showed me how much energy I could conserve when I just believed in myself. That if I was willing to be open to whatever showed up in life I could see it's all a gift. We almost made love together; but instead she showed me that I am already the love that I sought outside and that I was the nature that I sought to connect to.

I saw that the sacred wears a female guise. The jagged relationship that I had with my sex god was nourished by a remembering of lifetimes-past when deity was female and sex was for worship.

A few weeks into our time together she declared that it was crystal clear to her why she had come into my life. Not to be my partner or Devi, but to heal me so that I could manifest and welcome-in my very own Ben-perfect woman.

'You don't need to sleep with me Ben. The woman that will show up in your life will be so much more than I am Ben. How does that sound to you?' she asked.

She then went on to make it clear that my highest purpose would always supersede my relationship. As a man I had a soul-contract to go penetrate the world. Further compromise of my truth would cause everyone in my life to suffer and I would become a hollow and weak husk of man. She said that an ancestral healing was in my hands.

I integrated her teachings; they became the foundation of decisions that I needed to make in the coming months. I knew that I should walk the tight rope without a safety net. Tantra was to be my new path.

But I couldn't reconcile the fact that a departure from my marriage would bring untold damage to my daughters. It is all "for purpose" she said. I knew that my children would suffer if I continued to stifle my life; they needed parents who were totally and lovingly embracing life. Isn't the best example we can set for our children to live life totally in love.

There was so much pain.

Could Love really show up in that way? Could it?

Nemesis

Back for more titillation Reader? Maybe you're in the wrong place, cos it's about to get heavy. I may have been on a spiritual path but I was still addicted to sex; it couldn't be disowned. The Tantra teachings were certainly two steps forwards but medicine takes time to work, wise teachings take time to integrate.

I was about to take one step back; feeling rudderless I needed a fix. Something that sets sex addiction apart from most of the other addictions is that you need another person for a fix.

The dope had become heroine.

Old lovers feel like home, they're comfortable; they're an easy fix. I managed to track down Rene, it had been years since we were in touch. She was living just outside Rio in Brazil. A rendezvous was convened. She had made it quite clear that we weren't to be lovers again. She said there was too much heartache the last time we had an affair. We were simply to be "good friends catching up".

The sex god decided to hijack my equilibrium that sticky August night...

Her intensity arose.

Somehow we *were* doing it.

'Are you sure about this Rene?'

'Yes. It's okay.'

What she wants isn't what she speaks. A healthy feminine essence would never say "Yes" if she meant "NO".

She pulled me deep inside.

We gasped for air.

Full body contact, we fucked tightly.

Fierce grace.

The following morning we went our separate ways with a cheery adios. The sex god returned to its luminal-lair dripping with amrita; where it could digest, nourish and recharge.

Acting on desires may well be enlivening and exhilarating, but it sometimes ends up complicating your life – especially when you contact an old friend looking for sex.

Life goes on moving and changing.

Two weeks later a ball busting letter arrived.

"It's not okay. I'm not okay. How could you do that to me? I've been such a good friend to you for so many years. How could you take advantage of me, use me like that, you shit... You are so full of spiritual shit, where is the real Ben, the real man? You douche bag, you fucker..."

I hadn't intended to hollow her heart.

Her anger was her fire – there to keep her safe.

The sex god had breached another frontier. Friendship wrecked. I felt dark and out of control. Many emails with escalating disaffection arrived over the next year. New and incredulous wonders of the ways of Nature were revealed. Rene wasn't happy in the *hell hath no fury* way of being unhappy and my evolution had stalled.

My attachments must have created those circumstances; why else did I need to experience them?

Oh Kali. The whole affair was very confusing to me. She had told me "No Sex", but then she said "Yes".

But I had orchestrated the moment; as I'm not that irresistible.

My naive replies modulated through nervous humour and then gravity. Spiritual platitudes morphed into defeatism; "You are right" or "I am sorry I've always been this way, I feel out of control". But my sorry wasn't acceptable to her and the deluge continued. Huge pain moved in me as the deepest conquests of my life were privately fought at my core. I then implicated my father and all manner of childhood wounds, eventually settling with the swansong of "All men are bad, all men are shits". Addiction surely makes a man small. God help me.

My teacher has since taught me that I can access my healthy masculine by asking myself "what would I want from my lover if *I was the woman and she was the man*." I apparently should have been a big enough man to "Just say No". Brothers, when our masculine is healthy we would have said a resounding *"No"* to Rene. *That's* what she wanted to hear.

Maybe she needed to reveal the fervent toxicity of the sex god to me – my avaricious, grasping, weeny sex god. She had seen right through the cunning plan that facilitated our consensual fucking. She was the bright mirror that showed me what I was blind to. The sex god was called to account by Kali.

I knew it was a turning point. I needed to stare into the eyes of my dragon.

But how?

The mind can never be satisfied no matter how many pleasures it is fed. I was addicted to sex. Did I really need to get so sick in order to realise something, to process it or get it out of my body? I would rather release for an afternoon with some explicit eastern European porn than spend it relating warmly to my family. I was out of control and bereft of ideas as to how I could become a healthy-functioning man again. I knew that abstinence from the sex god would be a caustic condition. I was addicted to chemicals that are freely available and I would do anything it seemed to get a hit.

What was the methadone for that fucker?

Does the pain of addiction mask a gift from the soul?

Reader, is addiction something with which you can empathise? Or are you special? What's your secret? Addiction is a feature of the human condition. Maybe your addiction is food or complaining or computer games? Maybe you're an ex-crack-head or junkie? Maybe like me, its porn or sex? Perhaps it's none of those as there are more socially acceptable addictions to take you... Maybe you're just a socially-accepted alcoholic numbing your way through it all? Or maybe love is your addiction – perhaps you cannot be without your partner?

We are all addicted to air.

We like doing things that feel good.

But what if well-being was my truest nature? Where *was* the fucking pot of well-being at the end of my rainbow? Where was all my misery coming from? Misery appears with certain kinds of thinking; I was done with this life thing. All I wanted was to return to where I came from, to be inside the loving womb of woman snuggled up against the hearth of her feminine essence at Source.

I sought guidance from my Teacher. She said 'Ben, if you could totally accept yourself and take responsibility for everything that happened in your life then you could totally transcend yourself. You could unlearn your conditioning and become a Love phenomenon.' She held me, 'You are standing atop a cliff of self-acceptance and you have an inner knowing of what is possible for you... At the edge of any cliff, you have the choice to stand there frozen, scream all the way down, or learn.'

I could see that freedom would be mine when I took responsibility. I didn't need to be accepted by others, I needed to accept myself. As she spoke I vacillated between doubting then believing that I could tame the sex god.

She continued, 'Ben, maybe it is time for you to make your own world instead of succumbing to the one pressing on you from the outside. Don't surrender to anyone outside of you who is anything less than the divine... Be faithful to the mystery taking place in your heart Ben. Be faithful to that, rather than the ideas of others who might try, with the best of motives, to disempower you and make you theirs.'

Yeah, yeah, yeah.

The medicine tasted awful.

I understood that if I wasn't living my truth then I was living a lie. So what was *my* truth? How did *my* heart sing? What poetry arose from the stillness of *my* heart? I was ready (almost) to harden my practices to get to the bottom this challenge.

My deepest yearning was to know who I am. Perhaps that yearning will take me Home. I hatched a powerful plan to bring light into the abyss.

- *Divorce my wife*
- *Step into my purpose and align with the sex god.*
- *Start again as a ruthlessly honest man.*
- *Walk a spiritual path*
- *Be young, free and single again*
- *Perhaps fall in love again.*
  Perhaps I could fall deeper in love with one woman than I could ever believe possible. (But who would love an honest sexual man?)

But I needed courage to follow through with it. Where was my courage? How could I find courage if I still wanted more of something that I didn't need?

In spite of it all I needed to fall further to find my *divine courage*.

I felt lonely.

The heart of me wept.

No mud, no Lotus.

And there was more mud on its way.

Heart of Darkness

Satisfaction is always short lived... I had seen the path to freedom; but in spite of my best made plans I needed one more fix. I wanted some of the real thing. I needed to make love to a woman, to give myself completely to a woman. One more time. Oh Universe you were playing with me again, right – just for a laugh?

My teacher said "Those are just feelings, simply watch them, let them pass." I couldn't just watch them.

I called the splendidly colourful Aleska. My infidelity didn't faze her, as she too was in a sexless marriage. She knew of my war with the sex god and like a pusher she dangled free drugs in front of me. She also needed it badly; she knew what she was doing. Perhaps her sex god had made a deal with mine.

'Shall we do lunch or get a hotel room?'

'I haven't had any for a while Ben. My husband still repulses me. He isn't interested in my body. I'd sleep in another bedroom if we had one... It's obvious that we need each other's bodies, let's do it.' There wasn't any restraint; perhaps she was bored of saying "No".

'I haven't done anything like this before. You'll be nice to me won't you? I don't like painful stuff.'

'I promise we'll only go as far as you are comfortable. I'll take good care of you baby.'

'Mmmm, sounds divine. Let's get a room today!... No seriously, let's meet next week, during the daytime so my husband thinks I'm at work.' How threatening the unsexed married woman is to the married couple.

'Okay I'll make all the arrangements. How about the afternoon of the 23rd? We can get the room for 2pm.'

I loved the danger and the chase. Dangerous was utterly thrilling. We always have a choice to repress or welcome feelings. Intense feelings assured me that I was alive and not emptiness.

'I need to take a day off work, I'll confirm back to you.'

I was acting out again. There were a few cells within me that were beyond the sex god's realm, they *understood*, they loved me, they needed to help me. The glee expressed by the sex god soon gave way to an unusual inner soliloquy of vacuous and depressing thoughts. There was so much inner remorse at being so addicted. My house felt empty. I crawled upstairs to hide under the duvet and a *descente aux enfers* began.

My sex god used to be such a delicious energy; it allowed me to be pure Eros. But it had transmuted into a turbulence of aching human sadness. I feared that the sex god would consume me and ruin every friendship and loving relationship around me. If my divorce finalised I would be distanced from the most important people in my life; just so that I could step into my purpose – and go play sex god.

Pah.

The sex god was beyond control. Sex god you've gone and got another woman to shag. Well fucking done. Get over it, just go fuck her, it's what *she* wants anyway. Maybe I'd heal her or something. Maybe she would heal me? Perhaps she'd be the last one I needed? Maybe I'd get caught; maybe getting caught would sort me out. Then I'd have to check myself into SAA. I felt so out of control. Thank god I wasn't into S&M and darkest fetishes. Thank god I wasn't a rapist or a paedophile. Thank god I didn't have to pay for sex. The sex god was out of control. What if I needed to experience such darkness to balance all the light that I am? What if I had to have the dark so I could feel the light? But light and dark is all bullshit; there is only light. But how could my state of affairs be light? How could I see it as light? I was so wracked by its pain. What darkest belly ache. Was the sex god the devil? Is this what it's like to be evil? The sex god felt evil. I could fuck Aleska or numerous other women only a phone call away. I could call them up. They all wanted me, they called me an angel, a healer, a real man – as I serviced their empty little holes. Giving them my light such that I am depleted. I was a perished husk of a man, a decommissioned unhealthy man. I once was so much light-energy. I felt like human waste. Perhaps I'd be best buried under a mile of granite – that would put the sex god back to stardust, let it adamantly seep through some other soul; but not mine next time. Please...

Maybe even this story, this spill, is all a sex god wank after all. Recounting debauched stories is another clever way for it to indulge its conquesting self? I've sought to rationalise everything in this book, has it worked Reader? Has it fucking worked?

The sex god had become overwhelmed madness. I writhed as a flood of feelings coursed through my body. It was physical, emotional. It was a bad trip. I was freaked out. Flashbacks to beautiful girls. I cried. Why did I have to lie? Why couldn't I be honest about my sexual energy? Is addiction simply an excuse to lie? Why the loss of control? Why me? It's all Nature... But what if I was caught, that'd be nice, I could come clean. I'd lose my wife, my partner and she's everything to me. Isn't she? I just want her to love all of me. If I lost her I'd be mortified; I'd need to numb myself. I would become a full blown sex addict wanking myself to oblivious numbness. I would become a lonely old man wanking my way to death. I'd be using porn and prostitutes to the point of physiological harm of my body. I would abuse my remaining friendships to get the real thing. Do the swinging circuit to get it, do anything to act out and get my hit. I'd end up not sharing my life, not being touched and loved intimately. I'd be alone, lusty and grasping... But maybe I'd find another lover, women always want me after all... Then I could repeat the whole pattern again, eventually being exposed as a disingenuous using man. I was frightened of the loss of this world. Then one day I would be destroyed, I would be totally subsumed by the sex god. I would lose everything. I would be unloved and un-trustable, not even trusting myself. Whatever the sex god wanted it could never be enough. I would have no basis to relate to anyone. I'd have self hatred, aloneness and wretched removal from life. I was sad at the wasted potential of this man. I'd make the news, though I doubt you'd read about me. I would end up in the gutter, homeless, wanking over hags and crones, feeling them up; just so the sex god could get some stinky fungal pussy. Ha, that's how hags get it too – see I told you there's someone for everybody. The sex god always wins. I would despair, I would give up and embark on a long slow rotting aloneness.

I may then die in a gutter wanking over the prospect of taking Penny one last time.

Darker, harder.

Putrefaction, disintegration and death.

I was so sad; my inner child was so sad. Where was my wonder and innocence at all of the mystery of life? My healing presence for others, where had it gone? Where was it? Where was I?

Where was the fucking manual?

It wasn't supposed to be like that. My expectation over what my life was about swallowed me.

I sobbed uncontrollably.

Much time passed.

My next breath emerged. It was surely a gift.

Raised from the ashes of dread I knew it was important to keep allowing energy to move, evolve and release.

What was the outcome I was resisting or needing from all of this? Everything is an expression of a single divine reality; everything should be honoured and welcomed.

Gratitude for the beautiful sunshine appeared.

I remembered that I am not the experience itself, I am that which is beyond the experience, I am Love. Love isn't an external something I needed to get or give, *I am the Love* that I was seeking outside of myself.

I was ready to evolve and be my authentic self.

I was resolved to be more powerful than the sex god.

Alignment

We are dead for a long time; we may as well live while we
are alive, hey? Sex god let me align with you and let us be of
worshipful service to a woman. An experiment in truth was
embarked upon.

I sat in a classy bar surrounded by the postmodern contrasts
of wood and metal all highlighted with pungent-blue lighting.
I slowly savoured a large chilled glass of white Bordeaux. The
enjoyably awkward Aleska arrived rosy cheeked and fashionably
late. She was wearing her chic city-woman, almost masculine,
work clothes. She was half my age, and her blond hair and pale
skin made her look younger still.

'Hiya beautiful, so great to see you, I really needed to see
you.'

I reconfirmed that a young woman radiates such special
energy.

'Yes me too, I've been so excited. But now I'm really
nervous Ben, please take good care of me. Remember just touch
me first, hold me.' I could see her sizzling energy.

'Let's get you a glass of wine.' We sipped our wine faster
than usual and made some pointless polite chitchat. We giggled
about how many fantasies we'd had about each other; sordid
possibilities had already played-out many times. Anticipation
really was an exquisite aphrodisiac.

'Shall we?'

We went upstairs to the splendour of our suite. Nervously,
Aleska continued the chitchat.

'Shhhh.'

In spite of my meltdown the previous week, I felt that the sex
god was beautiful and something very special was going to evolve
between us in this little corner of the Universe. I felt my healthy-
masculine within.

'Wow the room is beautiful, you've made it magical.'
Ambient candles and colourful silks provided an embalming
energy.

'Ben, I feel so ugly, so unsexy, I'm not sure I want to take my clothes off for you... I just want to be touched.' She'd believed her husband's disdain for her.

'Hey it's okay sweetheart, we're going to come together as pure intimacy. Let's just be with that part of us that we have denied, denounced and disabled to fit into everyone else's view of normal. Let us step in together and claim ourselves.'

I was in my element as a lover, I had a clear intention to service her, worship her, savour her and give my sex god to her. I stroked her curves and traced the outline of her succulence. I proceeded to gently touch her, smell her and lick her. Exploring her with deepening intimacy, Eros adored her exposedness. She became docile, surrendering into the balm of our sex. She needed to receive – she wasn't inert, just at ease in her role as a receptive goddess. The feminine archetype is that of lovingly receiving; I was happy to give to her for as long as she wanted.

It was sacred sex.

Listen to our hearts roar.

The sex god's white-hot scintillation became furnace.

Sex magic happened.

When men give that kind of love, world peace can arise.

Emptying

The sufferance of love; I became certain that I couldn't make Jane feel safe any longer. I looked in the mirror at the man I love. I saw myself at seven years old. I smiled at him with my inner smile. .... Yes I do love me. I was still there for Ben.

What a paradox to hold, so much beauty, so much self hatred. I had acted up again albeit with conscious alignment with the sex god. It was an awesome experience. My darkness was simply the resistance of being myself. It was a disguise that I wore to hide my authentic self; a persona that I adopted so that I could fit the world; pleasing others at my own expense. If I wholeheartedly accepted my sex god, loved my body and my sex there wouldn't be a problem. The other side of my shadow was my strength.

Okay so I finally got it. I needed to become innocence again and align with my purpose.

Spirit shall have dominion over instinct.

I wondered for a moment what would transpire when my libido diminishes. I still had the mojo of a twenty-four-year-old. Someday surely the sex god would go find another soul to live through, lest I be masturbating in my grave... I hoped that young lovers would make-out on my gravestone... Or maybe another evolution would arise for me as my teacher told me that one day I shall go beyond sex for it is only when sex doesn't matter that I can truly know God.

On a day when I was free of my elders' wounding and conditioning of me, I was inadvertently brilliant. I knew that it was finally time to profoundly question my assumptions, my ethics and to open to new possibilities. I chose to step beyond my edge.

I was fed up living a life that suited everybody else; it was time to live my own life.

Empty

Beautiful, beautiful flower, stalk cut off n laid at the foot of the Buddha – its beauty will fade and it will die like my body.

Sacred - Peace

I am a sacred sexual being. I am ready to step into my healthy masculine essence. As I love myself, I am capable of truest love.

Pan can fly.

Authentic

The weaver of my tapestry changed yarns, selecting instead an embrace of rarest yarns in a bouquet of radiant colours. One day while in a profound gathering of friends I realised that life is so much more than a perpetual-reaction to my circumstances. I found within my soul the reservoir of courage that was needed. It was a special essence of courage that had long ago been jettisoned and left to sink into the abyss of my being. It was the courage of a child who would climb a large apple tree to get mistletoe for his mother. It was the courage of a child who would challenge his father to a go-kart race without brakes – and win. It was divine courage that enabled me to step into my very own cœur-age. In a split second I committed to a path of seeking my way back to Truth.

> *It was time for me to evolve to be my healthiest essence;*
> *my uniqueness apart from my wounds, my culture and my*
> *history. I was charged by my enthused-creative-authenticity*
> *to be a complete expression of my actuality.*

Reader, chewy I know, but let those words settle into your own psyche as a possibility for yourself.

As I stepped into my Ben-ness I dug up my buried treasures; wisdom and peace won from suffering life's experience were harvested. What a palaver of twisted Ben avoiding psychology had brought me to that place. The sex god had brought me there. My mind had convinced me that I was imprisoned and then went further to inflict violence upon myself. **My mind was surely a terrorist.**

I realised I was being asked to awaken to faintest memories of why I came to Earth; to be free. Free to dance with the one who brought me here while being free of fear and suffering; free from the idea that I'm lacking ANYTHING.

Thus my sex god had to be re-integrated for me to be whole. Sex was to be my resurrection. There was Work to be done. If

I have ease with every feeling within, only then can I be fully present and show up totally for my beloved. Another woman could only love me in totality when I loved all of myself.

I could only attract Angelica into my life if I became authentic Ben. I had some shagging around to do first.

Crucifixion

Women, men will eventually let you down. Be Love even when they do, for as we have learned, it isn't their fault.

My commitment brought power. I chose to divorce my wife and start walking my path alone. Jane had thought that monogamy would rescue her from the terror of abandonment. Twenty six years after I met Jane at Joy's party back in England our bobbin of golden cording ran out of thread. The north wind laid waste our garden[xii].

We often read about high profile infidelities. Celebrities and their children are forced to suffer the hurt and humiliation of divorce in the media spotlight. Thousands of people get divorced every day and mostly for the same sex god derived reasons. **The traditional marriage-container is broken as it cannot contain the ways of the sex god.** What is we were all honest about sex? What if we all re-designed and co-created new relationship containers that allowed us to be authentic?

There were many reasons why my marriage with Jane came to a close. I had often asked myself why ... and now I understand. We had grown into fundamentally different people and the container of our marriage could no longer hold us; it couldn't contain Ben and his sex god. The hostage situation of "I don't want him but you can't have him" together with my inauthentic dishonest ways had to end.

Freedom was imminent. But freedom was accompanied by the crucifixion of becoming an absent father. Such an exodus rumpled the fabric of my being; and the hearts of those who loved me. Could I ever surrender to the risk of love again?

Masters told me that a man needs two things, freedom and a mission. I had both.

My tears birthed a rainbow.

---

xii   K. Gibran – The Prophet, on Love

Liberated Libertine

Droplets of morning dew imbue magic over an awakening world; those tears from heaven freshly poured by the dawn goddess are utterly captivating and only ever with us for a short while. What a miracle it all is.

I was ready to be a libertine.

If you are out of your cage then by all means flap your wings. Copious yoga, dance, guilt-free sex and the heart-elixir mantra of Krishna Das became a way of life. I continued on my tantric path, moving into an expansive relationship with all of existence. Beauty became available to all the senses. And around that time pussy became Yoni[xiii] and cock became Lingam[xiv].

There was much Work to be done; Work that required that I sit with the pain around my stories. One day I travelled deep into the countryside to join a healing process.

A sacred space had been ritually opened amidst the large gathering of men and women. It was a healing space that allowed us to explore our wounds in the witnessing presence of the opposite gender. Earlier that day I had been surrounded by fifty women, all dancing their feminine nature – while I danced my wildest man in the middle.

My turn arrived. I sat inside a circle of nine women, nine goddesses no longer embedded in their old cultural story. Tantra practice asks us to be total – resolved to feel every arising emotion, resolved to sit in the fire of sometimes severe sensation. In some ways it is the yoga of suffering.

I sat in silence for a moment allowing my breath to settle.

I then opened my eyes. I was fearful as I looked into their eyes, was I being judged? No, I felt their love and I received their love.

---

xiii Yoni: The Sanskrit word for female genitals which translates to "Source of all life" or "sacred space".

xiv Lingam: The phallic symbol used in the worship of the Hindu god Siva or wand of light.

My soul became scintillated by wandering angels. I connected with each woman in turn through an open gaze from the heart of manhood. In each of them I could feel the possibility of all their ways of being. They were all women at once – mothers, whores, goddesses through all of time.

I could say or request anything, there were no limits. Fear moved through me.

In defiance of my fear the sex god spoke.

'I have a body that has colossal amounts of sexual energy in it. That energy rules me, I've resisted it, I've been unsure of it.' Perhaps the sex god just wanted to be loved. Maybe I wanted them to tell me off, to tell me to control myself, to tell me that I was out of control. I wanted them to tell me to be a real man and be powerful over myself.

There was a pause as my words penetrated their feminine core.

Then each of them spoke in turn, as words arrived for them.

'When I listened to you, the first thing that came to me was, I want your cock, I want your sexual man energy. Give it to me, don't hide it, don't be ashamed of it. I think it is amazing to sit before a beautiful shining sexual man.'

'That is just so beautiful that you would share this and ignore your fear. Your sexual energy, your manliness, is so so beautiful.' Tears fell from the two of us.

'You must share all that energy. You must give it to women. Worship them. You must use your power and your presence to create safety for women.'

'My divine feminine loves your divine masculine.'

'Or what about transforming it into some other creative outlet, like writing or making money or art?'

'I want your sexual energy, it is so good to hear a man who has so much to give. So many men are so closed down.'

There was a pause to allow their words to penetrate my masculine core. I sat with my body's wise response.

My koan was solved.

the sex god | 229

The breath that I am, moved with a healing quality throughout my body... My subconscious reclaimed the innocence of my sexuality. Letting go of my old story, integration took place. It was a transcendent moment that allowed me to step into the richness, fullness and wonder of who I am.

Subtle changes within eventually show up on the physical level.

When men re-engage with their divine masculine and feminine aspects within themselves *and* women do the same, then the World can heal.

The addictive grasping of the sex god fell away. Tears of loving relief gave way to shining joy; the fullest expression of myself. The sex god *is* loved by women-kind and was to be loved by me.

Alignment.
The Lotus started to open.
I love the sex god... No more lies.

Let us talk freely about our sex gods.
Let us embrace our sex gods.
Let us all celebrate our sex gods.

Then a new request arose within me.
'Thank you... Now would you all just lay all over me. I want to feel like I am in the womb of womankind.'
I curled into a foetal ball and they slowly and lovingly enshrined me in their form,
their fragrance,
their love,
which was all Love.

Angel from the Bonfire

Life is so fresh. I was ready to be in the unknown. It was Beltane, the midpoint in the Sun's progress between the spring equinox and summer solstice. It was a day that has been celebrated by Celts since antiquity. On that day I went dancing and Source arranged for a rare concatenation of circumstances to arise.

I was a participant at a weekend of conscious rave-like dance. Dance is always profound therapy, layers of pain fell away. The hot glow from a huge Beltane bonfire attracted me. For a good while I stared into the flames, burning off the remains of the old Ben.

We draw toward us that which is most compelling within us.

Then through the flames I saw Angelica smiling at me.

'Where have you been?'

'Where have *you* been?' It's also hard for a goddess to find a conscious lover. There aren't many around. Yet.

Fortune herself had come in quest of me. I knew that my heart was the safest place I could be. Angelica arrived at a time when I was prepared to crack open my heart and let go of that safety. I was no longer lost in relationship, but *found* in relationship.

Heart, sex and spirit aligned.

The Chapel

I am in awe of the capacity of my heart to contain the experience of so much joy and so much pain. Sometimes life deals us experiences where extreme joy and pain are held simultaneously. I found my heart holding the joyous feelings of falling in love with a new lover alongside the soul-impaling pain of departing from a life-long relationship. Feelings almost popped me. What extraordinary human capacity.

But isn't it the case that over time we develop a preference for the kinds of feelings we wish to walk around with? As a child I learned the life-sapping habit of avoiding vulnerability. My teacher told me that I must be *willing* to have my heart broken a thousand times if I am to truly experience the deepest Love. Only then can I realise that truest love doesn't hurt. The source of heart-hurt is the fact that I love, not the other person. It was actually okay for me to have all those paradoxical feelings; feeling got me out of my mind and into reality. Yes it was fine to *simply be* with whatever arose in my human experience. Feelings are a feature of being alive and I am grateful to be alive to experience them. What life "feels" like is all that really matters, thoughts are only ever illusory.

Angelica and I rented an old converted chapel in Wales to romance and deepen our connection.

The bell chimed, it was the second chime which signalled the close of our meditation together. We were bathed in the chimes warm piercing of the silence. I slowly returned my attention to my delicate belly-breath and then sipped a long slow inhale – which was then gently released.

Opening my eyes I witnessed the majesty of a sharpened vision. Beauty was more available to me. I took in the millions of subtle white fibres on Angelica's pashmina. I observed the effervescent clarity of the exotic weavings in her shawl and the spangled drapes of light kissing its downy surface. The celestial colours before me could be smelt, the sounds in the room tasted.

The vivid aliveness of all-life was touched with my eyes as we returned from a deep meditation.

My eyes levelled to meet the embracing gaze of Angelica who was sitting in Lotus across from me. Her dark eyes were illuminated with spontaneous goodness, like they always are. She was staring deeply into the emptiness that is me, there was a familiarity in her eyes. I knew the fullness of her soul as my own. I was what she was looking back.

The bell chimed again, her hands came together in front of her heart in the prayerful gesture of Namaste and she bowed forwards. I bowed forwards on top of her. We melted into our puddle of honey. We paused there for an eternity; until the certainty of all-is-change showed up. Change arose as a subtlest stirring of abject-horniness in one cell deep in my pelvic being. The sex god glow slowly grew. Tao arose from Source; I started to stroke the exposed skin on her low back.

Eros leads to gnosis[xv]. A mystical lovers-touch spontaneously and slowly evolved through us like a rare art-form[xvi]. Exquisite lovemaking can arise when there is no agenda. My keenly sharpened senses recorded every nuance of her smooth skin. It was heightened sensuality unfolding in a space of exquisite witness. Our mutual bows then crumbled into the liquid serenity of lovers entwine. My fingers toured her body, and her small hands mine.

The bell chimed again. Our hot breath communicated mutually held feelings which soon manifested as quixotic unifying love making.

I brought what I was bringing and received what was given. It was an energetic exchange. Unheard, the bell chimed again, and again. The world stopped for us as we mutually peaked and held each other tightly in a yab-yum[xvii].

---

xv   Plato

xvi   The ancient and exquisite practice of Latihan.

xvii   Yab-Yum: A symbolic representation of the male (Shiva) and his consort (Shakti) in a sexual embrace. When the male and female principles come together (Upaya meets Prajna), the false duality of the world can be overcome.

The bell chimed again. Our eyes closed and we fell back into meditation.

'Let's go get some fresh air as it doesn't look as though this rain is going to give up anytime soon.'

'Let's walk in the rain. Waheee!' The unfettered abandon of "young love" that we found ourselves within.

We strolled around the giant freshwater Lily-ponds just behind the beach. They were bathed in the same magical air that was sacredly transmitted through Monet. Rain strafed splashing crowns of water across the glassy surface of the pond. The bounty of Lily flowers growing across the pond reminded us of the Lotus that we had each seen on separate travels in India. The magic absorbed us.

When a Lotus (or a Lily) grows, it starts life as a small flower-shoot deep down in the mud at the bottom of the pond. It grows slowly towards the light at the water's surface. As the flower reaches the surface it starts to blossom, eventually becoming an exquisite flower. This symbol has for centuries represented life's struggle and shows us the opportunity to grow and move towards our own light. As Tantra flowered within me, it changed my relationship to myself, my lover and all people.

If there were no mud, there wouldn't be a Lotus.

No mud, no Lotus.

That summer of love was one of the wettest for decades, there was also record rainfall. Our path broke away from the ponds just as the rain intensified. It was warm rain that felt good on the skin; it somehow washed our souls. We walked past a tree of two twisted trunks that appeared to be hugging each other, mirroring our own pauses for sweet embrace.

The full breadth of a silver-sanded beach opened before us. The sea was fizzed with whitecaps and the horizon was brought closer by rainy mist. Skipping, cart wheels and more loitering embraces ensued. As we walked back up the beach path we collected bountiful herbs, camomile and mints. It was getting late, the last rays of sunshine faded out of the sky. They were replaced by Angelica's loving shine.

We ventured back to the chapel to warm up.

I fetched an armful of oak logs from the woodshed and set a larger-than-necessary fire going in the open hearth. The chapel had a Victorian four-legged bath that was big enough for three, it took an age to fill. I set hot water tumbling and placed chamomile and mint into the water, sweet aromas could immediately be tasted in the swirling vapours. Some candles, not too many, completed an ambiance worthy of my goddess.

We slid into the womb of water and assumed a lovers gaze through the steam and flickering amber light. We shared mutual stories of awakening, of the gentle heart-yearnings to find Truth, to go home. Our trust and intimacy of spirit was deepening.

'Stay here Angelica as long as you need to, I'll go and prepare the space down in the Chapel.'

The wood fire had burnt ferociously for the past hour and had become a golden glow, the vaulted chapel felt tropical. I lit a circle of candles surrounding two sheepskin rugs in front of the fire and then toured the room with a pyre of frankincense. The tall walls became a shimmer of shadow dances and reverence. Ethereal music filled the space with aurora. The finessed ingredients contributed to an atmosphere of delicious expansive intensity, our space was ready.

I sat with my eyes closed absorbing the sensory richness of our sacred space. The chapel had become a spontaneous worshipping and healing space; it was a space befitting the deepest love for my woman. I knew that I was entering a stage of life where my radiant man essence was to become its vast potential.

The chapel had been a place of worship for several hundred years; probably body-denying, fearful and belief-stricken worship. That night the Chapel was to host a supremely celebratory style of worship. Surely devoted worship of Love, sex and spirit through the feminine beloved is the highest form of worship. The goddess-mother is where we *all* come from, and that's a fact.

What arose for us and through us that night wasn't taught by masters or gleaned from text books.

Angelica made entrance in a short robe. Casting off her silk, she laid her petite body face-down. She was ready to receive my adoration, my sexual healing; she was gentle elemental syrup. My lifetime of intimate experience with all manner of goddesses was concentrated into a gift for that one woman. She was about to become all women to me.

I became transparent and beyond gender, yet fully male. My massaging touch was translucent and total as I toured her curves always giving and communicating my loving presence for her; simultaneously I received her. I gave her everything that I wanted her to give to me. Angelica melted in our time bending temple of worship. She was my beloved. I wished to be eternally fused with her, physically, emotionally, energetically and spiritually.

She opened her eyes for a moment as an unworthy thought bubbled to the surface.

'Why Me?' she whispered.

'Why not you Angelica?' Everyone is special. To me she was more special.

The worship of my woman was giving me everything I've ever looked for, and it was inside me all along. What a joke this life is.

A healing started. Each petal she yielded was a veil that covered her inner sanctum, her holy place where I could experience her infinite love. I was able to be fearless totality in the face of such love.

The obese veils of body and emotions fell first and then the veil of "others being responsible" fluttered to earth. Relaxing and expanding, her conditioning fell away along with her ego-mind including her once-positive ideas of dreams, reason, passion, bliss, courage, compassion, and knowledge. All cast off like petals into the cosmic wind of my worshipping witnessing presence.

Her idea of being a woman or a man melted away. The final fronds of her humanness were disowned along with the thought that she was separate from the divine Source. To the seed of her being she became her original Nature.

The portal and key to that place in love is only available through devoted worship of her divine feminine. Her feminine embraced the penetration of my masculine. In that moment I committed to her, I devoted to serving her and giving all that I am to her.

She allowed me to come closer and closer to touch her reality.

We had entered the place of union that unites opposites.

We paused in bliss.

Relaxing and expanding.

Her archetypal energies started to reveal themselves, surface energies at first, then wounds from her life. Then her little girl appeared. Then anger from her other lives appeared - it was ancestral wounding, impersonal and not of her.

Then wounded pages belonging to womankind's long forgotten souls followed.

Then the wounding of all women and the wounding of mother earth. So much pain is held in the pain body of a woman, there is no wonder a woman bleeds.

I continued to hold her in witnessing presence; she let me hold that space as she felt safe.

We paused in witness.

Full of emptiness.

Relaxing and expanding.

Breathing together, she had broken free of the patriarchal structures engraved onto her essence. A new possibility was born of Source as she became the goddess Venus, the all-pure feminine essence. It was the essence which all was born out of, the Source from whence it all comes. All of life is born out of the mother energy, including all men. Venus told of myths from antiquity, unspoken-but-known wisdoms from all time, in all tribes of people, in all of the cosmos. The wisdoms transmitted through and then dissipated.

Angelica is all women all at once from all of time. She is the same energy that brought us here to witness *herself* – the ALL. Our profound experience was all born of the devoted worship of my beloved. The experience was birthed by being the healthy masculine; a witnessing, safe, and trusted presence. Through my love for my beloved I can express my love for all peoples, all creatures, the earth and the cosmic all.

I had become the biggest Man that I could be.

For I am all Men.

Amen.

Falling Free

All is change. Angelica was a little testing this morning. While she is my beloved goddess, she also has the same ever-changing moods and emotions incandescent in every woman. She can be bossy, stroppy, ratty, critical, persnickety and testing; she has her egoic ways. And as the moon decides, she bleeds pain of womankind. She is in every way a perfection of woman, ever in the moment and flowing forth her myriad emotions. Such are the ways of the divine feminine. As I am all that I am, I have learnt to hold space for her ever changing energies, so that she can feel safe to be *all that she is*. Through holding space for her she can shed her outer sheathing-petals to reveal the full flower of her being.

Some energy moved and she soon got over it.

A short yoga practice bathed in Nag Champa opened the day. After which we went outdoors into a chilly early morning mist. The Sun soon warmed us as we wandered across the wheat fields. Some courting skylarks joined us; sex was everywhere. We offered our voices to the morning chorus by giving several Aum's into the still air; sharing our deepest gratitude for this life and all that is. We then strolled back to the chapel hand-in-hand via a causeway between two lakes illuminated by a billion dewy diamonds and our circuit was complete.

We were both in knowingness of the Absolute and the love-rainbow that was so resplendently arcing between us.

We then entered a day of silence.

A richly-toned clock in the entry hall of the Chapel chimed six o'clock and our period of silent togetherness came to a close.

Angelica and I were naturally good at practicing what we called Source and Sauce. Our relationship was a blend of austerely questing into the mysteries of life (Advaita, the male aspect) *and* celebrating our aliveness, living life and expanding sensorially into all that she had to offer (Tantra, the female aspect). **Our relationship is based on abundance rather than need.**

Life is to be lived.

It was time to party.

The champagne cork hit the vaulted ceiling then landed on the altar. Celebration had begun.

'Wooohoo!'

Over champagne and epicurean food we shared stories about past lovers with raunchy detail. But I was fearful of telling her something that had been festering in me through our day of silence... The time had arrived to broach the potentially incendiary subject of the sex god with her. I knew that authenticity required my openness, transparency and trusted bottomless intimacy. I also knew that our shared authenticity would allow us to be sexier than you can imagine together. If I told her upfront about the sex god's ways, then our relationship may be a long one. I was ready to say "this is how I behave", deal with it. My planned concise statement became a lengthy oratory.

'Angelica. You make me feel safe to be my sex, but I don't know if I can be the man you need me to be...' She motioned to interrupt. 'No Angelica, this is different, all the love, the worship, the healing, the awesome sex we've shared over the past few days is the result of a lifetime of being a very sexual man. You should know that I've had many experiences with many women... Angelica, I feel as though there are two of me, there's me and there's a part of me I call the sex god. I love the sex god, he lives somewhere beyond my groin, he has so much sex to give and is forever hungry for sex. If we are to be together I need to be authentic, to be truthful, as truthful as this man can be. I need to grow into being truthful to you and that may take time. You would need to love all of me including the sex god... *and* the lecherous fornicator that I can be... The sex god is mostly good in a giving way, but he can be bad, real bad, he gets me into all kinds of trouble.'

'I love your sex god Ben, I love all that he can do for me, *he* has blown my heart wide open and I know he can take us home.' She paused. 'But I feel fear Ben, fear that arises to protect my heart... If you are honest with me I can work with you.' Our unflinching eye-contact was held. '...If you can hold my fear, I can love you.'

I let her words integrate.

She loves my sex, she loves my sex god. My heart opened at the prospect of being loved in totality. If I could just be me, authentic me with this woman, then perhaps anything would be possible for us. I understood her well-founded fears though. *I am* a big enough man to hold space for the fear that moves in her. I can be a healthy man.

'I respect your fear Angelica... I don't want to be frightened of myself any longer... but I feel as though I can't just change. I have to grow into this new way of being. There will be gains and losses, I may act up, there will be tears... and much much joy as we share the possibility of journeying towards all that infinite love you can give me. I need to learn to be loved in totality; I don't think anyone has loved all of me before. I want you to have every cell of my being AND every cell of the sex god. I am all yours. But I feel there is a journey to get to that place. Will you join me on that journey?' I needed an insurance just in case the sex god were to consume me again.

'It'll be a dance Ben, and I'm willing to dance. Let's see where the dance takes us.'

'Let's celebrate our sexual energy Angelica.' I felt the vastness of her heart smother my smouldering fear. I felt her heart take mine and together we ran over the edge of the cliff of Truth.

The sex god was embraced and consumed and adored.

I danced in celebration of my sex god.

We were falling free.

That Feeling

All women have a divine essence at their core. It can be experienced by any Man. Any Man who devotes himself to her, who worships her and lets her smash his ego, lets her love his vulnerable little boy, lets her understand his ancestral damage and lets her love him beyond comprehension, beyond words.

What if my elders had whispered that wisdom, that possibility to me forty years ago, how different would my life have been?

How could I have ever taken a woman for granted?

How could I have ever taken Mother earth for granted?

I stepped outside the Chapel to fetch another basket of wood.
'Wow Angelica, you should see the stars tonight, let's go for a walk.' It was an inky-black moonless evening; the skies were frosted with an airbrush of Milky Way.
'I'd love to sweetheart.'
We carefully wandered down the lane, occasionally walking into the muddy verge or tripping on a pot hole. A river could be heard above our giggles at the bottom of the hill. Its soothing burble was a homing beacon to a large meadow where we could witness the full horizon of the miracle of Cosmos.
We embraced and looked up at the sky together.
The billion-galaxied night sky made me feel so small. The Universe swallowed all of me.
I also received the same feeling by being absorbed into the chest of my beloved angel.
I felt consumed by her infinite Love.
Love is a gathering and celebration of what it means to be alive, it is to be everything and nothing all at once. Love IS life.
There's no doubt that one of the most amazing becomings of manifest Nature is to be embraced by the feminine essence of

my lover. I became instilled and entered a time where I ceased wondering. I just was.

Soaking up and receiving the open heart of Angelica is a place where I don't want protection. I feel strangely free, ageless and excited there. I don't know where I begin or end.

The clock stopped and time did not matter.

In embrace we rested for a moment together as One. In our lonely existence.

'Take all of me Ben, I've got all you will ever need'

A soul contract was made.

I became nobody. No body and all things.

Two disappeared.

It was the end of distinction. No clouds, only sky.

The sex god had led me there.

That Said

Many miles had I travelled. The cause that was set going by Mrs. Honey had created a result. The closer I get to who I am, the closer I get to Angelica.

But as we embrace our tomorrows, how can we fall in Love beyond form? Peace is a transition from loving egotistically to loving from the Absolute. We were both attuned to the presence of Love (with a big L) that is the All, we were also aware that much of our playful chemistry was romantic love (little l). Attachment (I used to call it possessiveness) is so present in young love. What would it be like to go beyond attachment to each other?

Tantra is the yoga of relationship to everything, the yoga of energy and consciousness. It guides the practitioner towards deepest Love. Forget marriage, what if Love was the container! I decided to **commit to finding out what is the deepest Love possible between a man and a woman?**

From innocence to innocence by way of junk and treasure, my tapestry was now half complete. Reader, thank you for staying the course with me. Your own journey will surely be different but you may well tour the same realms. Life requires you to own your purpose and be true to your heart. What could you do today that would be for *your* highest good?

Let's not blame the past, let's understand the bigger picture. Through all of time damage comes from damage. If I am loved unconditionally and I am powerful enough to exercise choice over my way of being in this world, then I can break the cycle of damage. As I choose to be authentic and worship my woman she shall love me in entirety. An ancestral healing can take place.

We live in times of evolution not breakdown.

Nature has designed men to be dick-centric as male sexuality is of utmost importance for the continuance of the species. As the Goddess awakens in western consciousness, evolution is calling us men to align our dick with our heart. Experiencing the union of sex and heart brings meaning to our manhood. As we place our sexuality in the service of Love, the world shall become heaven again. We shall weep tears of joy as our pain heals. We shall dance in blessed wonder for the exquisite beauty of all of life.

And Mother Earth shall heal.

Angelica and I have embarked on our quest for deepest Love, but I must ask must I be alone to find the Truth of God?

That's another story.

The Teachers

Teachings of many wisdom traditions have influenced this book. Gratitude to all the Great Ones and the many modern-day sages, teachers and wise people who are here to show us the way, including:

The Truth that unfolds through me

Ramana Maharishi
Osho

Mooji
Mahasatvaa Ma Ananda Sarita
Eckhart Tolle
David Deida
Arjuna
A.H.Almaas
L'Origine Du Monde

Chameli Ardagh, Abraham Hicks, Brad Blanton, Robert Bly, Chris Bourne, Michael Brown, Paulo Coelho, Andrew Cohen, Anthony De Mello, Baba Dez, Nik Douglas, Piero Ferrucci, Mark Gafni, Gangaji, Geho, John Grey, Matt Guest, Sally Kempton, Krishnamurti, Mike Lousada, Shakti Malan, Thomas Moore, De Secretis Mulerium, Nirmala, Rob Preece, The Man Kind Project, James Redfield, Gabriel Roth, Sandra Sabatini, Erich Schiffman, The Shift Network, Penny Slinger, Chuck Spezzano, Neil Donald Walsh, Ken Wilbur, Jewels Wingfield

Reading books, essays and transmissions from these people may inspire you. A full listing of resources, book references, discussion and facebook community can be found at the author's website:

www.benbelenus.com

CPSIA information can be obtained at www.ICGtesting.com
Printed in the USA
LVOW120321140313

324217LV00001B/119/P